The
Arrogant
One

USA TODAY BESTSELLING AUTHOR
MARNI MANN

Visit my website at: www.MarniSMann.com
Cover Designer: Hang Le, By Hang Le
Editor: Jovana Shirley, Unforeseen Editing, www.unforeseenediting.com
Proofreaders: Judy Zweifel of Judy's Proofreading, Christine Estevez, and Vicki
Valente
Photographer and Cover Image: PaperbackModel, Daniel Jaems

This book is a work of fiction. Names, characters, places, and incidents either
are products of the author's imagination or are used fictitiously. Any
resemblance to actual persons, living or dead, events, or locales is entirely
coincidental.

ISBN-13: 979-8-9894377-6-4

It's one thing to fall for a man who looks at you as though you're the one who set his soul on fire ...
It's another thing to be the one holding the match.

PLAYLIST

"Everyone Bleeds"—Jelly Roll
"Up to No Good"—Warren Zeiders
"It Ain't Right"—Jessie Murph
"A Lot More Free"—Max McNown
"Upgrade"—Jessie Murph
"Somethin' 'Bout a Woman"—Thomas Rhett, featuring Teddy Swims
"Last of My Kind"—Shaboozey, featuring Paul Cauthen
"Pretty Little Poison"—Warren Zeiders
"Love Me Back"—Max McNown
"Sin So Sweet"—Warren Zeiders

Click here to check out the Spotify playlist.

PROLOGUE

Hart

"I don't know why I'm not the face of the company when I have the prettiest one in this whole fucking room." I eyed down my four siblings as they sat around the conference table at our corporate office, laughing, and I waited for their rebuttal.

Because I knew it was coming.

Of course, they knew I didn't want to be the face of The Weston Group—the umbrella that held our family's two brands of restaurants and nightclubs. I was just giving my oldest brother, Walker, some shit since he'd just ordered me to go check out our latest competition—a steak house in Laguna Beach called Horned.

That was what you did when you owned a worldwide empire of food establishments—you assessed every hot spot, taking note of what they had done wrong, and what they had done right.

Horned had been making far too much of a splash in the

1

steak house scene, so they were obviously doing something right.

It was a task that couldn't be assigned to Walker. His face was known across the globe as one of the top chefs in the world and was too easily recognized. Given that Beck, the youngest boy, was an NHL superstar, he couldn't go either. So, the task rotated to either Eden, our only sister; Colson, the second oldest; or me.

And according to Walker, it was my turn.

"You sure are the prettiest, you playboy," Walker groaned.

"Hold on a second, Walker." Eden, sitting next to me, turned her chair until her entire body was pointed at me. Her all-black suit and matching nails weren't what caught my attention. What was doing that were the sky-high red heels tapping the air. "The prettiest title has been mine since the day I was born. What would make you think you'd earned that slot?" She nodded toward me and winked. "Because you hold the family record for the number of women you've slept with?"

"But does he?" Beck asked her, running his hand over his beard, which he'd been growing since the start of this year's hockey season. A fucking bush that I was shocked didn't get stuck in his helmet. "If we're talking numbers, I think I could give that bastard a run for his money." He laughed.

I glanced at Colson, the most laid-back of the bunch and the only parent in the room, and said, "How about you?"

"What about me?" Colson inquired.

"You want to weigh in? And share your recent count?"

He hissed out a mouthful of air. "A true gentleman doesn't kiss and tell."

Eden snorted. "There isn't a woman in California who hasn't seen one of you naked. I wouldn't call any of you a gentleman when it comes to that department. And honestly, I don't know how I'm from the same womb as the four of you."

Eden was certainly the most innocent of our group. What didn't help was that she had a team of brothers who would destroy any man who hurt her.

Not that we had to. She didn't fuck around with men like we did with women.

She didn't even date.

I shook my head, chuckling. "And there are some women in this state who have had more than one brother."

"Dude"—Beck's hand went over his mouth—"do you remember the chick who—"

"You will not finish that sentence," Eden cut him off, pointing at him. "I don't want to hear about any chicks unless they're going to become my future sister-in-law, and I think I have a long time before that happens." She turned her chair straight. "I need to get back to work. Walker, do you have any more orders for Hart? Or can we adjourn this meeting?"

Walker leaned his arms onto the table, the sleeves of his chef's whites rolled up to his elbows, telling me he had stopped in for the meeting and was headed straight to the kitchen. "In the next few days, I want you to go to the restaurant in Laguna Beach. Check out the interior. The menu. Take some photos. Order an item from each course. Take more pictures. And report back to us." He ran his hand over his black hair that was just starting to gray along his crown—premature for a thirty-five-year-old maybe or pressure from being one of the most innovative chefs there ever was.

"Done," I replied.

He tilted his body against the lip of the wood. "If they put a loaf of bread in front of you, I want to know if it's brown or sourdough, if there are seeds on the crust, if it's been toasted or just warmed or if it's served cold—the butter, if it's whipped or if it's a pat and if that pat is dusted in flaky salt. If your steak is served on a plate, I want to know the temperature of the

3

stoneware. If butter is pooled beneath your meat, I want to know what it's infused with—rosemary, thyme, parsley, or a combination of all three." He attempted to push up the cuff of his sleeve even higher than his elbow, but it wouldn't go up anymore. "I want every detail there is, Hart. Don't leave anything out."

I rocked in my chair. "Anything else, Chef?"

"That should do it—for now." Walker looked around the table at each of our faces.

"I'd like to talk about Toro," Beck said. "What's the status of the Beverly Hills build-out? I stopped by the restaurant the other day and added about twenty items to the punch list. The place is a fucking disaster."

"It's mid-construction," Walker replied.

"It can't be mid-construction," Beck countered. "Because it's been under construction for the last four months and it opens in six weeks."

The Beverly Hills development of Toro—our seafood and raw bar—was one of the most expensive projects we'd ever taken on. Part of that was due to the space we'd chosen and having to frame a kitchen from scratch, the existing structure not having one. The other part was that even though this concept, along with the clubs, was new and we were still learning as we were going, Beverly Hills was projected to be one of our largest locations. With every square inch, more time was needed, and that meant more money.

And as the chief marketing officer of our entire brand, I knew we were far over budget.

"It'll be done," Walker assured him.

Beck—more of a silent partner since hockey took up much of his year, but he personally financed many of our build-outs—looked at Colson, our chief operating officer, and said, "Do you agree?"

Colson rested his arms behind his head. "Our contractor always gets it done whenever we put the pressure on him."

"Have we put that pressure on him?" Beck asked.

The room turned silent.

"And do you know how much pressure it's going to take to have that restaurant up and running by opening night?" Beck continued.

I could hear a fucking pin drop in here.

Which wasn't a surprise. We were all nervous as hell that six weeks wasn't enough time to get the restaurant in the kind of shape that our clientele expected.

Our brand had a reputation. If we didn't deliver, that could destroy us.

Beck tapped his hand on the table. "There's only one person who will give me a straight, honest-to-God answer in this room. And that's you." He directed his statement at Eden.

Eden stared at him, the tip of her short thumbnail in her mouth. "It's going to be tough. It's going to be tight." Her thumb dropped. "Is it impossible? No. Is it going to take every bit of manpower? Yes. And we're going to be down to the wire."

"We've set an opening night, and we've made that date known to the public," Beck said. "But we don't know if it's a deadline we can actually hit. So, what I'm hearing is ... we're fucked."

"We'll hit the deadline," I assured him. "Toro will be ready for opening night."

Beck's brows rose high. "How?"

"Because we're Westons." I clamped my hands together. "And when we give a date, we uphold it—because our word is our fucking bond."

ONE

Hart

Out of all the sounds I'd ever heard in my life, her laugh was easily the sexiest. It filled my ears after we reached for the door at the same time, our hands linked by accident.

"Sorry about that," she said, her giggle dying out.

"No reason to be sorry."

Especially when it came to touching—and a woman this beautiful could touch me all she wanted.

My fingers stayed on hers for a second longer than they probably should, squeezing her and the metal handle at the same time. And as we both pulled the restaurant door open, I took her in even more.

Hair that appeared black in the dimly lit entrance and eyes that were radiant and a vibrant blue. Lips that were thick and sparkled with gloss. Tits that were tucked inside a dress and then covered with an unzipped jacket, which also concealed most of her body, but the little I could see was perfect.

More than perfect.

It was enticing.

And that was just her body. Her face was fucking stunning.

As her fingers pulled away from the metal—and me—and hung at her side, she stood frozen in the entryway, as though she were waiting for instruction.

But unlike her, I hadn't let go of the handle, using it to keep the door open, and I waved her through. "After you."

"Are you sure?" Her question was toned in a way that sounded flirtatious. "Because you arrived before me, so I think you should go in first."

I took another dip to her heels and gradually worked my way back up. "Yes, I'm sure."

The whole reason I'd come to Horned in the first place was to fulfill Walker's wishes.

Was I sure I wanted to eat alone tonight? No.

I'd rather eat with her.

Or eat her.

But I was positive that a woman as gorgeous as the one I was staring at—coming to a restaurant on a Thursday evening, dressed as beautiful and as elegant as her—was meeting someone.

"Please," I replied. "Go ahead in."

She smiled as she walked past me. "Thank you."

That grin ... *fuck*. I hadn't anticipated it to be as powerful as it was or that it could make her look even more beautiful.

But I was wrong.

Her smile was breathtaking.

And it was compelling enough to get her anything she wanted.

At least with me.

I followed her in, smelling the fruity jasmine that wafted from her—a scent as captivating as her gaze. And despite how badly I wanted to keep following her, we parted ways as she went to the hostess desk, and I veered into the bar.

It was a goddamn shame too. I would have preferred a night with her to the one I had planned.

Once I took a seat, I inconspicuously snapped a few photos and thumbed through the drink menu the bartender had handed me. I already knew what I was going to order, but I looked at it to see its presentation, assessing the paper of the menu and the font that was used, comparing their prices with what we charged.

"How's your old-fashioned?" I asked the bartender.

"I make the best one in town."

I chuckled to myself.

Nah, man, our old-fashioned at Charred—our Michelin-rated steak house with locations all over the world, including one here in Laguna Beach—was the best. It had actually won awards.

But bartenders were usually on the cocky side; ours were as well. Considering Horned had only been open for two months, the man in front of me still had a lot of convincing to do in a market that demanded excellence.

"Prove it to me," I told him.

He smiled. "Happily."

"Make that two," someone said from beside me.

I didn't even have to look.

I smelled her the second she spoke, the fruit and jasmine taking hold of me and not letting go. And the voice—I knew that too. The only thing missing was the laughter.

As I turned toward her, she said, "Mind if I sit?" Her teeth were on her lip, biting the plumpness, inviting my stare.

There was only one vacant stool at the bar, and it happened to be the one next to me.

"I would enjoy nothing more," I told her.

There was that smile again.

The one that had rocked me in the doorway of the restaurant.

It was doing the same thing to me all over again. But this time, even my dick was reacting, my shaft turning painfully hard inside my pants.

She got settled in the seat. "When your date arrives—assuming you have one—I'll get up so she can sit with you."

An interesting statement.

And an even more interesting offer.

Because if I were meeting another woman here, I shouldn't be looking at her the way I was.

"No date. I'm eating alone. Right here in the bar. You don't have to go anywhere ... unless you want to." I paused, choosing my next words carefully. "I suppose I should say, I'll get up when your date arrives."

The bottom lip she was nibbling was now rubbing against the top one, once again drawing my attention to her mouth. To its lusciousness. Glossiness. Causing me to think of only one thing—the way those lips would look if they were sucking on the end of my dick.

"You should offer that, yes," she agreed.

"Except I won't. Because I'd like to eat dinner with you tonight."

"And if I'm meeting someone?"

I leaned back in my barstool, removing my arms from the bar top, to get an even better view of her. "Whoever that someone is, it doesn't matter. Stay with me instead. I promise you'll have a much better time."

She spread her lips wide, a smile but without any teeth, her head slightly shaking. "That's a confident thing to say."

"I'm a confident guy."

At a competing restaurant, where I was currently semi-undercover, I couldn't use the name everyone knew me by. It didn't matter if I wasn't the face of the company; the Weston brand was known everywhere, and my name was attached to that.

So, I reached out to shake her hand and said, "I'm Lockhart," which was my birth name, used only by my mother whenever I had gotten in trouble as a kid. "And you are?"

While she looked at my fingers, I knew without any doubt that she would be joining me for dinner.

That I would know her intimately before this night was over.

And that her pussy was already mine—she just didn't know it.

"Sadie." The heat of her skin soaked straight into me. "It's nice to meet you, Lockhart."

I held on like it was the door handle, a few extra seconds than needed, and slowly released her grip.

Once I did, she traced her pink-painted nails across the bar top and said, "No date. No friend joining you. Just a quiet Thursday evening out?"

"Sometimes, I like it quiet when there's far too much loud in my life."

"Oh, I hear that." She glanced at the ceiling and across the busy bar. "Except there are much quieter places to go than here."

"Are you suggesting we go somewhere else?"

Her hands lifted to her face, and she held her chin. "You're spicy. Has anyone ever told you that?"

"Not in those words, but I like your description." I waited. "Sadie, who's joining you tonight?"

"Are you asking because you want to prepare yourself for battle?"

I laughed. "I don't see a battle in my future."

"Really? No war?"

"No." I wrapped my fingers around the glass that the bartender had placed in front of me and held it toward her. "I see you and me sitting here until the restaurant closes and then going somewhere for a nightcap."

"You've just met me. The restaurant probably doesn't close for another four hours or so. How do you know you'll still be interested by then?" She clinked her glass against mine and took a sip.

"Intuition."

"Yeah?" She set her glass down. "What else does your intuition tell you about me?"

I didn't return my tumbler to the bar. I wanted to hold the liquor, and I wanted to keep it close in case I needed more of its taste. It was the second-best thing I could put down my throat—her pussy being first.

"Based on what I'm seeing and feeling, one of two scenarios is true."

She swiveled her stool just enough to move her legs out from under the bar and crossed them once they were free. "I can't wait to hear this."

"You're either in the area for a business meeting and you came here after, getting a bite to eat before you drive home or to your hotel, if you're an out-of-towner—although I get the feeling you're a Cali girl." I paused. "Or you're here on a first date."

She glanced down her body. "This is first-date attire?"

I smiled once I earned her eyes again. "Do you really want that answer?"

"Lockhart, I'm dying for it."

"The dress is just short enough to show some skin. Not too much, just the right amount, so both scenarios apply. The top of it hugs you in a way that reveals what you're working with, without throwing it in a man's face or giving it all away—again, that can go both ways. Your makeup is light and professional, and your heels are seductive—those two balance each other out. But your hair—that's what I'm torn about."

"Meaning?"

My head tilted, my grin growing. "Men like hair. They fantasize about it. For some, they can see the way the wind has blown yours and think that's how it'll be when they get done kissing you. So, you're either going for the ravenous look or you just haven't tamed it."

She released her chin and ran her fingers down her dark, curled locks. "Better?"

"Except I'm not like the men I just described."

She moved her hair to one shoulder. "You're not?"

I held my grin and glanced toward the bartender, taking a long drink before I leaned toward her. Not close enough to be in her personal space, but a distance that would allow her to hear me better.

"No, because if I kissed you, your hair would look like I just got done fucking you. That's the kind of power I have in my lips."

As I leaned back, her mouth opened to respond and then quickly closed.

A gesture that made me chuckle until I realized we were no longer alone. A woman was standing behind us, a tablet in her hand.

"Sadie, your table for one is ready."

"For one," I repeated. "Fascinating." I winked at her. "What are you going to choose, Sadie?"

Sadie held my gaze as she debated the question, finally replying, "I think I'm just going to eat at the bar tonight."

"No problem," the hostess said.

"I want to go back to the *hair and kissing* thing," she said

13

once we were alone. "You're telling me that would happen just from your mouth?"

I nodded.

"What, do you have the lips of a god or something?"

"I'd show you ... but we're not ready for that. This is just drinks. You get nothing from me until at least after the appetizer."

She licked her lips. "What makes you think I even want anything from you?"

"You're thinking about it ... I can tell."

She laughed. "I'd tell you you're full of yourself, but I think you already know that too."

"There're two types of confidence. Believing in yourself and believing what's about to happen."

"You've got the first one nailed." She took a drink.

I smiled. "I've got both nailed."

"Of course." She rolled her eyes with a grin. "What was I even thinking?"

The bartender stopped in front of us. "Can I get you a refill?"

"Please," I replied.

"And you?" he asked Sadie.

"I'm going to nurse this one for a bit longer. Thank you."

As she was tucking some of that wild hair behind her ear, I asked, "So, you never answered me. Are you here for a business meeting? Is that what brings you in? Since I now know it wasn't a first date—or even a date for that matter." I tried, but my fucking smile wouldn't leave my face.

That was what she was doing to me.

Making me dream about later tonight.

Making me into a grinning fool.

Damn it, this gorgeous woman had powers.

"Business-ish." She shrugged. "And no date. Lately, I've only been meeting Mr. Wrong."

"It's a good thing I'm Mr. Right."

She gave me a nip of her lip before she grinned. "Well then, I guess it is a really good thing that I met you, Mr. Lockhart Wright."

I had to laugh for just a second as I let my eyes wander, appreciating every second I could take in this view because it sounded like my joke had gone right over her head.

"Tell me more about you. What do you do?"

"I work in social media. How about you?"

"Hospitality."

"That's a broad answer."

I winked at her. "So is social media."

"Okay, you got me there. I just hate talking about it. It's a job that monopolizes far too much of my life. When I'm not actively working, I'm usually thinking about work. But sitting here with you, I haven't thought about it once. It's been a nice reprieve."

I shook my head, moaning, "I couldn't have said it better." I finished my drink and pushed the empty away. "You know what I like? You were in the area for business-ish. You could have pulled up to a drive-through or gone home—wherever that is—and had something delivered. But you came to Horned, a high-end restaurant. You'd even made a reservation."

Should I be pissed that she hadn't made a reservation at Charred, which was three blocks from here? I wasn't going to let that haunt me right now.

"That tells me you don't fuck around when it comes to food. I love that."

"My father would be highly disappointed if I went the fast-food route. That's one. Two, I love good, quality, healthy food, and fast food doesn't cut it."

I took a deep breath. "Is Dad in the food business?"

"No, nothing like that. He's just a foodie. My parents cooked when my sister and I were growing up. We weren't mac-and-cheese kids, we ate everything they made and learned to love it. The need to have a good meal is something I carried into adulthood. Don't get me wrong, I might throw together a bowl of ramen at home or a turkey sandwich, but it's going to be decorated with all the extras."

I pounded my chest. "Stop. You're making me fall. Hard."

She laughed.

"You don't mind coming to a restaurant and eating alone?" I rested my arm on the bar top and faced more of my body toward her. "I realize that's what you're doing tonight. I'm just curious if you do it often."

"I don't mind eating alone, and, yes, I do it often." She ran her finger around the rim of her glass. "I'm a good time and excellent company. I can easily entertain myself."

"You've been a good time ... and excellent company."

Her smile was coy, one I hadn't seen from her yet. "It only gets better after a second drink." She laughed. "Which I'm not having."

"No?"

"I'm driving back to LA after dinner."

"To fly home, or is that where you live?"

"It's where I live. You're right, I'm a Cali girl."

My breathing was coming in and going out much harder and deeper than it should. My heart was pounding faster than it needed to.

But the thoughts running through my head? Fuck, I couldn't stop my body from reacting.

I needed Sadie.

I needed to know what she tasted like.

I needed to know what she felt like.

And I needed to know just how she sounded and the way she looked when she moaned.

"What if you didn't have to drive back tonight?" I asked.

Her eyes narrowed. "What are you saying?"

Once I voiced these words, I couldn't unsay them, and she wouldn't be able to unhear them.

But that was a chance I was willing to take for one of the most beautiful women I'd ever seen.

"What if I offer you a different ... scenario?"

"You like these scenarios, don't you?" She adjusted the way she was sitting, changing how her legs were crossed. "Explain to me what this one is."

"I have a hotel room about a mile from here."

"Are you asking me to stay the night with you?"

"Yes." I pulled the drink back, sipping the liquor off the ice. "I'd say I've been asking you that question, in some way, since you touched my hand when we walked into this restaurant."

"*You* touched m*y* hand."

I chuckled. "If that's the way you want to look at it, then, yes, *I* touched you. And I loved every second of it."

"Lockhart"—her brows furrowed—"do you think I'm just going to leave here with a complete stranger, go to your hotel, and ..."

"Have one of the best nights of your life? Yes. I most certainly think that. And that's all I'm asking for, Sadie—one night. Nothing more."

She pushed her lips together. "You really believe you're that good? That you can convince someone like me, who never does that, to do it now?"

"I know I am." I nodded toward the bartender to thank him for leaving my second old-fashioned in front of me. "Send your location to your friends or your sister. That's if you're worried about leaving with me. But I assure you, the only bad thing that's going to happen is you being forced to endure orgasm after orgasm until you can't physically come anymore."

"I have been the good girl for too long." Her face flushed, and it was a color I couldn't get enough of. "You know, I've been offered many things in the past. A one-night stand isn't one."

"You're the most gorgeous woman I've ever spoken to. I'm shocked to hear that men aren't throwing themselves at you."

"I didn't say they're not." There was that grin again, the one I was becoming addicted to. "I just don't let things get that far."

"Because?"

"I want the happily ever after, not the happy for now." She smiled. "The men who want what you want"—she glanced down my body—"aren't going to give me that *ever after* I'm looking for. They're going to give me *the now*. Which I don't need. I have plenty of toys for that."

The thought of a toy pressed against her clit or one sliding into her pussy was making me even fucking harder.

"What if *the now* is the best sex of your life?"

"Do I look like a woman who's deprived, Lockhart?"

And I was the spicy one?

Jesus, I liked her.

"Not at all," I answered. "I just think you'd enjoy what I want to do to you."

"Which is?"

"You're telling me you want to hear about it? In detail? That surprises me, Sadie, especially coming from someone who isn't looking for a one-night stand." I paused. "But I get the feeling you're tempted. Tell me I'm wrong ..."

She licked the inside of her bottom lip. "You know, I just came here for dinner."

"And I'm offering you far more than a meal." I turned and pointed toward the hostess station at the front of the restaurant.

"I'm sure they still have your table available. You can go. You can eat. You can do what you came for. Or ..."

"Or?"

"You can come with me"—I shook my head as I took her in —"and let me eat you."

Her brows rose. "Now?"

"Right now."

"Without even having a steak?"

"I'm staying at the Cole and Spade Hotel. I'll order you room service once we're done."

She stared at me silently for what felt like at least a minute. "I can't even believe I'm contemplating this ... what the hell has gotten into me?"

"Listen, I can come up with a multitude of reasons, but let's face it—there's something about me that you find irresistible."

"Maybe it's your arrogance."

I chuckled. "I can't deny that."

"Or your mouth."

"Wait until it's on your pussy and you can really say that."

I reached for my wallet, grabbed a hundred and fifty out of the billfold, and set it on the bar. An amount that was more than enough to cover her drink and both of mine. I slid it toward the bartender who was walking by and said, "For you."

"Thank you, Mr. Wright."

I laughed to myself at the bartender's response since he'd overheard our conversation earlier. A laugh that quickly faded because I knew Walker was going to give me endless shit for leaving the restaurant at this stage—without taking a proper amount of photos and not even tasting the food. But I didn't fucking care.

I stood. "Let's go."

"You really are serious?"

"Did you think I wasn't?" I held out my hand to her. "I gave you two scenarios, Sadie. To go to my hotel room with me or go eat at your table in the dining room alone—or I guess you could stay right here. The choice is yours."

"But I believe you also said I don't get anything from you until at least after the appetizer. We haven't had that yet."

And she was feisty too.

"You're going to get that in the car," I promised.

She smiled.

"I'm not joking," I added.

Her feet hit the floor. "Do me a favor?"

"Anything."

"Make sure I don't regret this."

I clasped her fingers. "I'm going to make that happen in the next few minutes."

I led her through the restaurant and out the front, bringing her toward the back side of the parking lot to my car. As I escorted her toward the passenger side, she laughed.

"You're the type who parks in the back of the lot so your doors don't get dinged." Her hands went to her hips while I opened her door.

"I am when there's no valet parking." Which I couldn't believe for a restaurant of this caliber. But when you dropped almost two hundred thousand on an R8, nothing pissed you off more than a fucking asshole who rubbed their car door against yours, leaving either paint or a dent. "What, you didn't expect that from me?"

"I don't know what to expect from you. You've done nothing but surprise me since I met you tonight."

I helped her into the low, narrow seat. "Then take in this piece of information too." I leaned into the doorway to get closer to her. "I enjoy the walk to the back of any lot. Not a single part of me is lazy."

"From what I can see of your body"—her gaze dropped to my legs and rose—"I can tell."

I chuckled as I shut the door and got into the driver's seat, starting the engine and shifting into first.

But I didn't release the clutch. I wasn't even looking out the windshield.

My focus was on her.

"One thing you need to know about me, Sadie, is that if I tell you I'm going to do something, I'm going to do it."

"Okay."

"So, that appetizer ... it's going to happen right now. Lift the bottom of your dress."

She glanced out her window. "Here?"

"Yes."

"Because?"

"Because I want you to show me your pussy." I watched her chest rise. "Trust me. Everything I'm going to do will make you feel good."

"How can I trust you? I don't even know you."

"You got in my car."

She nodded. "I did."

"The door is unlocked, and you're still sitting here." I waited before I repeated, "Trust me, Sadie."

She slowly inched up the hem, revealing more of her thighs. Even though it was dark outside, a streetlamp sat over the car, allowing my stare to drag across the creaminess of her skin.

"Higher," I ordered.

Both sides of her jacket fell open as she hiked up the remaining distance, but she left the smallest piece of fabric to hide what was underneath.

"Show it to me, Sadie."

Her lips were parted, and I could tell she was breathing

rapidly through them while her fingers tucked up the remaining length.

My gaze met red lace. "Take them off." I held out my hand. "I want them."

"God, you're dirty."

"Just wait until I touch you ..."

She arched her back off the seat and wiggled the lace down her legs, bending to step out of them, and once they were in her hand, she hovered her grip over my palm. "Are you going to give them back?"

"No."

"Don't tell me you have a wall of panties that you've collected over the years."

"Would you be surprised to hear that yours would be my first?"

"Yes." She dropped them in my hand.

"Because they are." I immediately tucked the lace into the pocket of my sports coat, my fingers returning to the gearshift. With all the movement, that spot between her legs was now covered. "Let me see it, Sadie."

"You really want to see—"

"Yes, I really want to see it." I adjusted myself before my dick thrust straight through my goddamn pants. "I want your dress high enough that you can spread your legs. First, I'm going to look at it. And then I'm going to touch it the whole way to the hotel. But since I'll be driving, I won't be able to see it. I want that visual in my head while my finger is deep inside your pussy."

"I've never met anyone like you, Lockhart."

"And you won't again." I nodded toward the door. "Reposition yourself so you're facing me. I want my view to be unobstructed."

She turned toward me, leaning her back against the door,

and she moved the dress so she could gradually lift her leg, only stopping when her knee was halfway up the front of the seat.

An angle that gave me just what I wanted.

"Fuck me, you're so beautiful," I moaned. My throbbing hard-on was becoming intolerable as I stared at the most perfect cunt I'd ever seen. Tight, hairless folds hid the best present beneath them, and right below was a slit I was dying to rub my nose over, one that was practically fucking sparkling by the way the light was hitting it. "Damn it, Sadie. You're already wet."

"Did you get enough? Or do you want to stare at her a little more?"

I huffed. "Enough? No. Not even close. But you can put your leg down." As she shifted in the seat, my fingers went between her knees. "Just don't close these—my hand needs access."

She held my gaze as I lifted my foot off the clutch and pulled straight out of the spot, veering toward the exit of the parking lot.

"You know ... I might have lied."

"How?"

I pulled onto the street, and once I got into second gear, my hand returned to her leg, crawling toward the heat. "I told you that everything I'll do is to make you feel good, but asking you to show me your pussy was for me, not you." My thumb was the first to reach her. I swiped it over her lips, the dampness spreading to me. It made me fucking moan. "And this—what I'm about to do to you—is going to be just as much for me as it will be for you."

Her breathing was coming out in pants. "That doesn't sound like a problem or a lie."

I chuckled as I went higher, wedging in my thumb until I hit that sensitive spot at the very top. "You're dripping."

"You haven't even felt all of me yet."

"Now, that's one sexy reply." I kept my thumb there while I turned the wheel at the light. "Sadie, I'm going to need you to shift for me ... unless you want me to stop what I'm doing—"

"I don't know how. I've never driven a standard before."

"Put your hand on the gearshift." I waited until she followed my instruction, and that was when my pointer finger began to dip into her pussy.

"Lockhart!"

"Fuck, you're tight."

I dived in deeper, going past my knuckle, only halting because I'd reached the end of my finger and I couldn't go any further. I left it in her for a few seconds while she pulsed around me, and I began to bounce it inside her, in and out, each thrust aimed toward her G-spot.

"Oh my God!" she screamed.

The smile was pulling so hard at my fucking lips. "When I give you the signal, I need you to push up on the gearshift."

I stole a glance at her. She was clutching my wrist with her head tilted back and her eyes closed.

"Sadie ..."

"This feels too good to focus on anything other than what you're doing to me."

My thumb was now rubbing her clit, the combination causing every one of her breaths to come out as a moan. Even the inhales. And each one echoed through my chest as though they were entering my mouth.

"Do you want me to stop?"

"No!"

"Then you have to shift. Put your hand there. Get ready." As my foot pressed down on the gas pedal, my finger moved faster as well, my thumb matching its pace.

A move that wasn't really fair—all it did was work her up

and make the multitasking nearly impossible for her—but I couldn't help it. I wanted her yelling even louder.

Which earned me a, "Fuck!"

And knowing I was the cause of that reaction was so hot.

"All right, Sadie, shift."

She followed my instruction.

And because of that, I rewarded her, twisting my finger, pumping my hand in a way that added even more pressure than what she was already feeling. But that was only half of it. The other part was what I was doing to her clit. I wasn't pushing hard enough to grind against it. I just gave her the kind of friction that one of those toys she had spoken about would do.

What I got was a scream. One that came out in waves. And a hissing of, "Don't stop," followed.

I wouldn't.

Not until her pussy squeezed me from the inside. Not until she got so fucking wet that I knew she was having an orgasm.

But I could tell she was close to having one—by her breathing, by her moaning, by the way she was stabbing her nails into the skin around my wrist.

Even though I had all intentions, I still wanted to play, so I said, "Do you think I should let you come?"

"Yes," she cried.

"I don't know ..."

"Lockhart, don't you dare stop—"

Her voice cut off when I increased the speed once again, my finger pounding into her, my thumb circling.

It only took a block.

And the second my front tires were passing through the next light, she was shouting, "Yes," and writhing and shuddering. "Oh, yes—ah!"

I took a peek. I had to. And, fuck, she looked even more gorgeous than I'd thought she would with her hair just as wild as I'd imagined and her lips open and a feral look owning her expression.

"Hell yes, you're giving me everything I want," I told her. "So wet. So tight."

I slowed as much as I could without asking her to shift. And when I was sure she was done, I carefully pulled my fingers away and stepped on the clutch, getting the car into the right gear before I licked her wetness off my skin.

"Shit, you taste good." I glanced at her. "I need more of that on my tongue. One taste wasn't enough."

She bit her lip as she slid her dress down. "Are we at the hotel?"

"We are." I turned the wheel and pulled up to the entrance, where the valet attendants were waiting. "You finished just in time." As I came to a stop, I sucked off the last of her from my hand. "Just so you know, that was only the beginning. Upstairs, in my room, you're going to get a lot more. And you're going to get it again and again."

She smiled. "That good girl I mentioned before? I think she just got a sample of being bad."

"Do you like this new side of you?"

Even in the darkness, I saw the heat spread across her cheeks.

"I think so."

"Being bad was step one. Naughty is next."

TWO

Sadie

Lockhart had a penthouse suite at the Cole and Spade Hotel—the most luxurious hotel chain in the world. He drove an R8. There was a Breitling Premier Tourbillon watch on his wrist, worth over fifty thousand—I only knew because I'd recently attended an event and Breitling was a sponsor—with a black leather band and a silver face. He wore a sports jacket over his striped button-down, jeans that were the right kind of fitted—not ones he'd have to peel off, but ones that showed just how muscular his legs were—and leather loafers.

Details that, to me, screamed money.

There was quite a difference between new money and old. The two had distinct flavors.

New was someone who drove the cheapest Range Rover that had been made just to have "that kind" of vehicle, they had the diamond-encrusted watch band, an outfit where the label was either visible or the designer's name was printed some-where on the clothes. They wanted to be seen.

Old money—they were already seen.

They chose speed and performance over the manufacturer's name, they preferred the sophistication of leather to the bling of diamonds, their labels stayed hidden, but tucked beneath that collar was a brand that came with a several-thousand-dollar price tag.

Lockhart was old money.

Which raised the question, *Who is this man?*

Born and raised in LA and fairly active in the social scene, I knew names. I knew faces. But his wasn't one I recognized.

That was what ate at me while I stood in the center of his suite, my hands on the back of the couch, watching him as he watched me.

Feeling him as he watched me.

There wasn't a part of my body that wasn't tingling from his gaze.

It was like we were animals of prey, waiting for one to make a move so the other could attack. But it wasn't claws that were going to come out. It was teeth, tongues, bodies, naked and sweating.

This was a sexual energy I'd never felt before, which was what I'd tell Bryn, my best friend, when I called her in the morning to explain why I'd texted her a few minutes ago with my location and told her to keep an eye on me. A story that would make her entire year since she'd been begging me to let loose and finally get laid.

Maybe dropping this good-girl persona had something to do with how handsome he was. If I was going to have my first one-night stand, I wanted it to be with someone as sexy as him.

He had thick hair the color of a dark coffee roast, deep green eyes, a nose that didn't get lost on his face, and wide lips that framed the most perfect smile, with a height that had to be around six-three. Above his clothes was a broadness, which told me that beneath were all kinds of muscle and grooves that my hands were dying to touch.

And his scent.

Dear God.

A combo of citrus and cedar, like the one spot in the middle of the woods that had a little less branch coverage and the warmth could seep through.

Lockhart was positioned with his back to the bar, his hands in his pockets. "Are you going to come over here?"

I dragged my fingers over the hard backing of the couch and across the top of the pillows. "I like it over here."

"But I'm not over there."

"No." I drew in air and couldn't believe how hard it was to do that. "But I can still feel you. Don't forget, your finger has only been out of me for a few minutes." An admission that made me blush.

Not because I couldn't believe he had done it, but because I couldn't believe how good it had felt and how quickly he had gotten me off.

"I could never forget … I can still taste you."

Would I ever be able to get that visual out of my head—of him licking me off his fingers? When, every time I zoomed in on his mouth, that was all I could see?

He turned toward the bar. "Do you want a drink?"

"Are you going to have one?"

He faced me again, his arms holding the counter behind him, which tightened his button-down against his—*oh damn*—chest. "Sadie, the only thing I'm drinking tonight is you."

I smiled. "Sounds like you can't get enough."

"I'm sure you'll be saying that to me again after I've tasted you."

I pulled my hands up and crossed my arms. "Haven't you already?"

29

"What happened in the car? That was just a tease."

"Maybe for you." I fanned my face.

"And for you."

My fingers halted midair. "But I came."

"It won't even compare to the way I'll make you feel with my tongue. Or my dick. You can have them both, or you can pick your poison. What do you want, Sadie?"

I shook my head. "The filthiest mouth I've ever heard."

"A mouth you're going to love." When I didn't respond, he added, "And a mouth you're anxious to experience all over your body." He nodded toward me. "Show me where you want it."

"You want me to point? To a spot? On my body?"

"I don't care how you do it. Just guide me." He shifted his weight. "Unless you want me to make that decision for you. In that case, I'll toss you over my shoulder right now and bring you to bed."

"What if I choose the first scenario? The pointing."

"If you do, the rule is, you have to be naked."

I laughed. "Oh, there are rules now?"

"Yes."

"And you want me to just strip off my clothes. Right here. And show you the part of me that's aching for your lips?"

"Fuck yes."

I let out a quick laugh. "The thing is, I get the impression you're serious."

"What would make you think otherwise?" He smiled. "I'm happy to strip off my clothes and point to the spots where I would like *your* mouth."

"You would?"

"Hell yeah."

I couldn't stop biting my lip—was that to hide my smile? I didn't know. I couldn't even think at this point, not when every part of me was on fire.

He put his hands behind his head. "Go ahead. Ladies first." His stare dived as low as it could go since the couch was hiding half of me. "Start with your jacket and then your dress. I know you have nothing on underneath, except for a bra—unless you don't wear those. You can leave the heels on."

I held the sides of my coat. "Do you always get everything you want?"

There was an oversize bucket-style chair across from the couch—a seat that faced me—and that was where he just sat. He crossed his legs, and a grin moved over his expression.

"It's funny you think this is about me. When, really, this is all about you." He skimmed his thumb over his bottom lip. "There's nothing I want more than to make you come over and over tonight—I've told you that. But in order to make that happen, I need you naked. The longer you wait, the longer you go without coming."

This was certainly a one-night stand I would never forget.

"Just so you know, I've done things for you that I've never done for any other man."

His foot tapped the air. "I must have quite the power over you."

"Or you just turn me on so much that I can't help myself."

He moaned. "Or that. Which I really fucking like." He leaned forward, putting his forearms on his legs. "Show me how much I turn you on, Sadie. I want to see if that pussy is wet again."

The jacket—a raincoat style—was long and bulky, and I was eager to shed it. I draped the heavy fabric across the top of the couch. The dress wouldn't be as easy to take off with a high neck and a zipper that ran down the side. Once the zipper was lowered, I would have to lift the dress from the bottom to bring it over my head, leaving me in only a bra.

I wasn't shy of my body. I worked hard to keep myself fit. I just wasn't used to getting naked in front of strangers.

But Lockhart knew me intimately now, so could I still call him a stranger?

"I'm so fucking hard."

My hands were at the bottom of my dress, holding the thick material, getting ready to take it off. "But I'm not even naked yet."

"You don't have to be. It's from the way you're looking at me. The scent of you. The taste ..."

"The scent?"

"A fruity jasmine. I smelled it the second I met you at the door of the restaurant." He put his hand up to his nose. "I can even smell it on me." He paused. "Does all of your skin smell that way?"

"It's my lotion."

"So, the answer is yes."

I nodded.

"Take it all off so I can smell more of you."

I pulled the dress up to my chest and heard, "Jesus fucking Christ," before my head was even through the hole.

I could feel his eyes boring through me as I dropped it on top of my jacket. My skin grew warm as that same gaze traced over me.

"You're breathtaking. Every goddamn inch of you. Wow ... I don't even have words that would do your body justice."

I could barely breathe—his stare was so intense.

"Come here."

My heels clicked on the wood floor as I made my way around the couch and onto the area rug, stopping a few feet in front of his legs.

This wasn't the gaze of a hungry man. This was the gaze of a man who had never eaten.

"I can't believe I get to fuck you tonight." His eyes roamed to my heels and slowly rose. "Take off your bra."

There was something so sensual about the pace of this and how it was all unfolding. About his orders. About the way he wanted to inhale me, but he kept his hands to himself.

I reached behind my back and unclasped the red lace, freeing each breast before I let the bra fall to the floor.

"I didn't think you could look more gorgeous than what I saw a few seconds ago, but I was so fucking wrong." He rubbed his lips together. "You, naked, is a whole different level."

Each second of silence made me hotter.

Wetter.

"You have my mouth." He nodded like he was confirming what he'd just said. "Where do you want it?"

The pointing.

I'd almost forgotten.

My hands were hanging at my sides, and I lifted them to circle my breasts.

"Fuck yes," he groaned. "Your nipples ... right where I wanted to start."

The only way to give him those was to straddle him.

So, I walked toward his knees, separating my legs to fit around his thighs, his cologne wafting up my nose as I lowered onto his lap.

This was the closest we'd been.

And I found myself holding in my breath, my heart pounding in my chest, my arms not knowing where to go, so I set them on his shoulders.

The unfamiliarity of all this made me study his face—hair, eyes, nose, mouth—to get acquainted. Every feature was new. Fresh. Inviting.

Achingly sexy.

"Hi."

I smiled at his greeting. "Hi."

His teeth ran across his bottom lip as he took me in. "You know ... I haven't kissed you yet."

"I know—"

His hand was suddenly on my cheek. Although the movement was fast, his touch was gentle. "I want to change that ..." Before he even finished speaking, his mouth neared, and when his voice trailed off, his lips were on mine.

Where his grip was soft, his mouth was fierce. A tongue that had no trepidation about coming in, lips that molded between mine and sucked until he pulled away and I found myself leaning in for more.

Because whatever that just was, it wasn't enough.

He chuckled. "My mouth isn't done with you, don't worry."

The breathlessness—where was it coming from?

The pounding in my chest—why was it increasing?

Who was this man, and how did he have this kind of power?

Something else he hadn't done since we'd arrived in this room was touch me. But it finally happened, and I heard myself draw in air as his palms massaged my hips, rotating to cover the sides of my stomach and again toward my lower back. A path he followed several times.

"Pinch your nipples for me. Get them even harder before I lick them."

My thumbs ran across the pebbled buds, each pass causing my breathing to climb before my index finger joined to clamp them. "Ah!"

He kept his gaze locked with mine, so confident that I would follow his order that he didn't need to see the action—he only wanted to see the reaction. "My turn."

His mouth approached, his speed unhurried, as if he was testing his control. When he reached me, he ran his nose across the side of my chest, avoiding the middle and going straight to the opposite section. "You smell so fucking good."

I could feel his quick inhales and his slow exhales.

I gripped the wide, fabric-covered armrests and arched backward while he locked our stares and took one of my nipples into his mouth.

There wasn't any music playing, but I swore I could hear a beat as his tongue flicked. As his teeth nipped. As he sucked the end, pulling without releasing.

"Lockhart ..." My head fell back, and I was no longer able to watch his movements, each one coming as a surprise—and that was just what they did, causing the air to sigh through my lips. "Agh."

"More?"

"Yes," I cried.

So, that was what he gave me.

A throb that he was supposed to be alleviating only grew. The churning between my legs became so feisty that I slid my hand through his hair and tightened my grip, my head straightening so I could look at him.

And with my other hand, I pointed to that nagging spot. "Here."

The smile that came across him made the feeling inside me burst.

"You know, I've been dreaming about the taste of your cunt."

I swore his eyes were smoldering.

"I want you to sit on my face."

"Where? On the chair?"

He held on to my ass, and he slid us down so his head was resting on the very edge of the top cushion, his long body extended across the seat, his knees bent, holding what was no longer supported by the chair. "All you have to do is straddle my mouth."

He was right. The chair was low enough that I could balance in that position with my legs hanging over the fabric sides.

He tapped my butt cheek. "Get up there. I want to fucking eat you."

His statement didn't cover me like a blanket. It lit a match beneath me, and I wasn't running from the fire; I was sprinting toward it.

I climbed up, wiggling past his chest to spread out my legs, and when I got to his neck, I realized the only things I'd be able to hold on to in this position were my thighs.

But the second his mouth was on me, I lost all sense of where I was anyway because the only thing I could focus on was his tongue.

"Oh my God!"

I couldn't distinguish what direction he was even licking me in; I felt it everywhere. At the top, bottom, swiping the middle, movements that weren't slow. He was lapping me as though he wanted me to come.

And I was lost, drowning in pleasure, screaming out moans. "Oh! Yes!"

I'd never been with anyone like him. Someone this experienced. This knowledgeable.

This man didn't need a map. This man was the author of the map.

So, I couldn't stop the orgasm from building. I couldn't even attempt to slow it.

It was coming on fast, hard, and with a ferociousness that was completely taking ahold of me.

"Lockhart—"

"I know. And I want you to come on my face."

His demand came with puffs of air that sent me even further over the edge. But that edge was a dangerous place. If I wasn't careful, I'd fall off the chair, and if I rocked too hard, I would tip us right over.

A scary scenario, considering I no longer had control of my body and the feeling that was rising through me was making every bit of me shudder.

"Fuck!" I held on to my thighs while the waves of tingles exploded through my abdomen. "Don't! Stop!" I heard myself say, then shouted out his name.

I felt my body swaying forward and back to the rhythm of his tongue. I sensed his hands on the bottom of my legs and the hardness of his chest beneath my ass.

But the only thing that was really holding me, shackling me, imprisoning me, and not letting me go were the tingles. The way they lifted through me, the way they burst, and the way they finally trickled to a whispering stop.

"*Mmm*. Yes," he moaned, which sounded like a growl, especially as his licking turned to kissing, giving me tender pecks along my clit. "You're the best thing I've ever tasted."

My eyes fluttered closed. "I—"

"You're coming with me." He picked me up, my legs now straddling his waist, my arms flopping onto his shoulders, and he carried me through the suite. "I want you to know how good you taste. Kiss me."

My wetness was all over him—on his lips, the tip of his nose, the skin on each side of his mouth, even his scruff was glowing.

I smiled, but I didn't move.

"Kiss me, Sadie."

My fingers spread over the back of his head, sinking into his hair, and when I went to lean in to simply press my mouth to his, he didn't let that happen. He dived into me, parting my lips with his tongue, dominating me the same way he'd just done between my legs.

There was that match again, igniting a flame that I'd thought, after my second orgasm tonight, couldn't be relit.

But I was wrong.

He laid me on the bed, and while he continued to kiss me, he got to work on his clothes. I helped, kicking off my heels so I could use my feet to push down his jeans once he unbuckled his belt and button and zipper. I pulled the lapels of his sports coat to free his arms and at the buttons of his shirt, each item flying to the floor as they were freed from his body.

Once he was naked, he got off me and reached toward the ground, returning with his wallet and the two condoms he took out of it. As he stood straight, tearing off the metal corner with his teeth, I got a direct view of his body.

Every suspicion I'd had didn't compare to what I was seeing now.

A chest that was etched, dusted with the perfect amount of hair to run my fingers through, pecs and abs that were defined, dips of muscle that wound around his arms and across his shoulders. My stare dived, and what it met caused my jaw to drop.

"What are you?"

He chuckled as he aimed the condom at the tip of his large, erect dick. "What kind of question is that?"

"Well, you've turned this good girl into a bad girl—something I didn't think was possible. You've got a body to die for. You're hung." My eyes widened to emphasize that point. "Lockhart, you feel like a dream. Am I going to wake up tomorrow and that's what this is all going to be?"

"Let me tell you why that won't be the case." He grabbed the outside of my thighs and pulled me toward the end of the bed. "When you wake up and squeeze your legs together, you're going to feel soreness from what I did to you. You don't get that from a dream." He lifted my hand and placed it on his abs, rubbing it up and down each groove.

God, this guy was all kinds of arrogant.

"And this—this body—it's too real. Nothing can feel this good when you're asleep." He pointed his crown at my entrance, his eyes holding mine as he slowly slid into me. "Or this—fuck." His Adam's apple bobbed as he groaned. "But I'll give it to you—it's hard to believe anything can be this incredible." He hissed out an exhale. "Or how you could be this tight. But, fuck me, you are."

I'd thought I was lost with his tongue, but that was an aimless wandering compared to this.

"Damn!" I drove the back of my head into the mattress while I took in his full length, my body swallowing every inch. "This isn't just incredible, this is wildly the best."

Did that even make sense?

I had no idea; my brain was mush.

He let out a chuckle and lifted me again, holding me around him in the air while he pumped into me. "Wildly the best, huh? Let's see if I can make it even better."

I didn't know how better was an option.

But I quickly learned he was looking to achieve it as he placed my back against the wall, holding me there with his weight. "You're about to have round three." He was twisting his hips with each plunge, arching upward so he wasn't just hitting my walls; he was grazing my G-spot too.

"You're not going to make me come again that fast," I panted.

"No? Because I can feel it." He put his lips by my ear. "Your cunt is closing in around me and getting extra wet. Your clit is getting hard. Your breathing is labored."

I moaned in response.

"Exactly." His mouth went to mine. "Are you going to deny it? And say I don't know your body?"

"You don't."

"But I've made you come twice tonight. About to be a third. I'd say I know it well enough."

I hauled myself up, the paint and texture and hardness of the wall burning my back as I bounced, trying to meet each of his thrusts. The pleasure was just spreading faster than I could handle. "You're not wrong."

"I know."

I let out a gasp as I neared that familiar place. "I want you to come with me."

"That's what you want?"

I hugged his chest against mine, using his shoulders to lift and drop. "Yes."

"Only if you make me a promise."

"Which is?"

"After I come inside you, I can take you into the shower and fuck you again in there."

My hand spread across his cheek. "You only have one condom left. That's where you want me? In the shower?"

"I can have more delivered in less than ten minutes, so I don't have to choose where I want to have you. If you let me, I can fuck you over and over and over again."

"Negotiations during sex—something else I've never done." I smiled. "Deal."

As soon as the approval left my lips, something triggered inside him. Because everything I'd experienced so far was now entirely different.

And I didn't know how, but it was even better.

"Oh! *Ohhh!*" I couldn't stop the sounds from coming out of me.

Because he was going deeper, faster, grinding against me in

a way that hit my clit at the same time.

I couldn't meet him in the middle anymore. I couldn't turn my hips to buck into him. All I could do was hold on.

So, I gripped his shoulders and pressed our mouths together and let his words, "I'm going to fucking come," fuel my orgasm.

It was already there.

As his strokes turned rougher, which I was begging for, it peaked, and I yelled, "Lockhart!"

"Let me fucking feel it." His thrusts turned short, sharp, and rapid. "Sadie, yes! I'm coming with you!"

I was shuddering, the crests shaking my chest, my stomach; they were even going through my thighs. My breaths came out in blows. My fingers lost their strength, my body too numb, and they were unable to hold on.

But within a few seconds, he started to slow, his mouth devouring mine until he eventually came to a stop. He pressed our noses together while we breathed against each other.

"No dream could ever compete with that," he whispered.

When I pulled back, I snaked my finger through the sweat on his forehead. "No. It certainly couldn't."

"Are you ready for that shower?"

"I could use a little cooling off." I smiled.

He laughed. "You think I'm going to let you cool off in that water?" He pulled me off the wall. "I realize you don't know me, but you should know *that* by now."

CAT

I'm on my way to work. I know it's early, but I also have a feeling you're up. Can I call you?

ME

Are you okay?

CAT

> No, I'm far from okay. I think I'm getting fired the second I walk into work. The whole situation is a disaster, and I have so much I need to get off my chest. Please, I know it's the ass crack of dawn, but I need my sister.

My sister's last message came across my watch, and I carefully maneuvered Lockhart's arm off my chest and tiptoed into the living room.

ME

> Give me 5 minutes, and I'll call you.

CAT

> Hurry!

My dress felt different as I slipped it back on in a rush. So did my jacket and purse. I hadn't remembered taking off the latter, but it was on top of the couch with everything else. Everything except for my heels. I found those on the floor by the bottom of the bed, quietly sliding them on.

Now that I was dressed, I silently stared at Lockhart in the barely lit room, the sun beginning to work its way up the sky. He was on his stomach, stretched out across the mattress. His right arm was still lying in the spot where I had been just moments ago. Only a thin white sheet covered him, showing the hump of his perfect ass, and where it ended on his lower back, the ripples of muscle began.

Amazingly sexy, even when he slept.

CAT

> CALL ME. I'm losing my shit. 6:30 a.m. road rage is a real thing, ya know.

Do I leave the suite without saying goodbye to him? Do I go into the hallway to call my sister and try to find a way back into

the room? Do I wake him up and tell him I'm going out for
privacy and that I'll be right back?

So many options.

And even though I didn't know what was right or what to
do, I knew that this was the morning after, and that part felt
kind of strange. Lockhart and I had only discussed one night.
Breakfast—unknown. How I was going to get back to my car
since I'd left it at the restaurant—unknown. The whereabouts
of a room key that I could use to go to the hallway or lobby and
back—also unknown. I wasn't on the reservation. Waking him
up was the only possibility.

As I stood here, debating the different scenarios, I
couldn't drag my stare away from that bed or stop thinking
about the woman who had helped ruffle up those sheets and
toss that comforter to the floor, along with most of the
pillows.

He had turned me into one bad girl.

Or maybe I was just a good girl who had turned bad for one
night.

One long, naughty night.

My teeth found my lip as the first scene started to rewind
and replay in my head—the feel of his leather seat under my
bare ass, the coldness of the window as I'd pressed my back
against it.

The sensation of screaming in his front seat.

God, last night was the best sex I'd ever had in my life.

CAT

SADIE!

My teeth released my lip, and my cheeks puffed out with
air as I could hear my sister screaming through text.

She needed me.

And it didn't matter how tempted I was to wake him—he

43

had emphasized how long things would last between us, and I'd heard him loud and clear.

I turned around to let myself out, and as I took a step toward the door, I felt it.

The soreness between my legs.

If I wasn't trying to keep quiet, I would have laughed.

Damn that man.

THREE

Hart

The door to the suite slammed behind me as I rolled my small suitcase down the hallway toward the elevator, taking it to the first floor and stopping by the front desk to hand back the key.

"Thank you, Mr. Weston," the front-desk clerk said, taking the thin piece of plastic I had slid toward her. "Checking out, I see."

The personal greeting was always noticed and appreciated whenever I stayed at a Cole and Spade Hotel. My face was known at these establishments since we'd built Charred into a majority of their lobbies.

"I am."

"How was your stay?"

I tapped my finger on the counter. "Too short."

"Well, hopefully, we'll see you back soon. Can I get you a bellhop to assist with your luggage?" She lifted the receiver of her phone.

45

"That won't be needed. Thank you."

"Does the valet know you're leaving? I'll call and get your car—"

"Already taken care of."

She set the phone back down and nodded. "Have a wonderful day, Mr. Weston, and thank you for staying with us."

I thanked her and walked out of the lobby, where my car was waiting out front. I handed the valet the bills that I'd tucked into my palm, and while he put my suitcase into the small trunk, I got into the driver's seat.

I hadn't even reached for my seat belt, the door not even closed, when I smelled her.

The fruity jasmine.

The scent wasn't strong, like she was sitting in the car with me, but strong enough that my eyes closed and the hottest breath exhaled through my nose.

Immediately, my brain went back to last night.

When she'd stripped off her clothes and revealed her body. When she sat on my fucking face on the chair in the living room. When I held her against the wall in the bedroom. When I tasted her again in the shower. When I'd positioned her on the dresser, using the second condom before I had more delivered.

An evening of fucking.

That was all it had been.

So, why had there been disappointment when I woke up this morning and reached for her and she wasn't there? And when I had seen that she hadn't left a note? And why was I aching for her now?

"Can I get you anything, Mr. Weston?"

My eyes opened. The valet was standing outside the driver's door, holding it like he wanted to close it for me.

"No," I replied.

He shut my door, and my hand went to the gearshift, my foot on the clutch, my gaze pointed at the driveway ahead.

But I didn't move.

At least not forward.

What I did instead was reach for the button to roll down the passenger window and got the valet's attention as he stood a few feet away.

"When did you start your shift this morning?"

"At six, sir."

"Did you see a woman come out here? I don't know if it was around that time—earlier or later. She was wearing an emerald-green dress, long black jacket, sky-high heels. Black hair." My jaw tightened. "She's gorgeous."

"A woman who meets that description did come down."

My chest tightened. "And I'm assuming she was picked up?"

"Yes, sir. By a rideshare."

I nodded and rolled the window back up, shifting into first to pull out of the entrance and onto the road. I wondered why she had preferred to take a rideshare rather than waiting for me to wake up and take her to her car at the restaurant.

An answer I was sure I'd never get.

I wasn't even a mile past the hotel when Brady Spade's name came across the screen of my dashboard. He was one of the owners of the hotel chain, a longtime business partner, and one of my best friends.

I connected the call. "Brady, what's good, my man?"

"Just checking to see how your stay was in our Laguna Beach location. You know, since I'm Mr. Customer Fucking Service."

I laughed. "You're hardly that, my friend."

The Cole and Spade Hotel brand was made up of seven equal partners. Three Spade brothers, their cousin, and three

Cole siblings. Out of all of them, Brady and Rhett Cole certainly took the crown for the grumpiest.

"And we both know that's not why you're calling. Is everything all right?"

"Everything is great. I just wanted to let you know I'll be back in LA in a few weeks. It's been a while since my family, the Coles, and your family have all been out. Let's put something together and hit up the town."

Most of the partners, when building or renovating a new hotel, ended up living on location until the construction was finished. My buddy had been all over the world with brief stints in LA between build-outs. And since he'd gotten married, I had seen him even less.

"Send me the dates," I told him, turning at the light. "Maybe Beck will have a home game that night. We can start the evening in our suite and go out from there."

"I like the way you think."

My phone beeped, the dashboard showing Walker's name on the screen. There was no doubt in my mind why he was reaching out this early.

"Fuck me," I groaned. "I've got Walker calling on the other line, and I'm sure he's about to ream my ass out."

"Is it over a woman?"

I chuckled. "Isn't it always?"

"Single and reckless—things I don't miss." He laughed. "I'll text you the dates, brother."

I said goodbye and clicked over. "Walker—"

"How did it go last night?"

"Jesus," I sighed. "How about a *good morning*? Or, *Hart, are you on your way back to LA*? Or, *Did you get in safely—*"

"Whether you're still in Laguna or on your way back doesn't concern me in the slightest. Stay there all week if that suits you. I want to know about Horned, which is why I sent you there in the first place and why I'm calling this early."

I turned down the volume to the speakers. "Did something crawl up your ass this morning?"

"The second I opened my eyes and lifted my phone off my nightstand, there was another glowing review for Horned on my fucking screen, saying how delectably ingenious of a restaurant it is. That's one. Two, I have a tiny fucking window to talk to you before I'm headed into meetings all day, and then I'll be in the kitchen for the unforeseeable future. And three, if you think I get off on calling you this early, I don't. I'm tired, I'm overworked, and I want shit to get done the way I want it done. Since I can't clone myself, I have to rely on the four of you. So, patience is not something I possess at the moment, Hart."

Walker in the kitchen was like a surgeon in the operating room. A space where he was fully focused and didn't want any interruptions. He was also the inventor of every dish that was served in our large collection of restaurants. Without him, we wouldn't have a product or a billion-dollar empire. But that wasn't where his attitude came from. That was because the man never slept.

"You have exactly six minutes to give me every detail," he continued.

I glanced at the time on my dash. It was 7:54.

I slowed at the light and exhaled. "It's not going to take me six minutes. It's not even going to take two minutes."

"I don't like the sound of this, Hart ..."

"What I'm going to say next, you're going to like even less." *Fuck.* Listening to him lose his shit wasn't how I wanted to start this day. But I knew it was coming—and I supposed, in some way, I deserved it. "I didn't eat dinner at Horned. I left after my second old-fashioned."

"Explain yourself."

It would be easier to tell him I hadn't felt good and gone back to the hotel to crash. But I didn't lie, and I especially wouldn't lie to my brother.

I shifted into third, the engine revving at the same time I said, "I met a woman."

"You're fucking kidding me."

I waited until it felt right, and when that moment never came, I replied, "I'm not."

"You're telling me you went to Laguna Beach for the night, booked a hotel so you wouldn't have to drive home, went to a restaurant I'd assigned you to eat at—not as a personal assignment, but as a work one—and you aborted the mission. For a fucking woman."

"That's what I'm telling you."

"Hart ..." His tone was sharp and unforgiving. "I asked you for one thing, and you chose pussy."

"It wasn't just pussy. It was the best pussy I've ever had in my life." I rubbed my hand around the leather of the steering wheel, like it was the skin of Sadie's navel, and I smiled. "I'll head back to Laguna sometime in the next week and have dinner at Horned."

"Don't bother. I'll send Eden. At least I know she won't find some random dude and go home with him instead of completing the task."

"Walker, that's a little extreme."

"Call it anything you want, but I'm not giving up our placement as the best steak house in Laguna to some fucking no-name chef and a backer with a large bankroll. We've worked far too hard to get to where we are."

"We're not losing anything, don't worry." I huffed out some air as I slowed for the light, knowing I needed to change the mood. "For what it's worth, she was gorgeous. I'm talking the most gorgeous ever."

50

"Do you think that helps your defense?" He waited. "It's not like she's going to become your wife or, shit, even your girlfriend. Knowing you, you didn't even get her number."

"Says the dude who's forever single ..."

"Because if I'm not in a goddamn meeting, I'm in the kitchen. How the hell am I supposed to find a woman when I'm married to a fucking gas range?"

I laughed. "Just don't stick it in that gas range, please."

"Asshole."

I came to a stop at the red light. "I want you to know, the only reason I didn't get this one's number is because she'd left this morning while I was still asleep."

"You're telling me, if you'd been awake, you would have asked for her number?"

Those images that had come into my head earlier, the ones that recapped last night, reappeared. "Maybe." I bit my lip, remembering another interesting twist to the evening, and I reached into my pocket, pulling out her red lace panties, and held them to my nose. Goddamn, that scent. If she was in this car, I'd pull over right here and eat that pussy. "But if I could be guaranteed a repeat of last night, fuck yes."

"I'm sure you can find her. There's this thing called Google, you know."

"I never got her last name."

He laughed. "Of course you didn't." He continued, "Do you regret that?"

"Doesn't matter."

"I don't know, Hart, I think it does. In all the years and all the women you've slept with, I've never heard you talk about getting one of their numbers."

I tucked the panties back into my pocket as the light turned green and shifted into first. "There's no way I can get it, so there's no point in even talking about it."

"Just like I thought, you regret it."

"First you come at me about not eating dinner, and now you're making me feel like shit that I didn't get her fucking number." I shook my head. "If you were in front of me, I'd flip you off."

"And since I'm not?"

"I'm going to hang up on you ... dickhead."

FOUR

Sadie

M y fingers tapped on the keyboard while I sat at the desk in my home office, but not a single one of those letters appeared on the screen. Because I wasn't actually pushing the keys. I was just gently clicking my nails against them, hoping that the article would miraculously write itself.

Next to my monitor, my phone sat on a holder, showing the most recent article that had been written about Horned, describing it as delectably ingenious. Whoever the writer was, they were creative. I swiped my thumb across the screen to toggle to the other three articles I'd found on the restaurant, hoping they would inspire something for me to write. Each one mentioned the cuisine was divine, the space was modern and inviting, the cocktail list was original.

What could I write?

That I had seen the entrance and a little of the vibe of the bar—most of which I hadn't paid attention to since I was too focused on Lockhart—and I finished half of my old-fashioned before I was swept into his car.

But this article was due yesterday, and I was avoiding my boss at *Seen*—LA's most-read publication—like the plague, and he'd already emailed me twice.

How could I write this though?

I hadn't eaten there. I'd done nothing more than smell the food, and even that hadn't stood out because my nose was too mesmerized by Lockhart's cologne. Giving my opinion on anything that related to the restaurant—something I did for a living—wouldn't be fair. Or honest.

And I prided myself on writing the most genuine, unbiased food reviews.

I'd email my boss back once I thought of a way to tell him the truth. An excuse that could only be encouraged by an extremely strong martini, which meant I needed to text Bryn and convince her to go out with me tonight.

And just as I was about to, I caught a glimpse of the far side of my office, where I filmed some of my content, and stared at the neon sign that hung on the wall, showing a name that was famous in this city.

Dear Foodie.

The name of the most popular food critic from Santa Barbara to San Diego. She had her own weekly column in *Seen* and an online following of over five million, where she showcased her brand deals, food-related traveling, cooking, and love of eating. She was a woman with an eclectic palate and a desire to consume all cuisine.

With a face no one had ever seen, she was as mysterious as she was in demand.

And not a single person—other than my boss, Bryn, my parents, and my sister—knew she was me.

Beneath the white neon sign was a very tall, very unsteady

pile of boxes, and I scanned the exterior of them, trying to locate the one that housed the cookware I would need for today's shoot. A brand had sent me their pots and pans with a six-figure check, and contractually, I was obligated to post their cookware at least four times over the next month.

On today's agenda was an instructional cooking video, using two of their frying pans that I needed to have shot, edited, and uploaded for tomorrow's morning post.

I walked over to the stack of boxes, the cookware most definitely on the bottom, given the size of the cardboard, and I moved the top one, going box by box until I reached the last one. They'd sent their full line, so there was no way this could be the only box. I checked the other four stacks in my office, and as I was about to go into my living room, where there were another five mountains of boxes, my phone rang.

Shit.

He was going to murder me for not responding to his emails.

Can I send him to voice mail?

How horrible would that be?

It would be horrible, considering he was already furious with me, and if I didn't answer, that would only make things even worse.

Bracing for impact, I held the phone up to my ear. "Hi—"

"Oh. You're alive. I was wondering if my next call was going to be to the local hospitals to find out if you'd been admitted."

I winced. "I know. I wanted to reply to your email—"

"But you didn't." He exhaled loudly. "Sadie, when I email you, I expect a response. When I email you twice, you either need to be admitted somewhere where they've confiscated your phone or you're too ill to look at it, you're on a silent retreat in a town I've never heard of, or you're in the morgue."

I deserved that and said, "Understood." I swallowed. "And I'm sorry. It was so wrong of me. It's not because I couldn't make my deadline—you know how I am about turning things in on time, I'm always the queen of rocking every deadline."

"Which is where the confusion comes in. This isn't like you. So, what's going on?"

I took a deep breath, thinking of that evening. "I went to Horned ... but I didn't end up eating. I left after having a cocktail. And I didn't see enough of the restaurant or engage with the staff or even sample the food, therefore, I don't feel qualified to write the article."

"And you didn't know how to tell me."

My head dropped. "Yes, and I feel terrible about that. I'm sorry."

He sighed. "You know we've promised our readers that Horned was getting reviewed this week. We've been building it up, teasing it. Our readers trust us. And because they trust us and they know we deliver on our promises, they're loyal."

I wrapped an arm around my stomach. "Which is another reason I didn't reach out."

"Is there a reason you haven't gone back to Horned to eat? You didn't mention why you'd left, so I'm unsure if something happened in the restaurant or—"

"No, nothing like that. I left"—I glanced around my large office, trying to think of what to say—"for personal reasons. Reasons that had nothing to do with the restaurant. And I haven't been back because I've been slammed. I had an event last night, and I've been filming content and ..." My excuses sounded weak, but they were the truth.

I needed an assistant and to stop saying yes to everything and to find a balance; work was dominating almost every part of my life. Even though it should have been a priority, driving back to Laguna Beach was the last thing I wanted.

"Sadie, help me out here. What am I going to tell our readers when your column is one extremely glaring section of emptiness?"

Silence ticked between us.

"I'll go to Horned tonight," I told him.

"What?" He laughed. "You'll never be able to get in. They're booked out for months."

"Then I'll eat in the bar. Or I'll find another way in. Trust me, I'll get it done." I waited, and he said nothing. "Please, let me fix this. I messed up, I was wrong, and I want to make it right."

"If the article is in my hands by tomorrow morning, I'll forget we even had this conversation. I won't forget that you didn't respond to my email—don't let that happen again—but you'll be forgiven."

"Deal."

The phone went dead, and I continued to hold it in my palm, staring at the home screen, my brain reeling with everything I needed to accomplish tonight. Dear Foodie could get into any restaurant in the state within a second. Sadie? Not so much.

But I would figure this out. I had to.

My weekly article in *Seen* had been the start of my career in the food business, and it began the foundation of my social media following. Without them, I wouldn't have grown into what I had today.

I would never forget that.

I pulled up my Contacts and my Favorites, hitting the number for my best friend, and as soon as it started ringing, I returned the phone to my ear.

"She's calling me midday rather than texting," Bryn said as she answered. "Which tells me this is going to be major. Hold on. I need to sit down." She paused. "Okay, I'm ready. Hit me with it."

I laughed. "I love you."

"I love you more. Are you all right?"

My stare wandered over my office as I calculated how much time it would take to film the cooking video and have it edited, and then wash and dry my hair for dinner because the way I looked at the moment was terrifying. "Do you have plans tonight?"

"Sounds like I do now. What kind of trouble are you going to get me into?"

I rolled my eyes. "Because I've got Miss Trouble written all over me."

"Miss Bad Girl is more like it."

"Oh God, stop. We're not going there *again*. We've talked out the whole Lockhart night forward and backward and sideways."

"And I could hear it one more time, and it would feel like the first."

And I could repeat it over and over, and it would never be enough.

I wondered if Lockhart thought about that night the way I did. If he wished I'd woken him up before I left.

If he regretted not getting my number before we fell asleep.

"Moving on," I groaned. "So, because I was a bad girl that night, I didn't get enough info to write my article on the restaurant, and my boss isn't happy with me. That's why I'm calling. Do you want to go there with me tonight?"

"You know I'd never say no."

"Well, you need to know what you're getting into. You might just rethink that answer."

"Okay ..."

I moved back to my desk and took a seat. "I don't have a

reservation. We could be waiting there all night and still not get in."

"Nonsense. We'll get in. I'll pull out some sorcery if I have to."

I shook my mouse, watching my inbox refresh with brand deals and social media notifications. "I'm afraid to ask what kind of sorcery you're talking about."

"Just make sure you have cash on you. Like a hundred-dollar bill. You know, in case we have to tuck it into the hostess's hand."

"Good thinking." I smiled. "So, what you're saying is, you're still in?"

"Babe, I was never out."

I danced in my chair. "I'll pick you up at five. Mwah."

Is Horned worth the three-month waiting list to get in? Is their signature filet, served Pittsburgh-style with a charred exterior and a medium rare interior, worth twelve dollars an ounce? Is the old-fashioned as sinful as I've heard?
Yes, yes, and absolutely yes.
Sinful on the tongue and heavenly all the way down. And I'm not just speaking about the old-fashioned. That's the way I would describe Horned.
An exquisite meal, flawlessly executed and wickedly satisfying.
Make your reservation, Foodies.

I'd written the two-hundred-word article and let it simmer on the screen while I went into my en suite and got ready for bed, returning to my computer to make sure the last few paragraphs were as strong as they needed to be. I was always hyper-fixated on the conclusion of every piece. Since it was the summary that mattered most—the wrap-up of my final thoughts and whether I believed my readers should take the chance—I normally rewrote it several times before I submitted it to my boss.

I read it one last time and emailed it to my boss, relieved that I'd made things right and this whole incident would be behind us.

Before I could go to bed, I had to confirm that tomorrow's video was scheduled for the morning across each of my channels. Pleased with everything I saw, I returned to Instagram and loaded a new post, choosing one of the photos I'd taken tonight that showed my fingers wrapped around an old-fashioned. My followers knew I tested out the restaurant at least a week before I posted about it, so no one would suspect I was just there this evening; most importantly, Horned's staff wouldn't try to piece anything together. My anonymity was as important to me as the authenticity of my reviews.

I stared at the picture until a caption came to me, and I began to type.

Horned: Is it sinfully delicious? Or overpriced and overhyped? My full review will be in Friday's edition of Seen. See you there, Foodies.

Within seconds, hundreds of likes began to flutter in and the comment section exploded. The hype was already there, and come Friday, the readers would be too.

I hoped to hell this made my boss a happy man.

FIVE

Hart

When Walker started blowing up the family group chat at six this morning, before I even opened my eyes to head to the gym, I knew Dear Foodie had reviewed Horned in *Seen*, and the feedback—based on the tone of Walker's texts—had to be stellar. He requested we all be in the office by eight when our normal hours started at nine. And there was no question in my mind what this meeting was going to look like.

Everyone in my family followed Dear Foodie online. In this business, specifically in Southern California, she could make or break you. That was the power this one woman held, that was how well she was trusted, and that was how honest she was in her reviews. If she gave your restaurant full praise, your reservations would double, even triple, overnight, which made me fear that Horned was about to take over our title as not only the best, but the most popular steak house in Laguna Beach.

Since Beck had practice, that left Eden, Colson, and me sitting around the conference room table, twiddling our goddamn thumbs as we waited for Walker to join us. By the sound of everyone's exhales, the deepness of our sighs, and the size of our to-go coffee cups, we knew this was going to be one hell of a start to an already-shitty day.

"Have you guys checked out Dear Foodie's Instagram this morning?" Eden asked, looking at Colson and then me.

I nodded.

"Sure have," Colson replied.

"Have either of you seen her review?" Eden inquired.

Dear Foodie never posted her weekly *Seen* reviews on her social media. She only teased them there, directing her viewers to the source of her article.

"I haven't," I admitted, and Colson signaled that he hadn't either. "I wanted to hear it from Walker."

Eden laughed. "Because we all know he's going to read it to us."

"We'd be idiots to think otherwise." Colson sighed again. For the most laid-back man I knew, there was an edge of worry in his expression. "He's concerned, you guys. And Walker doesn't get concerned easily. But this one, it's really getting to him."

I thought about what my brother had just said. "That's because he knows something we don't."

"What gives you that impression?" Eden asked.

I turned my chair toward her. "A new restaurant opens up every day in this area, and he doesn't sweat it. Only a handful have come in over the years that have really ruffled Walker's feathers. For each of those occasions, there's one common denominator."

She pushed up her glasses, the thick black frames only worn when she was too tired to put in her contacts. "The opportunity to franchise."

"Yes." I ran my hand over my scruff. "You nailed it."

Colson adjusted his tie, pulling it down a few inches and unbuttoning the top of his shirt. "The last thing any one of us wants, especially Walker, is a Horned opening in every market that Charred is located."

I smiled. "There's one way to solve that—"

"*Sinful on the tongue and heavenly all the way down*," Walker barked after the door to the conference room flew open and he came in, reading the printed publication that was in his hand. "*And I'm not just speaking about the old-fashioned. That's the way I would describe Horned. An exquisite meal, flawlessly executed and wickedly satisfying. Make your reservation, Foodies.*" Standing at the head, he let the paper drop to the table and took a seat. "You have got to be fucking kidding me!"

"With the buzz surrounding this restaurant, none of us should be surprised," I said. "But take it from someone who's been there—there's a lot left to be desired."

Walker set his arms on the table. The buttoned sleeves of his chef's coat didn't make a sound when they landed; the noise had come from his hands as they slammed down. "Like?"

"They don't even have valet parking." I chuckled. "What fucking five-star restaurant with prices like they charge doesn't offer a parking service?"

Which had certainly come in handy that night. The back row of the lot was the perfect spot to sink my finger into Sadie's pussy—a pussy I hadn't stopped thinking about—so I hadn't complained then about the lack of valet parking, but I was definitely complaining about it now.

"Because they don't have to," Eden said softly. "Take it from someone who's *actually* been there and sampled the food." She glanced at me and smiled. "It was quite the experience."

She pulled out her phone and tapped her screen, which turned on the TV in the conference room. The photos from her phone then appeared on the flat screen. "I took pictures of everything I could." As each photo flipped to the next, she made sure we knew what we were looking at, saying, "The exterior of the building, the entrance, the hostess stand, the bar, dining room, and finally the ladies' room." A few seconds passed. "And now, onto the food." At least fifteen shots followed of a meal that looked incredible.

At the end of the slideshow, Colson said, "The interior looks nothing like Charred."

"I think that's part of the appeal," Eden replied. "Where we have a classic steak house feel with a modern, elegant twist, Horned feels nothing of the sort. I dare say, it's almost an overly sexy vibe. We have traditional decor with garnet and mahogany accents, dark wood, and dim lighting. Horned is chrome and mirrors with furnishings done in emerald and sapphire."

Walker let out a whistle of air in response.

I crossed my hands and set them in my lap. "What they've done—and it kills me to fucking say this—is by creating a non–steak house feel, they're attracting people who are coming in for everything but. Seafood isn't just an alternative, it could be the reason they're walking through the door." I leaned back in my chair and stared at Walker. "An environment with ambiance that welcomes all eaters."

"You're not helping the situation," Walker said.

"I'm being honest. When you come into any Charred, you know the main attraction. You see it in the colors, you smell it in the air. There are no surprises. Our eaters enjoy that."

"But is the temperature changing?" Eden questioned. "Are we not advancing with the times?"

The room turned silent.

"But we've implemented changes," Colson voiced, holding out his hand to check off each item I knew he was about to mention. "We now offer a vegan option as well as a vegetarian course. Allergens are listed beside every dish—something you hardly find in any restaurant in America and never at steak houses. We offer more health-conscious staples and side dishes, we've tweaked recipes to eliminate high-saturated fat fillers and seed oils, and in many of our locations, we're farm to table."

"But is that enough?" Walker asked.

His voice boomed across the room, and a quietness followed.

"The opening of Toro is going to give us that answer," Colson said. "It proved to be true in our first location in Denver, but that's an unfair assessment because there, it's a market we dominate. Same with Banff—there's nothing like it in that part of Alberta. But here, in LA, there are some heavy hitters in the seafood and raw bar space. It's going to be very telling if the concept is embraced and the feedback is positive."

"That doesn't fix what's happening with Charred," I countered.

"Nothing is happening with Charred," Walker shot back.

Eden crossed her arms over her chest. "And who knows what Dear Foodie's review will be when she eats at Toro?"

"And there's that," I replied.

As Walker looked at me, I could see his brain reeling.

"We need her there."

As the chief marketing officer, one of my many tasks was getting us reviews and ratings, so it was up to me to promise, "She'll come."

"How can you be sure of that?" he asked. "She never reviewed Charred."

I pushed back from the table and crossed my legs. "Because we were established long before she came on the scene. Her focus is on new. And we're going to be new." I rubbed my hands over my knee. "Don't worry, I have some ideas on how to ensure she's there."

"Ideas?" Walker asked.

"You know this is where I thrive." I nodded toward him. "Just trust me."

"And what if her review of Toro is a repeat of the post she did of the bar at Charred Manhattan?" Eden asked.

Walker groaned, "That would be my worst fucking nightmare," and covered his face with his hands.

"I could think of worse situations," Colson chimed in. "But, yeah, that was bad—I can't lie."

As we all gazed at each other, we remembered the one and only time Dear Foodie had given us a shout-out.

She had happened to be in Manhattan and stopped at the bar at Charred. Whether she ate there, we didn't know; her post on Instagram only included a photo of her espresso martini. That was something she did often when she traveled— she shared pictures of food and drinks and all things restaurant-related. They weren't reviews; they were just teases of her life in photographs. In the one she did for Charred Manhattan, the glassware looked fantastic in her hands, which were wrapped around the thin stem, the coffee beans shaped like a clover as they floated across the dark liquid. Even her caption—*My second coffee of the day*—was fantastic.

But when one of her viewers asked in the comments how the drink was, she replied, *Average.*

A response that sent Walker into a spiral.

So, the next day, I had gone into Charred LA and had an espresso martini—a drink I'd normally never get—and, goddamn it, Dear Foodie was right.

The martini was mid—at best.

I had worked with our lead bartender, and we had come up with a whole new recipe that was enforced across the entire company, at every one of our locations.

We listened, we tweaked, we mastered.

I focused on my brother, who was silently losing his shit at the head of the table. "Walker, tell us why this one is fucking you up so badly."

A question none of us had asked him, and it was long overdue.

"I've been doing a little digging, reaching out to my sources, talking to vendors." He rubbed his hands together. "Horned isn't just a restaurant. It's a concept. They're testing it, and if successful—and it has been—it will be launched nationwide."

I mashed my lips together. "Who's they?"

I knew what he was going to say.

I could see it on his fucking face.

"The Gordon family."

"Shit," I moaned.

"I was afraid you were going to say that," Eden added.

The Gordon family, our biggest competitor. Like us, they had started with steak houses, and where we had branched out into seafood, they had gone with Italian. Wherever we built a restaurant in a new territory, a Gordon restaurant wasn't far behind and normally within a few miles.

"They're financially backing the place," Walker explained. "They somehow met the chef, liked her ideas, and decided to bankroll the build-out. If it goes well and the Gordons want to move forward, the chef has the option to partner with them, or they can buy her out. But the chef owns the recipes and the concept, so the Gordons can't move forward unless she wants to."

Colson put his hands behind his head, rocking in his chair. "What you're saying is, Horned is up for grabs."

"And it's ours if we want it." I licked my lips.

"Why the hell would we want it?" Walker asked. "We're in the midst of building out Toro Beverly Hills and scaling it the same way we did with Charred. We're growing Musik at the same time, adding more locations to Cole and Spade Hotels. We have our fucking hands full."

"This hand isn't full." I held it up in the air. "Walker, just hear me out. The Gordons know the restaurant business as well as we do. If they're bankrolling Horned, they believe in the model. It's nothing like what either of us has. It's more boutique in a sense. Where Charred only goes into major metro markets across the world, this could hit small, hip markets that are in need of something eclectic. Think Portsmouth, New Hampshire; Sarasota, Florida; Santa Fe, New Mexico—you get the drift." I lowered my hand to the table. "Just think, we could give them something good, reliable ... and wickedly satisfying."

"Don't ever say those words to me again," Walker warned.

I laughed. "Just think about it."

He got up from his chair, leaving the publication where it had dropped. "Let's get Dear Foodie into Toro. Let's get a glowing fucking review. And if I'm still alive at that point and I haven't died from a goddamn heart attack, we can discuss the future of Horned." He walked out.

I turned to Eden and Colson. "What the hell are we going to do with him?"

"Take him out. Get him to relax. Get him laid," Colson said.

"Speaking of going out," I began, "I talked to Brady. He'll be back in town in a couple of weeks, and he wants us all to hang. The night he picked, Beck has a game, so I'm going to reach out to the other Spades and Coles and get them on board. We'll take over our suite at the arena and have dinner and drinks there, and then we'll go out." I looked at Eden. "You're coming. Don't even tell me you're not."

Her brows rose. "It's not a guys' night?"

"Brady's married now," I told her. "Where he goes, Lily usually goes, which means it's an everybody night."

She nodded. "I'll think about it."

With the door still open and our employees in the hallway outside, I kept my voice down and said, "I want you to give it to me raw—really, how was Horned?" I tapped my foot, the suspense creating a buzz inside me. "I didn't even know you had gone. You didn't say anything in the family group chat about going."

She twirled a long, dark lock around her finger. "You mean because you couldn't keep your dick in your pants, so your baby sister had to come to your rescue."

I laughed.

"I ended up eating at the bar," she continued. "It was the only seat I could get since I couldn't get a reservation. But it was as good as Dear Foodie described. I was blown away—and you know I'm fussy." Her hand stilled. "I want to know something."

With her eyes still locked on mine, I knew the question was directed at me. "Okay."

"Now that you'll never talk to her again, like all the others from your past, was it worth missing out on that meal? Or if you were going to do it all over, would you make the same decision?"

"*Oooh.*" Colson chuckled. "Little sis is coming in hot."

I smiled as I stood, leaning the top of my thighs into the edge of the table and pressing my palms against the wood. "I'd do it over and over and over." My head dropped as the image of Sadie's naked body came into my mind. "She was the best fuck I've ever had."

"Then that's a phone number you should have gotten, big brother," she said. "You really fucked up that one."

69

SIX

Sadie

I lifted the lychee martini up to my mouth and breathed in the aroma. The scent was so yummy that my eyes closed as I took a sip. The sweet, almost-floral taste circled my tongue while the vodka and vermouth burned—a combination I craved at the end of a long day.

Or a week that felt as if it had lasted an entire year.

Like this one.

"This drink is hitting so differently—am I right?" I said to the girls.

Cat was to my right, and Bryn was to my left, the three of us at a high-top table in the bar of a popular sushi restaurant.

Dear Foodie wasn't on duty tonight. This was all Sadie.

Of course, I'd still snap some pictures and share it on my social media with a cheeky caption. When food was beautiful, it deserved an audience, and that was why I fed it to mine. My brand wasn't just about reviews, although that was a large part of it; it was also about celebrating all things culinary. So, when I got home, I would choose the best picture from this evening and schedule it to go live in a few weeks.

The girls knew that when I was at a restaurant, my phone would stay on the table, and I'd be snapping photos throughout the evening, even asking them to take some of me, neck down, to guarantee I wouldn't be recognized.

"This honestly might be the best thing I've ever put in my mouth." Bryn laughed. "Okay, maybe that's a bit extreme, but, yes, it's hitting in every way." She nodded toward my sister. "So, fill me in. How are things with Mom and Dad? Sadie told me they're driving you cray."

"Cray is an understatement," Cat replied. "I'm really thankful Sadie talked me off a ledge and tried to make me feel better, but the way they constantly weigh in on every situation and pretty much let me know that whatever I'm doing, I'm doing wrong—I could do without all of that."

"I'm thirty, and my parents still do it to me," Bryn told her.

I lifted my hand in a wave. "Same to the age and same to hearing the constant opinions of our parents."

"But you're kicking ass," Cat said to me. "You're making a ton of money, you own your own condo, and you did it all without our parents' help. What exactly do Mom and Dad have to say to you? You're making all the right decisions."

"I didn't make all the right decisions, little sis. I made decisions that just happened to work out after lots and lots that didn't." I offered a gentle smile. "Mom and Dad harp on my plan B. You know, on what I'll do if social media goes away or shifts and influencing no longer pays my mortgage. My gig at *Seen* pays well for a publication, but it doesn't compare to the brand deals I get checks for and my earnings from the social media giants."

Bryn moved her hair off her shoulder. "Your followers aren't just going to disappear."

"No, they won't, but that doesn't mean I'll get paid to have so many," I countered.

Cat shook her head. "Mom and Dad will forever worry about every single thing."

"Remember, it's kinda their job, and we have to love them for that," Bryn said. "Just because we left the nest doesn't mean they'll cut back on parenting. I swear, girl, it only gets worse."

"Ugh," Cat groaned.

"Wait until you have a kid," Bryn offered. "You're going to hear everything that they did and why it was right and why you should do it too—at least, that's what my sister tells me."

Cat rolled her eyes. "I can't wait." She held the wide glass of her filthy martini up to her lips. "Stop me when I try to convince the waitress to get me a pitcher of these. Because that's how many I'd like." She swallowed down half the contents. "Two martinis I can handle. Three? Things have the potential of turning a little wild."

I laughed. "Three is, by far, my max too."

Bryn smiled at me. "We've heard about Cat's week. Now it's your turn." She ran her finger around the rim of her glass. "Work-wise, I'm sure it's been a doozy since I know how busy you've been. But personal-wise, I'd say the end of last week wasn't so bad for you." Her grin grew.

"She's talking about the Horned guy, isn't she?" Cat asked.

"Oh, he was horned all right." Bryn laughed.

My sister didn't know all the details. Some things didn't need to be mentioned to family, regardless if we were best friends. Cat knew I'd broken my dry spell and that, for once, I'd become a bad girl. She didn't know how many times I'd had sex with Lockhart and where. The gist of it was that I might have turned bad for a night, but the good girl had returned.

"We were both horned," I added.

"Tell me again why you haven't already fallen in love with

this man and spent every night with him this week?" Bryn asked.

"You know why," I replied.

"It's me," Cat said, raising her shoulders in defeat. "I'm the problem."

I put my hand on one of those shoulders and rubbed it. "You are not. You called me that morning. I made a decision, and I left his suite. I could have woken him up, he could have gotten my number the night before. Lots of different scenarios could have played out, but none of it is your fault."

Every word of that was the truth. Still, I had regrets. Even though I didn't know how I'd feel if I'd woken him up and things turned awkward and he didn't want my number, at least I could have said I'd made the effort. Because I hadn't, I opened my eyes every morning since and wondered about what-ifs.

And now, as I sat in the middle of a bar that was full of what most would think were good-looking men, not a single one did anything for me.

Because physically, they didn't compare to Lockhart.

"I still feel terrible," Cat voiced.

"Don't." I continued to rub her. "You didn't know. You couldn't have even guessed. I mean, when have you ever called me and I was in a guy's bed?"

Bryn snorted. "It should happen much more often."

"It's probably never going to happen again," I confessed. "I'm truly not cut out for the one-night-stand thing."

"Why?" Bryn asked. "Random sex would be the perfect stress reliever for you." She winked. "Honestly, it would probably be the best stress reliever for all of us."

I squeezed the stem of my glass. "Because if you were a fly on the wall, you would have thought he was into me. That this wasn't the first time we'd met. That we'd already known each other's body and what the other was craving. Our connection was *that* sizzling." I sighed. "Which is where the problem lies. I can see myself catching feelings—and one-night stands aren't conducive for catching anything."

"Aside from orgasms," Cat said.

I groaned, "Yep."

Bryn moved her drink out of the way so she could reach across the small table and put her hands on my forearm. "You have feelings for him."

She didn't phrase it as a question.

She was confirming what she suspected.

And it triggered an immediate reaction in me. A thumping in my chest, a pounding so hard that I had to cover it with my fingers to attempt to slow it. When that didn't work, I released my heart and lifted my drink, holding it to my lips and swallowing. I wasn't even tasting. I was chugging as quickly as I could, my eyes wandering at the same time. Because staring at my best friend would only confirm what she already knew. How could I admit out loud and to myself that I had developed feelings for a man I'd spent less than twelve hours with?

That I'd caught more than just orgasms.

Which was the most idiotic thing I could have done, considering I had no way to get in touch with him. I'd looked up Lockhart Wright, and there wasn't one listed who lived in LA—at least according to Google. I had no idea what he did for a living and no clues that could lead me to him—besides that he was a rock star in bed.

To make matters even worse, not a single thing I looked at was holding my attention. Nothing in the bar. Nothing in the entrance. Nothing in the dining room or toward the back, nothing—

My gaze halted on the table in the corner, where a foursome was sitting.

The face of one of the men was achingly familiar.

So familiar that I almost choked on my martini.

I blinked, trying to correct my vision, making sure what I was seeing was real.

I blinked again and again and again and—

Shit.

The view didn't change.

It was him.

Lockhart.

He shared the table with another man and two women, and it looked like he was on a double date, staring at the lady beside him, smiling and laughing at her in a way that reminded me of the way he had looked at me.

I wished I were in that chair, not her.

But did I?

He was the kind of man who went on a date only a week after he slept with me.

Or maybe, even worse, he was dating her.

Or—*oh God*—what if he was married to her?

My brain was spiraling, and everything inside me started to burn.

I felt sick.

I slowly returned my gaze to Bryn, filling my lungs, holding in the air as I silently replied to her question, *I had feelings for him, yes*, but the words never actually left my mouth.

My heart rate was even higher than it had been before I saw him in the restaurant; now, it was making my entire body shake.

I put down the glass and raised my hand to point. "Look over there, in the corner—do you see the foursome? The guy who's facing us, in a black button-down, with heavy scruff on his face and deep green eyes that are so bold you can see them all the way over here?"

"Yep, I see him," Cat said.

"Me too," Bryn agreed.

I sucked in another breath. "That's Lockhart."

"What?" Bryn gasped. "No way ... he's with ..." Her voice drifted off, as if she didn't want to say the words I was already thinking.

As soon as she turned quiet, Lockhart's gaze shifted. It was as though he had heard her, but that was impossible; the bar was too packed, and the dining room was extremely loud.

But he was looking straight ahead now.

And his eyes were directly on mine.

SEVEN

Hart

Iff there was such a thing as a dream come true, it was happening right now. Because less than fifteen yards from where I was sitting in the dining room of the sushi restaurant, Sadie sat in the bar. She was positioned at a high-top, a martini glass close to her mouth, her hands wrapped around the thin stem.

She had been visiting me in my sleep since my lips had kissed her pussy, and every morning, I'd wake up, wondering if I was ever going to see her again.

Hoped was more like it.

But instead of looking at me like she wanted to get on her knees to suck the cum out of me, matching my desire to lick the orgasms out of her, she was glaring at me as if she wanted to fucking kill me.

And that expression intensified with each second that passed.

What the hell?

What the fuck did I do wrong?
She's the one who left that morning, not me.

She said something to the other two women she was with, and then she set her glass down and got up from her chair. She didn't look at me as she crossed the bar and went through the front of the dining room toward the hallway, where the restrooms were located.

I could eye-fuck her for the rest of the night and play this little back-and-forth game of bullshit, trying to figure out what was on her mind, or I could ask her myself.

Given that direct was the path I preferred, I said to the group, "I'll be back in a few minutes," and I went to the hallway.

Since this was a restaurant I frequented with friends, I knew the restrooms weren't onesies. At least in the men's room, there were several stalls and urinals, so I cracked open the door to the ladies' room, checking if there were other women in there besides Sadie.

From here, I had a clear view of the stalls, where there weren't any feet, and of the sinks, too, where she was standing. She gripped the sides of the porcelain and was staring at herself in the mirror.

Fuck, she was beautiful.

She wore a dress—not like the other night, this one simpler and a bright red, shaped like a long, oversize sweater—with knee-high boots.

A color that looked ravishing on her.

And a dress I wanted to tear off with my goddamn teeth.

Pretty confident that she was alone, I walked in and locked the door behind me.

Sadie immediately connected eyes with me through the mirror and turned toward me. "What are you doing in here?"

"Coming to say hello." I paused. "And coming to get some much-needed answers."

She laughed. It wasn't the kind of sound that came after a joke. This was a sound that told me she was shocked to see me, and this was the only noise she could muster. "Answers regarding what?"

"Why I woke up that morning and you were gone."

She searched my eyes, a slow back-and-forth pattern, before she said, "Why does it even matter?"

An interesting response, given that I'd sworn she was into me. That entire night, I had fed a passion inside her, but I was positive it went deeper. I'd felt that shit straight in my chest, and I thought she had too. But the look on her face as she had glared at me from across the bar and in here was entirely different from the way she had gawked at me the other night.

"Why does it matter? How about I give you some honesty? Because that's the only way I know how to give it. I've thought about you every goddamn day for the last week. How much I want you. How much I fucking need you." I went to loosen my collar, realizing the top two buttons were already undone. "Maybe that's a little dramatic, considering I only knew you for one night. But that's what you did to me, Sadie. That's the impression you left. That's how you made me feel."

"It was a one-night stand. Nothing more." She clenched her fingers as they hung at her sides, her tone and stance so cold and turned off. "That's what you told me, remember?"

"Is that all you wanted from me? One night? Is that the reason you left?"

She shook her head. "No."

"Now we're getting somewhere." I gripped the back of my neck. "Have you thought about me?"

"It doesn't matter."

I didn't like that response at all, not the first time I had heard it or the second.

My brows pushed together out of frustration. "Why didn't you leave me your number?"

"That doesn't matter either."

"All of this matters, Sadie. Please stop saying that." I released my neck and shoved my hands into my pockets. "Why are you looking at me like that?"

Her arms crossed, which pushed up her tits. "It amazes me that you don't at least know the answer to that. I can understand why you're clueless as to why I left and didn't give you my number or—"

"You left without even kissing me goodbye."

Her eyes narrowed, and she stayed quiet.

"I wish you had woken me up," I said. "I had a hell of a good time with you, and I didn't want that good time to end. I wanted to get breakfast delivered and ..." The thought of what would have happened next made my lips pull wide. "Then I wanted to—"

"No, no, no." Her head shook again. "Please don't tell me what those plans were. I honestly don't want to hear them."

Jesus, this was getting confusing. She hadn't wanted a one-night stand. That wasn't the reason she'd left. But I should know why she was looking at me this way? Yet I didn't have a fucking inkling.

Did she regret hooking up with me?

Had I fucked up somehow?

Or was it something else?

I pulled my hand out of my pocket and brushed my thumb across my lips. "You suddenly don't want to hear about what I wanted to do to you, yet when I was whispering against your pussy in the shower, telling it just how I was going to fuck it when we got out, you didn't complain then. And when we finally lay in bed and I wrapped you in my arms and your face was on my chest, you fell asleep in seconds, more content than anyone I'd ever seen. Tell me, what happened between then and now?"

Her head fell back, exposing her throat. She stayed just like that for several seconds until she looked at me again. "Everything."

"What?" I waited. "What the hell is everything?" I studied her eyes, trying to understand what she wasn't saying. "We spoke about it being only a one-night stand—I get that. You left —I don't get that. And now I'm standing in the women's restroom, attempting to talk to you about it, and you're not saying anything. You need to just say it, Sadie." I shifted my weight. "All I want to do is get past this so I can get on my fucking knees and put your pussy in my face." I smiled, hoping the diversion would lighten her mood.

"You really are that clueless, aren't you?"

It hadn't worked.

I ran my hand over the top of my head, feeling the hardened, gelled pieces. "Please tell me what's going on."

She mashed her lips together, her chest rising as she took deep breaths. "The woman you're with tonight."

"What about her?"

"You know, the one you've been heart-eyeing. I get the feeling she'd be extremely upset if she found out you were in here, saying these things to me." Her voice started to get sharper. "That you've been thinking about me. That you've been wanting me. That you want to eat me out in this bathroom." She ran her stare up and down the length of me. "That's a slimy move, don't you think?"

My neck protruded back while every single one of her words hit me.

Again and again.

"It's a ... *what?*" I asked.

"You heard me."

The woman I was with.

Slimy.

Oh fuck.

It finally clicked.

I knew exactly what was causing this. It hadn't dawned on me at first, and I hadn't even considered the way things looked. Now it made perfect sense.

But before I addressed that elephant, I had a few things I needed to uncover.

I took a step toward her and then another, and on my third, she raised her hand and said, "Stay there. Don't come any closer."

"Fine, but let me ask you this." My hands returned to my pockets so I wouldn't be tempted to reach for her. "You were the one who left. You gave me no way to get in touch with you. So, why does it bother you that I'm with a woman tonight? It's clear you had no interest in seeing me again."

I didn't just observe her stare. I felt it.

In every part of my fucking body.

"That is," I continued, "unless you have regrets about leaving. Knowing that by now, we'd be on our second or even third date."

The words had fallen right out of my mouth, and I was taken aback by them. I'd already admitted things to her that I didn't ever say to women, things I never felt about women. What I knew was that when I'd woken up that morning, I wasn't done tasting her. And when I realized she was gone, the disappointment came over me, and I'd wanted more. But hearing myself admit that we'd be on more dates was taking it one step further.

And, shit, I didn't hate that at all.

"Lockhart, why would I have regrets about leaving? Clearly, I'd have to share you—that became obvious tonight—and I don't do threesomes."

Jealousy made her spicy.

Delicious.

And I wanted to inhale every fucking layer.

I smiled. "I don't either ... especially with my sister."

Her brows rose. "Your ... *sister?*"

"That's the woman you think I'm with. The other couple are business associates who happen to be married. I'm not on a double date, Sadie. I work with my sister and the associates also happen to be my good friends."

She was silent. Processing. Her expression lightening, even if there were hints of confusion mixed in.

"Jesus ... I thought ..."

"I know what you thought, but that assumption wasn't even close to being accurate." I let that settle. "That's only the first issue. The second is that I still don't know why you left."

She stared at the ceiling, licking the gloss off her lips, her head shaking. "I needed to make an important phone call, and I didn't want to do it in the suite." She finally looked at me. "It was a rushed decision and ... not the right one."

Not at all what I'd suspected.

Regret was a word that had been haunting me, and I needed to use it again. "You're telling me you regret it?"

"You're not going to let this go, are you?"

"Why should I? You leaving changed everything. Tonight is luck, but what if we hadn't been so lucky?" I pulled my hands out of my pockets, ready to touch her.

"I don't know. I've been thinking about that. And ..." Her head tilted to the side. "Yes, I regret it." Her voice was soft. "Yes, I've felt horrible about it." Her voice turned even quieter. "And, yes, I've wished every day that I could have a do-over."

I took a step, and this time, she didn't stop me, not even as I slowly closed the distance between us, my hands going to her waist, pulling her against me. "You've got that do-over. Right now."

Her fingers pressed against my chest. "I was hoping for a moment like this. Maybe not exactly like this—I certainly didn't want our run-in to go down this way. But out of all places, I can't believe you're here at the same time as me."

I brushed my nose over her cheek. "What if I weren't?"

As I pulled back, her eyes glued to mine. "I wouldn't know how to find you. I wouldn't know how to fix it."

"And we'd go forever without seeing each other again."

She nodded. "I hate that thought."

I stretched across her hips toward her lower back. "About that do-over ..." I leaned into her neck to get more of her scent. "I wouldn't mind hearing a little, *I missed you, Lockhart. I'm happy to see you, Lockhart.*" I smiled even though I was out of her line of sight. "*My pussy is tingling and wanting you, Lockhart.*"

She laughed. "You are ..."

I leaned back to stare at her. "I'm what, gorgeous?" I licked across my lips as I took her in. "I have to say, jealousy looked so fucking sexy on you."

"Dick." She laughed. "You enjoyed that bit, didn't you?"

"Once I figured out what was happening and the cause of it, I did. Getting there was just a little painful."

She arched into my fingers. "But let's say you had seen me with another man tonight. That I had looked at him the way I'd looked at you. Smiling. Laughing. Would that have bothered you?"

I didn't know why, but I didn't like the thought of that.

When I had been between her legs, the idea that I'd made her scream the loudest fucking owned my mind. That no one had ever licked her like me. That she would wake up craving my dick the same way I dreamed of her pussy.

Those were the thoughts that made me reach for her face and hold it. "If I'd looked out into the bar and seen you with another man, tonight would have played out the exact same, except for the conversation we're having right now. That would have looked different."

"How so?"

"I'd have asked you if he could make you feel as good as I could. If the answer to that was yes, I'd have left you in the restroom. If the answer to that was no, then ..."

There was a rattle on the door, followed by a knock and a, "Hello? Is someone in there? Why is the door locked? Excuse me, do you know why the bathroom door is locked?"

I glanced toward the door, seeing if it budged by someone sticking in a key, and then glanced at Sadie again, her eyes gradually returning to mine.

"Then what would you have done?" she asked.

I smiled. "Do you really want to know that answer?" When she nodded, I added, "Or would you rather me show you?"

She winked. "I want you to surprise me."

EIGHT

Sadie

This man—*my God.*

The way he led me out of the restroom with an urgency that told me nothing and no one could stop him. The way he hurried me around the front entrance, to the side and back of the building with my hand clasped in his. The way he stopped in the middle of the narrow, dark alley to put his palms on my face and kiss me.

But it wasn't just any kiss.

It was a kiss that made up for the last week that his lips hadn't been on mine.

When he finally pulled his mouth away, taking all the air from my lungs in the process, he backed me up until I was against the brick of the building. His tall, broad, massive body hovered over me in a way that made me feel tiny and completely protected.

"I'm going to make that regret of leaving hit even deeper."

"It already is," I admitted.

He ran his nose across the side of my face, his lips dragging too, the heat from his breath making me go from hot to scorching. "There are so many things I want to do to you that this alley just won't allow."

"I want all of it." I put my finger over the center of his mouth. "But there will be plenty more times in the future for you to do things like ... get on your knees."

He nipped the back of my finger, his hands flattening on the wall above my head. "You're saying you're going to give me your number this time?"

I laughed, but it wasn't straight from humor; it was sex-filled too. "For the record, you could have gotten my number before you had me strip in the suite."

"I could have, yes. But what if we had gotten to the suite and things weren't working between us and I wasn't into you?" His lips grazed my cheek. "And I didn't end up becoming fucking wild over you, so I would have gotten it for nothing." He licked the bottom of my earlobe, and a shiver ran through me. "Instead, I didn't get it, and I've ached for you every day since. What are you doing to me, Sadie?"

"How hard have you ached?"

He moaned, "Feel my hard-on."

My hands were already on his stomach, caressing a set of abs I still dreamed about, so they only had to lower a little before I was on his bulging erection. "You weren't kidding," I whispered. "You do need me."

"Jerking off to you isn't the same as getting to fuck you. It doesn't matter how much I pump my dick. It won't ever feel as good as your cunt."

I'd never met a man with such a filthy mouth, and I'd never thought I'd appreciate it as much as I did.

"You jerked off to me?"

"Yes."

"And what did you visualize?"

"You. Your body. Your wetness." His mouth lowered to my breasts, and even though I was still in my heavy, thick dress, I could feel his lips graze my nipples. "The way your pussy hugs my dick." He looked up at me from my chest. "The way it pulses when you're coming."

"You're going to get that tonight."

"And I want to savor it. I want to put you in every position and see which one makes you scream the loudest." He rose back to my lips. "Since that's not going to happen right now, this alley will have to do."

I stroked the outside of his jeans, cupping his full length, rounding my hand over the top. "I want it."

"Take it out. Make it yours." He kissed the base of my neck, a spot that was my weakness, sending immediate chills across my body. "Show me how badly you want it inside you, fucking your pussy."

I pulled at the clasp of his belt, and once it was open, I unbuttoned his jeans and lowered his zipper, stretching down his boxer briefs just enough to free his dick. With both hands, I surrounded his shaft and pumped him.

With his lips in front of mine, he groaned, "Wait until this is in you. That regret is really going to slice through."

I believed him.

He reached behind his back, pulling out his wallet, where I knew—because of the last time we had been together—he kept a condom in one of the flaps. He removed the foil and tore off the corner with his teeth.

The movement sent me the warm, woodsy scent of his cologne. A smell more perfect than I remembered.

A scent that, I swore, had me panting as I rubbed my finger over his tip, urging the bead of pre-cum to bubble out.

I needed to know what he tasted like.

A desire so deep that as soon as I felt it, I wiped it off and brought it up to my mouth. And even though it was mostly dark, I could feel his eyes on me. Watching. Waiting. His stare growing as I licked the small drip, tasting the burst of saltiness once it hit my tongue.

"The hottest fucking sight I've ever witnessed," he growled.

There was no tone in this world that was as sexy as his.

As someone who listened to audiobooks, I was positive about that.

"That wasn't for you," I told him. "That was for me."

He rolled the condom on and grabbed the side of my neck. "How did I taste? Enough to make you want to swallow a mouthful?"

"With pleasure."

He let out a deep, gritty chuckle. "Keep this up, Sadie, and I'm going to fucking marry you." He kissed me. Harder this time. With a roughness to his lips that told me just how much he wanted me.

Marry?

I didn't know why, but his reply sent me toward an edge I hadn't seen coming.

He released my face and lifted one of my legs, wrapping it around his waist before he slowly slid my dress higher.

"You could have brought me anywhere. Why here?" I asked.

"I can't do what I want to do to you in my car. You know that."

I heard his smile based on his sound, and I felt it against my lips.

"I suppose we could have stayed in the ladies' room, but we

risked the chance of someone unlocking the door, and there was no way I'd put you in a position like that."

"A position like what?"

"Anyone—even a woman—seeing you naked. Having them hear you moan. Or risk the chance of you feeling any kind of embarrassment. When I fuck you, it's us. No one else."

"Keep that up, Lockhart, and I'm going to marry you."

"Then we understand each other."

I wrapped my arms around his neck. "What I understand is, you're going to fuck me so hard that I'm going to want privacy so no one hears me or sees me." I straightened my back against the wall. "Prove it."

Within a second—and I had no idea how—my panties were ripped off, literally shredded from my body, and he held them in front of me.

"You're really making this a habit," I said.

He put the lace up to his mouth and swiped the fabric under his nose. "I can't help myself. Your pussy smells so fucking good, I want it to stay with me. Forever."

"Do you still have the other pair?"

He put them somewhere, probably his pocket, and his hand returned to my face, tilting it up to his. "What if I told you they were in my home office?"

"I would ask you if they were in a desk drawer."

"And if they were?"

I smiled. "I'd wonder why they weren't framed on top of your desk."

"Is that where you want them?" He laughed. "So every time I sit there, I think about your cunt?"

"You should be thinking about it anyway. You shouldn't need the reminder."

He moaned, *"Mmm."* And then he said, "You're not wrong."

My eyes closed as the tip of his dick teased my entrance, and I sighed, "You're torturing me."

"Consider it your punishment for leaving that morning."

"Fair. But you're still an asshole."

He laughed, a sound that quickly turned to a grunt as he slid into me.

"*Ahhh,*" I exhaled. "You feel so good."

The taunting was gone, and now the only thing between us was pleasure. With zero hesitation in the way he moved, the satisfaction was coming in fast.

He wanted me.

And it was beyond clear that he was tired of waiting to have me.

"Considering how many times I fucked you that night, you would think I'd already know how tight you are. But, goddamn it, it comes as a surprise every time I thrust into you. And"—he let out a loud moan—"not only are you tight, but you're so wet too."

I could feel it.

I'd been turned on since I'd found out the woman was his sister, and every bit of conversation that followed was just verbal foreplay. By the time he had walked me out of the ladies' room, I had been soaked.

"It's what you do to me," I admitted.

He picked up speed, going faster and deeper with each stroke. "I'll never be able to get enough of you."

My nails went into his shoulders. Despite him wearing a button-down, I swore I pierced the material and went straight into his skin.

Especially as his power increased and he hissed, "Fuck yeah," and that caused me to buck against him.

My body couldn't fight what was happening. The tingles, the tightness, the wetness—I could sense it all. It was as though

I hadn't been touched in years. That was how strong this felt, and that was the intensity in which this moved through me. I was just so tuned into him, so overwhelmed by what he was bringing out in me.

He wasn't just holding me against the wall, fucking me.

He was grinding his hips in a circle, hitting spots that I hadn't even realized were sensitive, positioning me in a way where every time he dived forward, he hit my clit. And when he was all the way in, he twisted again, tapping my G-spot.

The combination was almost too much to bear.

"Oh!" I shouted. "Yes!"

I didn't know if there were people walking by the entrance of the alley. I didn't know if there were employees coming out the back of the restaurant to smoke who could hear us.

I didn't care.

I was lost.

Inside him.

Within him.

And I didn't want to be found.

"Harder." My nails dug down even more. "Please."

The bricks were stinging my shoulder blades as I scraped against them, the feeling like rug burn, even through the sweater. But I didn't care. Everything felt incredible, even that.

"Are you sure you can handle it harder? I know that's what you asked for, but I don't want to break you."

I panted, "Break me."

He aligned our lips. "Don't tease me, Sadie."

"This isn't a tease. This is me begging you. I need you, Lockhart—"

The air left my lungs as he gave me exactly what I'd asked for.

But I didn't need to breathe.

Because the tingling was building, and I was no longer in control.

Not of the sounds coming out of me.

Not of the air that was or wasn't moving through me.

"You're tightening." He shot forward, giving me the deepest, fastest slam. "You're going to come."

I was, which was why I demanded, "Don't stop," and then I screamed, "Please, oh God, don't stop!"

How did he know my body so well?

How could he make me feel this amazing after only sleeping together one other night?

Why did it feel like I'd been with this man my entire life?

"Come with me," I pleaded. "Please, Lockhart, I need you to. I need to feel it."

As soon as the words left my mouth, his lips silenced me from saying anything else. And once again, this kiss was different from the others.

It was hungrier.

Needier.

Far more demanding.

And it came with a promise.

Because within a few more dunks, he was giving me everything I'd asked for.

"Ah!" My scream lasted for several seconds as I neared the peak. "Oh my God, Lockhart, I'm there! I'm coming!"

"Fuck! You're making me come too!"

We were shuddering together. Our shouts mingled, our moans intertwined, our movements matched as we rocked into each other.

When his orgasm formed, his pumps became sharper, his grunts deeper, and when he yelled, "Sadie," I knew he was feeling what I was.

"Yes!" I gasped. "Lockhart!"

I clung to his shoulders, and he gripped my hips, hurling into me, driving back, and sinking in. And as fast as we built, we slowed just as quick, until the stillness and quietness completely took over.

He kissed me, softly at first and then a little bit more passionately. "I'm going to make a deal with you."

"Okay."

"I'll put you down, only under one condition."

I tightened my grip around him. "I can't wait to hear this."

"You give me your number."

I laughed. "And if I don't?"

"You'll be stuck out here with me, in this position, until I get you to change your mind."

I nuzzled against his cheek, breathing him in. My eyes automatically closing as the biggest wave of contentment passed through me. "Sounds like you're grounding me, Lockhart."

"I'm not leaving it up to luck anymore. I think you like being bad." He gnawed my lip. "And I think you want to be a bad girl again."

As I rushed back to the table, taking a seat, there was concern etched across my sister's face.

"Where have you been? Unless you've really been in the restroom for the last fifteen or so minutes?" she asked.

Bryn was gazing at me, too, assessing me, her eyes covering every inch, as though she could piece together where I'd been.

I wasn't sure if my face was red, but it felt heated. I hadn't gone to the restroom before coming here, so I had no idea how I looked. If my hair was a mess. If my makeup was smudged. If they could smell sex all over me.

"If I told you, you wouldn't believe me." I lifted the refill one of them had ordered for me and downed the entire martini in one shot.

"You had sex with him, didn't you?" Bryn smiled, waiting for me to confirm after I swallowed.

I stayed silent, although I couldn't hide my smile.

"Oh my God, you did, you little minx." She gently hit my arm and kept her fingers on me.

I set the glass down. "That's his sister he's with, not a date. I learned that when he followed me into the ladies' room and locked the door."

My sister's eyes widened. "You did it in *there?*"

"No." I laughed as though this were something so normal for me when it was the complete opposite. "We did it outside. In the alley behind the restaurant."

"Whatever he's doing to you, I like it." Bryn squeezed the spot she was holding. "I like it *a lot*, a lot."

"Me too—and tell me you got his number this time?" Cat asked.

I pulled my hand back from the glass and wrapped my arm around my stomach. "I didn't have my phone on me since I'd left my purse here on the chair. But he took mine."

"You know this is the start of something huge, right?" Bryn's smile was as big as I'd ever seen it. "Huge, as in a full-blown relationship by the end of your next date."

The excitement was there. The emotion too. The tingles hadn't even come close to dying down.

Even though I'd heard every word he said and those words hit my heart in the most powerful way, I also knew Lockhart didn't date. He did one-night stands. And I worried that if the commitment bug bit him, he would have second thoughts and change his mind and bail.

So, I replied, "We'll see ..."

"We'll see what?" Cat countered. "Look at you. I've never seen you happier, which makes me the happiest."

"That makes *us* the happiest," Bryn added.

I smiled at my girls. "I don't know ... I do have a good feeling about things. It all feels a little"—I glanced over at the table where he was sitting, and as if he could sense my stare, he looked up and gave me the sexiest grin—"perfect."

NINE

Hart

ME

Hey, beautiful. It's Lockhart.

SADIE

Took you long enough to text me. A whole
day? I expected more from you …

ME

I just got your number last night.

SADIE

And I'm just playing with you. 😉

ME

I want to see you.

SADIE

So soon?

ME

I can't think of a single reason not to. Unless you're sore. That I can accept. Although I'd still want to see you. I just don't know if I could keep my hands off you. Or if you told me the world of social media was keeping you too tied down and you didn't have a night to come up for air.

SADIE

LOL. It does keep me busy, as I'm sure hospitality keeps you busy, but, no, I can make time.

As for the other part, I'm sore-ish. But not enough to stop me from seeing you.

ME

I must not have been hard enough on you.

SADIE

Ha! But I asked for it—and, no, you weren't, LOL.

ME

Shit, Sadie. Then just wait until next time. I won't be kind to her at all.

SADIE

Oh, I'm waiting, and I'm more than ready.

Tell me the plans. Drinks? Dinner? Or are you taking me straight to bed?

ME

Food usually comes first, except in your case. We can't seem to ever make it that far. I think it's time I change that.

SADIE

Does that mean you're taking me to a restaurant?

ME

How about you come to my place? I don't want to be too far from a bed ...

SADIE

I like this idea.

ME

Saturday night. 7 p.m. I'll send you my address the day of.

SADIE

Are you sure you can wait that long?

ME

It's going to be hard ... I can't lie.

ME

One more night.

SADIE

You have a countdown going—I like it.

ME

I just really fucking want you.

SADIE

I might want you too—you know, just a tiny bit.

ME

We're not going to make it through dinner, Sadie.

SADIE

Not at this rate, no.

ME

Let's make a promise to each other. No touching, not even kissing, until we're done with dessert.

SADIE

Dessert? That's quite the commitment. The main course, I get. But the dessert could come thirty minutes after, maybe longer. You're sure you can hold off that long?

ME

Fuck no.

SADIE

You still want to make that deal then?

ME

Yes.

SADIE

LOL. What are we betting?

ME

I'll give you anything you want. The reward is meaningless.

SADIE

Anything?

ME

Anything.

SADIE

You're dangerous, Lockhart.

ME

I think you like that about me.

SADIE

I'm staring into my fridge, wondering what I should bring tomorrow night. Any ideas?

ME

I wouldn't bring a new pair of panties. I'm starting quite the collection.

SADIE

Sigh. You're the reason I'm running low.

ME

I'll buy you hundreds of pairs, don't worry.

SADIE

It would be interesting to see what you picked out. Color, fabric, that kinda thing. What are your favorites?

ME

Are you asking out of curiosity or because that's what you're going to show up in?

SADIE

Both.

ME

I like you in red. The bright red you wore to the sushi restaurant.

SADIE

Fabric?

ME

The lace was cool. It hints at what I want to see, and it makes me work for it.

SADIE

So interesting. Now, back to what I'm bringing. Wine? An appetizer? Dessert?

ME

I've got it all covered. You're good.

> **ME**
>
> Twelve hours. Now, that's a countdown I can handle.

> **SADIE**
>
> I'm not going to lie—it's gone by rather slow.

> **ME**
>
> Don't remind me.

> **SADIE**
>
> You're texting me at 7 a.m. on a Saturday. Are you telling me you're an early bird?

> **ME**
>
> Are you? You're awake. LOL.

> **SADIE**
>
> No. Not even close. I'm a grump in the morning. The only reason I'm not sleeping is because I forgot to silence my phone and your text woke me.

> **ME**
>
> Fuck, I'm sorry.

> **SADIE**
>
> Don't be. I love waking up to a text from you. And I want to talk.

She wanted to talk. She probably meant through text, but I wasn't going to miss out on the opportunity, so I hit the button to call her and held the phone up to my ear.

She laughed as she answered, and I could hear the morning thick in her voice.

"You took those words literally, didn't you?"

"That, and I really wanted to hear what you sounded like when you first woke up. That chance was stolen from me before."

She let out a moan. "Are you a romantic, Lockhart?"

"You want the honest answer?"

"Always."

"I don't know. I never get far enough to even test it out. I'm usually gone before the sun rises. But this morning, I wanted you in my bed. I wanted you in my arms. And when you said you wanted to talk, I couldn't pass up the opportunity of knowing your sounds."

As I walked into the kitchen to make some pre-workout carbs, I glanced through the hallway of windows, the sun hitting my face as it peeked through the clouds.

"Do you know what else I'm craving to know about you?"

"Tell me."

"To see how soft you look in the morning."

Her laugh was gritty. "Soft?"

"Your skin. Your smile. The feel of you against me—all things that I assume are extremely soft." I stopped in front of the coffee maker. "I suspect you look different in the morning than you do at night. I don't mean because of the lack of makeup. I mean because dawn makes everyone a bit more vulnerable. I want to know how that vulnerability appears on you."

She sighed. "God, you are a romantic."

I positioned the cup and hit the button for one shot. "Is that a bad thing?"

"No. It's a very, very good thing. It just means I'm going to be a heaping pile of goo. All the time. Like I am right now."

"Even in the morning?"

"Ugh. A tough task, but you just did it, so it's possible." Her tone backed up her words.

"What's your beef with mornings?"

I could hear the rustle of sheets as she said, "I tend to stay up late—sometimes working, sometimes not—so when my alarm goes off, it feels like I haven't gone to bed yet, even if I've gotten six or so hours of sleep. It takes me a while to pump myself with enough caffeine to get going."

"Social media never sleeps."

"It truly doesn't."

I held the shot of espresso to my lips. "Are you a coffee drinker?"

"Coffee, followed by a late morning energy drink, and I'm not opposed to an afternoon latte either."

I chuckled. "That's one hell of a caffeine dose."

"When I said it takes a lot to get me going, I wasn't kidding. Where does your love of mornings come from?"

I left the cup on the counter and popped a piece of sourdough bread into the toaster. "Well, I wouldn't call it a love. I would call it a routine. I get up early to work out. I don't have it in me to do the afternoons or evenings, and since I have a home gym, it's easiest to get it done and go to work." I scratched my bare chest. "The earliness carries over into the weekends. Shit, I wouldn't even know how to sleep in past six."

"Ugh."

"Don't worry, I won't wake you tomorrow morning—but if, at any point, you've questioned whether you're staying the night, the answer to that is yes."

Her laugh was small but powerful. "I figured."

"Back to what I was saying. I won't wake you unless you want me to. Or unless you want breakfast. In that case, I'll serve it to you in bed."

"In bed?"

"Of course."

The air she exhaled was filled with pleasure. "Hands down, the sexiest thing a man has ever said to me. So is the thought that you can cook."

"Listen, I'm not the best cook I know—that spot is reserved

for a few of my family members—but I can hold my own in the kitchen."

"Same. I'll never be as good as my mother, but I can also hold my own."

I took out the bread and went to the pantry to grab peanut butter and honey, along with some dates. "You're going to get a taste of my cooking tonight."

"I can't wait." I could hear her smile.

I set everything on the counter, and since I didn't believe in speakerphone—the most annoying setting ever made—and I needed both hands to finish this breakfast, I said, "I'm going to let you go back to bed. I'll see you tonight, gorgeous."

"See you soon."

SADIE

Let's say I was going to ignore what you said and bring a dessert. Is there a flavor you're dead set against?

ME

Ah, she's awake and caffeinated.

SADIE

LOL. I'm two coffees AND an energy drink deep.

ME

Jesus. Are you all right?

SADIE

You mean, am I on the verge of a heart attack? Nope. I'm perfectly good, I promise.

ME

Good. I don't want you dying on me, Sadie. Not when things are just getting started ...

SADIE

I like the sound of that—the just getting started part, not the dying, ha ha.

Back to the flavor question. What are your hates?

ME

Lemon. Yeah, nothing lemon sounds good to me.

SADIE

Does that mean you don't have a favorite?

ME

My favorite is the flavor that I smell on you.

SADIE

How do you make everything sound so perfect?

ME

I'm just being honest.

SADIE

So, you don't have a favorite, and you don't like lemon. Does that mean if I brought pineapple cupcakes, you'd eat them?

ME

The fuck?

SADIE

Ha!

ME

Is that your favorite?

SADIE

I'm a chocolate girlie, but I'm really open to everything. I wouldn't turn down a pineapple cupcake. I'd taste it. I'd taste anything.

ME

Then bring me what you want to taste, and you can lick it off me.

I held my phone in my hand, staring at Sadie's texts, my thumbs hovering over the screen. I never invited women to my house. The last thing I needed was every one-night stand knowing where I lived and how to get through my gate.

I didn't enjoy chaos, and that would be a direct invitation.

But when it came to her, things had been different from the start. I didn't know why, I didn't know how. I just knew I wanted more.

I typed my address and hit Send, hoping tonight was only the beginning of that.

The beginning of us getting to know each other more.

The beginning of us starting something more.

And the beginning of us exploring each other's body even more.

Within a few seconds, her response came in.

SADIE

Ohhh, you live in the Hills. Fancy. 😊 See you soon.

With Beck's name on the screen, I held the phone to my ear and said, "I have about ten minutes to talk," as I answered his call. "You good, brother?"

"I'm sitting on our team's plane, waiting to take off."

I skipped the dramatics of making an old-fashioned and

poured myself a scotch, holding the tumbler not far from my mouth as I sat in my living room. "I would have thought you'd already be in New York for tomorrow's game."

"I should be, but the weather held us up. What do you have going on that you only have ten minutes to talk?"

Damn it, that fucking smile was sweeping across my lips.

"Sadie. She's coming over. I don't think I've told you about her."

He chuckled. "Is she the woman from Horned?"

Since Beck had had practice and not been at the family meeting that Walker had dragged us in for, when he brought up my night with Sadie, I knew someone had talked.

"Which one of our siblings told you?"

Even if there hadn't been a meeting, there were no secrets in this family.

"Who do you think?" he asked.

I bit my lip. "Walker."

"Bingo." He laughed. "Hold up. You said she's coming over?"

"Yeah."

"Bold move for you, isn't it?"

I stared out the windows, looking at the homes that sat on the edge of the canyon. "The first date to ever walk through my door."

"Jesus, Hart, who the fuck are you?"

"I don't know," I exhaled. "There's something different about her. We click in a way I haven't felt before. And she calls me Lockhart—all the rest called me Hart. There's something about it that feels bigger. Special, I guess you could say." I placed the drink down, my eyes closing as I added, "I like this one, Beck. A lot. And I don't even know her as well as I want to, but, fuck, there's just something so addictive about her." My eyes opened. "She's got me thinking about her nonstop, and if I'm not awake, I'm dreaming about her."

"You've got it bad, my man."

The feeling in my chest told me he was right; there was no reason in denying it.

"I think so, and what's fucking wild is that I've only seen her twice. Tonight will be the third. Mix in a bunch of texts and a phone call, and this is what she's done to me. A month from now? Shit, I can't even imagine how I'll be."

"I remember when the Spade brothers all fell hard for their women. Each one going down that rabbit hole of love, and I recall what they all said to me when they talked about it."

"And that is?" I asked.

"Sometimes, all it takes is a glance."

"They weren't wrong."

"Are you saying that's all it took for you?"

I nodded to myself and voiced, "I'm not saying I'm there yet, spiraling down that rabbit hole of love. I need time to reach that level. But I can see the entrance, and I'm open to it for once."

"I'm happy as hell for you, my man."

The smile finally faded, and I lowered my drink. "Enough about me. I know that's not why you called. Talk to me. Tell me what's up."

"I'll keep it simple. I've been thinking a lot about Horned."

"The restaurant?"

"Yeah"—he laughed—"and that's partly because Walker won't shut the fuck up about it. And partly because some of my teammates went there the other night and told me how good it was. I spoke to Eden, and from the way she explained things, the restaurant is up for grabs. The Gordons don't own it, they're just financing it."

"That's right."

"So, what do you think?"

I blinked several times, rubbing my finger across the rim of the glass. "Are you telling me you're interested in buying it?"

"That's why I'm coming to you. Walker is too fucked up about it to have that conversation. I think he wants it, but I think he's got too much on his plate, and he's weary. When it comes to this one, Eden is indifferent, she'll go either way, but she'll also support whatever is decided, and she'll help. Colson? You know him—he works to live, not the other way around. That leaves you, Hart. What the fuck should we do here?"

I hissed out a mouthful of air. "Do we need it?"

"Fuck no."

"Even if Horned exploded, bigger than it already has, it doesn't matter, we still don't need it."

"True." He paused. "And if the Gordons buy it and turn it into something? Something like Charred?"

"Are you asking me if I'll have FOMO?"

He chuckled. "You could say that."

As I stared out across the canyon, there were houses I recognized. One was Beck's. Another was Walker's. Colson's and Eden's homes were close by, but they faced in a direction I wasn't able to see from here. We shared the canyon with celebrities, other athletes, multimillionaires, and billionaires.

The Westons were doing all right.

"You know, Beck, when I walk into our corporate office every morning, I can't believe what the hell we've built. The number of restaurants and clubs we own. The empire that's now an international brand. All of it because Dad had a dream of owning his own restaurant, and that's what this has turned into."

"You appreciate it all—I get it. I also know there's a *but* coming ..."

I laughed. He knew me way too well.

That was why he had called me—because of that *but*.

"We have something in common," I told him, pounding the back of my hand on the arm of the chair.

"And that is?"

"We don't like to lose anything."

"Just what I thought." The eagerness was thick in his voice. "I'll make some calls."

TEN

Sadie

Lockhart stood in the open doorway of his house and watched me walk across the remainder of his driveway and up the three large front steps before I stopped in front of him. It wasn't just a normal look he was giving me. It was a stare made of pure starvation that covered every inch of my body—from the toes of my knee-high boots to the hint of my chest that stuck out from the top of my coat.

But where he was taking me in, I was doing the same to him. At the scruff on his cheeks and the way his deep green shirt—the same color as his eyes—parted at the top, revealing a tease of his muscular chest. How his broadness, the way he was leaning against the side of the door with his arms crossed, took up almost the entire space.

There was absolutely nothing small about Lockhart.

Not his hands. Not his feet.

Not his body.

And not anything beneath his clothes.

112

"Hello." I smiled.

"Hello." His gaze took another dip, and he moaned, "*Mmm*. This is the second jacket I've seen you in, and you're even more stunning in it than the first one you wore—and that was a coat I'll never forget because I got to watch you strip it off."

"Yeah, well, this is a special one too." I touched the collar, my hand then falling back to the glass dish in my arm. I was close enough that I could smell him, that warm, woodsy scent triggering memories with each inhale. "Beautiful house."

It was quite the mansion, full of glass on the two-story exterior, and due to where we were, I knew the view out back had to be spectacular. You lived in the Hills if you had money, and it was clear from everything I was seeing that Lockhart had plenty.

"I'll show it to you in a second." He nodded toward my hands. "I told you, you didn't have to bring anything."

"This"—I glanced down at the plastic lid—"is nothing." I laughed. "Just some pineapple cupcakes."

"You really made them?"

I continued to smile. "They're not straight-up pineapple. They're piña colada. I found the recipe online, so we can both be daring tonight. I hope you like coconut."

"I don't."

"Sounds like you're going to love them, then." I winked.

"My hatred for coconut won't stop me from eating them." He held out his hand. "Come here."

I closed the distance between us, and he took the dish from me, his other hand going to my face, tilting it up toward him.

"God, you smell good."

"So do you."

"With a little hint of scotch mixed in. I pregamed."

My eyelashes fluttered as I took in more of his breath. "I just so happen to love that smell too."

"Kiss me."

"I think you're forgetting the promise we made to each other. No touching, not even kissing until we eat these cupcakes."

He let out a deep exhale. "I don't know what you're talking about."

I smiled, the biggest one I'd had on all night. "Really? Have you gotten amnesia since we spoke? Which must mean you've also forgotten that we made a bet. We just didn't wager anything, so I took it upon myself to up the unknown ante a little."

His eyes narrowed. "How?"

I pulled at the tie that held the sides together, making sure it was tight. "The only things I'm wearing under this jacket are red lace panties and a matching bra."

His head fell back, and he groaned, "Sadie ... fuck me."

"Oh, I'm going to. I've decided that will be your present if you can go the next couple of hours without touching me."

"You're telling me that you're giving yourself to me?"

"I think I've already done that in the past, haven't I?" I paused. "But what I've decided is that you can have me any way you want me."

He licked across his lips, and when his tongue reached the end, it stayed out, pulsing against the corner. "You trust me that much?"

"I think I do."

"Enough so that I can do absolutely anything to you?"

"There are things I haven't done, but I'm willing to experiment, and I think you're the perfect person to do that with."

He chuckled. "And what happens if I do touch you in the meantime?"

"That touch won't lead to anything because then you won't get me at all. Which is going to be quite painful since the moment your fingers graze me, I'm going to take off this jacket and torture you for the rest of the evening."

He pulled at his hair. "You're fucking mean."

I smiled. "Do we have a deal?"

"I don't know," he growled.

"You're telling me you can't go a few hours without touching me?"

"Yes, that's what I'm telling you. I'm fucking dying right now, Sadie. All I want to do is pull you against me and hold you in my arms and press my lips to yours."

Deep within me, I was swooning, but I said, "You'll get to," and I tapped the air as though it were his chest. "Just not yet." I waited. "Do we have a deal?"

It took several seconds, but he finally moved back a few inches. "Yes. Now, come in."

I stepped into the foyer, and my stare immediately rose to the tall ceiling and heavy metal lighting and lowered to the artwork and the black floor beneath my feet. "Gosh, it's even more beautiful on the inside."

"You and my home have that in common." Our eyes caught, and he grinned. "I'll give you the quick tour." He took my overnight bag off my arm, hung it on his, and pointed at the doorway we were approaching. "Home office is in there, where I try to spend the least amount of time, but the motherfucker sucks me in."

I huffed. "I know that feeling."

I took a quick peek at the black wooden desk and the accolades that were hanging—words too small for me to read—but what I did see was the large letter on the wall behind his chair. A giant *W*, made of what appeared to be metal and painted black. *W* for Wright. It made perfect sense. I could feel his gaze on me before I even glanced in his direction.

"Sexy office," I told him.

He chuckled. "We will christen that desk—mark my words."

"I have no doubt."

I followed him into the living room and kitchen, spaces that were completely open, dripping in masculinity through texture and color and feel. Hues I wouldn't have picked due to their hard edginess, but they were still designs and shades I was obsessed with.

"Did you build this house?"

He set the dish on the counter and placed my bag on one of the chairs and turned toward me. "I did. It was a hell of a process, too, knocking down the previous house that had been here and starting fresh."

"You didn't design all of this, did you?"

"I worked with an architect, a contractor, and an interior designer." He moved closer, but not within reach. "I didn't just tell them to do their thing. I have a strong opinion when it comes to the places I live. I don't like frills. Fluff. And I don't like a fucking mess of shit where there's something on top of everything. I need my shit tight and clean and preferably very cold."

"You're the warmth in this space. You don't need the structure or filler doing that for you."

"An interesting way to look at it."

I continued to study the room. "And the view—that's full of heat as well." I glanced back at him after consuming layers of the canyon and the homes that sat within it. "I'm assuming that's the reason for all the glass?" It was everywhere; although this wasn't a greenhouse in a sense, it gave that feeling—at least from in here.

"The view is what sold me on the lot. I wanted to be able to see it from anywhere inside this house. Walls are to block things out. Up here, I want to let it all in."

I hugged my stomach. "I agree. Why waste something so breathtaking?"

He slid his hands into the pockets of his jeans. "It's funny, my sister said the same thing when I showed her the blueprints."

"Knowing how women think, I would say every date you've ever brought up here said the same."

He shook his head. "You're the first to see it."

"Because you just moved in?" My brows rose.

"Because I don't bring women into my home. Ever."

I let those words simmer.

They shouldn't come as a shock. He was a one-night-stand kind of guy. Men like that didn't bring women home; they didn't want their address and whereabouts to be known, and inviting them in would be revealing far too much privacy.

But to hear that I was the first? That hit.

Not just my stomach, but my chest too.

"Another funny thing is," I said, "we have that in common. I bought my condo three years ago, and a man has never stepped foot inside."

"Why?"

"First, I don't do one-night stands. Second, I haven't dated a ton over the last handful of years. Work has pretty much owned me. I've gone out on dates, and things have progressed, but they've never turned serious enough for me to invite him over."

There was another reason. One I just couldn't get into yet.

And that was Dear Foodie.

Part of her appeal was her anonymity, and having someone in my condo—aside from Bryn and my family, who knew all about her—would reveal her identity since much of the interior was constantly set up for filming. The second bedroom had been fully converted into an office and studio, and my kitchen had stage lighting and multiple tripods. The living room was also where I filmed content and housed the overflow of PR packages. If things had lasted with those men, I would have brought them over. But a few weeks, even a couple of months, wasn't enough time to ask them to sign an NDA and unveil that part of my life.

So, I never risked it.

"Is that a cherry you're going to let me pop?" He smiled.

"You're asking if I'm going to let you into my home?"

He nodded.

"Maybe." I winked. "I'm not as forthcoming as you are. I appreciate that you let me in—don't get me wrong, it just takes a little more for me to get there."

"Like your mornings. Multiple sessions of caffeine until you're feeling it."

I nodded. "Yes, like that. With a focus on the multiple part."

"I'm not worried. I'll be inside your place in no time." He walked to the bar that was on the far side of the living room. "What can I get you to drink?" When he reached the long strip of counter with the glass and mirrored shelves above it, he turned toward me. "I have everything. Name whatever you want."

"You're having scotch?"

"I was."

"No old-fashioned?"

"I was feeling lazy. But if that's what you want, I'll make you one."

My skin felt like it was on fire from his gaze, and I moved my hair off my shoulders. "How about a martini?"

"What kind?"

"Vodka, not gin. The rest, surprise me. My only request, besides the alcohol, is that you shake it so well that there are ice chips floating on the top."

"That's how I like mine too." He pulled a bottle of Tito's off the shelf. "For the record, I skipped the rest of the tour for safety reasons."

"Safety reasons?"

He poured some of the vodka into a shaker. "There are five bedrooms in this house, a gym, movie theater, man cave—all rooms that have nothing but surfaces to lay you on. The living room with the two couches and multiple chairs isn't safe either, but it's beside the kitchen, so there's no way to avoid this area." He looked at me over his shoulder. "Plus, it's where the liquor is housed—if we're not counting the man cave—and that's the only reason we're in here and not standing in the middle of the kitchen."

I stepped back until I felt the counter and gripped the edge with both hands. "You're being such a good boy, Lockhart. Although we're only about ten minutes in. You have a very long way to go."

Into the shaker went squirts from a few different bottles, followed by a scoop of ice. "I'll stay that way until after dessert —mark my words."

"You think you can make it?"

"And pass up the opportunity to do whatever I want? Only a fucking idiot would do that." He began to shake the concoction, and the movement tightened his shirt around his biceps, showing off the power in his arms.

God, this man was jacked. I hadn't forgotten the feeling from when I held his arm, when I felt it around me, when it hauled me up into the air.

When he finished, he poured it into a stemless martini glass and walked it over to me. "Do you see where my fingers are holding this?"

I looked from his eyes to the positioning of his hand. "Yes."

"Do me a favor? Don't touch them."

"You're taking this seriously. I like it." I laughed. "I'll do my best." I avoided his fingers and took a sip. "Extra dirty, and, man, is that good."

He eyed my mouth. "That's not the only time you're going to say that tonight. I promise."

ELEVEN

Hart

While Sadie gripped her dirty martini between both hands—hands I miraculously hadn't touched since she'd come over because there was no way I was losing this bet —I returned to the bar and poured myself another scotch. With a tumbler that was several fingers full, I walked back over to her. I knew I was standing too close. My fingers normally had a mind of their own, and there was a chance, without me thinking and unable to stop them, that they'd reach across the short distance between us and graze a part of her.

But I just needed to be in her space. I needed to be close enough that I could smell her with every breath. I needed my lips on hers. Would the martini taste better on her mouth or in a glass? I was fucking desperate for that answer.

Goddamn it, this bet was bullshit.

But there was a prize—a hell of a good one too—and I was going to earn it.

I held my drink in front of hers. "To getting to do whatever I want tonight."

She laughed. "You mean, to hoping that comes true. We're not there yet." She grinned. "Truthfully, we're not even close to there. But I'll still cheers to it."

"You don't have to remind me of the timeline. It's going to be the most painful couple of hours of my life." I swallowed a small amount of the liquor and nodded toward the kitchen. "Go. I need you away from these couches."

"You're telling me the counters are safer?"

Her smile was so beautiful; I wanted to eat it off her.

"No." I dragged my hand through the top of my hair, disregarding the gel that was in there. I just needed to fucking pull something. "So, I'm going to hold this glass and stand on the other side of the island and pretend I'm not stripping that jacket off your body."

"But you're mentally stripping it off."

I moved to the side farthest from her, set the drink on the stone, and flattened my hands on both sides of it. "Mentally, my tongue is on your clit, and there're two fingers in your pussy, and the only thing I can hear is your screams." I shook my head. "But we're not going to talk about that. We're going to talk about everything but that."

"Fair."

With her light-pink nails, I watched her lift the drink to her mouth, her lips surround the edge of the glass, and her throat bob as she swallowed. I didn't know what it was, but there was something so familiar about it all. Like I'd seen her do the same move before. Which I had, when I had sat in the dining room and she was in the bar of the sushi restaurant.

But was that what I was remembering?

I didn't know.

She returned the glass to the stone and chewed the corner

of her lip. "For the record, I want that mouth. I want that tongue. And I want those fingers."

My head dropped, and I hissed out all the air I had been holding. "You're fucking killing me."

"I know." She pulled out one of the stools and took a seat. "Let's shift gears before your hard-on becomes so intolerable that you pounce over the island." Her tongue tapped her top lip, taunting me. "Something that will kill your hard-on, like ... your sister." She winked. "Tell me about her. Are you guys close?"

"Perfect gear to shift into." I laughed and adjusted my dick, already feeling my erection start to soften. "Eden's her name, and, yes, we're super close. But I'm just as close to my three brothers. Eden's the youngest—my parents weren't stopping until they got their girl."

"Wait." She leaned forward. "You have four siblings?"

"I do."

"Holy crap. What's that like?"

I shrugged. "Exactly what you'd expect. A house full of chaos when we were growing up, kids everywhere, never a quiet moment. We're probably an even tighter family now than we were back then. I'd say that's because we're not under the same roof anymore. Space is a good thing when you have a family that large and you didn't have enough bedrooms for everyone to sleep in, and there was endless sharing when it came to food, clothes—everything." I gazed up at the ceiling and across the living room. "We didn't grow up like this. Or anything that even remotely looked like this."

She nodded. "I get it."

I pointed at the glass that framed the view outside even though it was almost too dark to see what I was aiming at. "My brother's house is straight across the canyon, and another brother's place is off to the right—both visible from here. Eden and

Colson live right around the corner. And what's funny is that not only are our houses in the same area, but we work together too. I see most of them every day."

"It's just my sister, Cat—spelled like the animal—and me and our small family of four. I'm trying to imagine having three other Cats while growing up"—her hands went to the top of her head—"and I can't. Chaos would be an understatement." Her eyes were wide and stayed that way. "Where do you fall in the age lineup?"

"Directly in the middle." I swiped my thumb over the side of my scruff. "Is that what you would have guessed?"

"I haven't guessed anything. I'm still in shock that your poor mother was pregnant five times and four of those were boys."

"And each of us was born about two years apart."

She took a deep breath. "That's so many months of being pregnant and feeding and changing diapers and—just whoa. I mean, I love it, but it's still a lot."

"All the power to the people who want a team of children. I wouldn't change the way I grew up for anything, but it's not something I want when I get married. Two is the perfect number, in my opinion."

"So, you want kids ..." Her teeth were back, this time grinding across her bottom lip.

"I do. You?"

"Very much so." She linked her hands together. "Growing up, I wanted to be married by twenty-five and pregnant soon after so I had my kids young. Not that thirty is old—I'm not saying that at all. I'm also not saying I'm ready to have kids now. I'm just saying life didn't play out according to my plan." She glanced down at her fingers. "But I'm honestly so happy with the way things unfolded. It's just ironic how you have this vision and the path you think you're on and things never seem to go that way."

"In my experience, things tend to go better."

She rubbed the top of the glass with her thumb, and I couldn't stop watching her fingers, something about them keeping my gaze locked.

"I thought I'd go to the University of Southern California and ended up at Arizona State University—the best decision," she said. "I thought I'd live in Scottsdale after graduating, and I came back to LA instead—another decision that worked out incredibly well for me." She smiled. "So, yes, Lockhart, I agree, things tend to go better."

"You're a Sun Devil, huh?"

"And proud to be one." She laughed. "Are any of your siblings married?"

"None of them are."

"Stop. You're kidding?"

"No, we're all single." I crossed my arms. "Some because of choice, some because they're married to work, and some, just like me, who prefer playing the field. Or the old me, that is— until I met you and you changed my opinion." I pushed up the sleeves of my shirt.

"Instead of a one-night-stand kinda man, you're a two-nighter." Her expression told me she was challenging me.

"Excuse me, this is night three." I stretched out my fingers, fucking dying to put them on her, and placed them back on the counter. "And I'm hoping there are many more after tonight."

She slowly dipped her head in agreement. "How about kids? Does anyone in your family have them?"

"Colson, the second oldest, has a little girl, Ellie."

"I bet you go wild for her, don't you?"

My thumbs tapped the stone beneath them. "We all do.

125

There isn't anything that little one can't get from us. I'd buy her a car if she asked me to."

"A car? Hold on. How old is she?"

I chuckled. "Four—and I know it's extreme, but that's how much she owns me. There's no limit when it comes to her. We spoil the shit out of her."

Her brows pushed together. "Didn't you say you guys all work together?"

I nodded. "We do."

"What do you do—"

The sound of an alarm came through the kitchen, which cut her off and sent me to the oven, nearing where she was sitting.

"Dinner's done." I put on the mitts and opened the door.

"I know I haven't mentioned anything about the scent, but I've been breathing it in since I arrived. Whatever you made smells delicious."

"It's something I've never made before." I pulled out the large, round cast iron pan and set it on top of the range, removing the foil from the top. I turned a little to the side to show her the masterpiece. "Greek-style meatballs with Parmesan orzo."

The meatballs were spaced around the pan, the orzo filling the open gaps with slices of lemon resting on top.

"As for the lemon hater, I'm good if it's a garnish or a hint of a flavor or worked into my cocktail. But for dessert, fuck no." I laughed as I reached into the oven again and pulled out the foil-wrapped rectangle, placing it beside the cast iron. "A fresh baguette that I even baked myself."

"It looks amazing, especially for someone who's never made it before. And freshly baked bread? All right, Chef. I'm impressed." She raised her hands in the air.

"I came across the recipe a few weeks ago, saving it for the perfect moment. That just happened to be tonight."

"I'm always hunting for recipes too. Where do you get yours?"

I slipped off a mitt and reached into the drawer next to me and took out a fork, slicing into the side of a meatball to make sure it was the color I was after. Pleased with what I saw, I took that chunk and some of the pasta and held it not far from her mouth.

"I got this one from Dear Foodie."

She stopped halfway to the tines, her eyes locked with mine. "You did?"

"This isn't the first recipe I've made of hers, and every one has turned out great. Shit, I made her stuffed manicotti a couple of weeks ago for my whole family, and they were blown away."

Since she still hadn't moved, I brought the fork even closer to her. She stared at it for a moment before blowing on the meat and parting her lips wider to take it in, immediately covering her mouth after.

"It's excellent," she said softly.

"Do you follow her?"

"Who?" She coughed as she swallowed and reached for her drink.

"Dear Foodie."

"Oh." She ran her tongue over her teeth and set her glass back down. "Yeah."

I took the rest of the meatball and popped it into my mouth, the burning worth it—it tasted so good. "That lady knows food. How to make it. Where to eat it. She's got quite the influence on the food scene around here, wouldn't you say?" I paused as I reached for two plates. "It's fucking crazy to me that she's been able to keep her identity a secret all this time. Everyone wants to know who she is, and no one can figure it out. Genius, if you ask me."

I set the fork in the sink, and just as I was turning toward her, her hand cuffed my wrist.

Since I'd pushed up my sleeves, the feel of her hot hand made quite the impression. It also forced me to smile.

"Are you sure that's allowed, boss? I thought this was a *no-touching* zone?"

She stayed silent as she stared at me.

"Someone broke before me. It's a fucking miracle." I laughed.

"I changed my mind."

"About what?"

Now standing, she pulled at the tie that was knotted at her waist until it was loose, the sides of her jacket then falling open.

"Fuck," I moaned, taking in her breathtaking body, covered in a red lace bra and matching panties. "That set looks gorgeous on you."

"I guess I'm the one who can't wait until after dessert."

My gaze rose to hers. "What are you saying?"

"I'm saying you can do anything you want to me, Lockhart. Starting right now."

TWELVE

Sadie

I pulled into my parking garage and turned off the engine of my Jeep, and with the strap of my bag dangling on my shoulder, I got out. I waved the fob in front of the lobby door and took the elevator to my floor. Once I was inside my condo, I tossed my bag onto a chair and flopped down on my couch, wincing at the slight pain between my legs.

But it was a good pain.

A delicious pain.

A pain that made me smile as I attempted to catch my breath from the last fifteen or so hours.

What had really kicked off the gasping and wildness of the evening was Lockhart's mention of Dear Foodie. Her following had grown so tremendously that I wasn't surprised when people talked about her in front of me, not knowing it was me. But hearing him discuss her with such high regard and that he'd used her recipe—one she'd filmed in this very kitchen with an altered voice-over—was too much.

So was the fact that his meatballs were better than mine.

But that was the first time I'd ever been in a situation where a man I liked—a man I was basically dating—discussed Dear Foodie with me.

And when it happened, I freaked.

I didn't know what the hell to do, so I did the only thing I knew that would stop the conversation, and that was untying my jacket and dissolving the bet and allowing him to touch me.

Something I wanted as well.

And it certainly worked.

Because from that point forward, my body became possessed by what he was doing to me. His touching. His licking. His thrusting.

There wasn't a spot on me that wasn't caressed by some part of him.

Oh God, it was everything.

And when we eventually peeled away from one another, we ate the meatballs and orzo with the freshly baked baguette, and I was in literal heaven. We had more of it for breakfast, and I left shortly after we finished eating.

But the whole time I was there, I didn't dare take out my phone from my bag, for fear that a notification would come across my screen and he'd see it.

I had been dying to though.

I wanted a glimpse of his online presence, and I wanted to learn more about him through pictures. Since that was the very way I expressed myself, it was how I related most to people.

I wanted that connection with Lockhart.

And I couldn't wait a second longer.

I unlocked the screen and clicked on my Instagram app, scrolling to the Greek meatball reel, and I pulled up the likes. There were over forty thousand, but there was a search bar directly above the likes, allowing me to look up by name who had double-tapped the video.

I typed *Lockhart Wright*.

Nothing came up.

I then typed *Lockhart*.

Not a single like, out of over forty thousand, is named Lockhart?

That was odd.

But this wasn't the first time I'd attempted to find his account on Instagram. It was, however, the first time I'd looked him up as someone who liked my posts. I repeated the same process under my total list of followers, but that didn't produce anything either.

There was possibly a way around this.

Under my followers, I typed *Eden*.

Six accounts loaded, and I studied each of their last names.

Smith.

Kelley.

Filla.

Lowery.

Swift.

The final one didn't have a last name mentioned, but there was a *W* that followed Eden in her username, along with a mix of numbers.

That was her, Eden Wright—it had to be.

On her profile, with a bio filled with relatable emojis, I slowly moved through her collection of pictures. In many, she was alone, doing things around LA—hiking, sunbathing, eating. And in the ones where she wasn't alone, she was with other women. Looks-wise, she was the complete opposite of Lockhart with beautiful, long blonde hair and blue eyes. She was most likely in her mid-twenties, which would fit the age description he'd given to me. But blonde? Her roots were too well covered to see if it was natural. I scrolled back up and dug through her followers, searching for Lockhart and Colson—the only other sibling he'd mentioned—and nothing came up.

So, Lockhart's sister followed me.

But what about him? The way he'd spoken about Dear Foodie gave me the impression that he was a follower too. Did he not use his name online? So many people didn't because they didn't have to.

Shit, Dear Foodie wasn't my name.

As I returned to Eden's pictures, a text came across my screen.

LOCKHART

Did you make it home safely?

I immediately exited out of her account, feeling as though I'd been caught red-handed—something I knew was impossible, but the coincidence was uncanny.

Still, the smile that pulled across my lips, the sigh that came through them—he was the only one who could trigger those.

God, I liked this man.

But things were suddenly ... messy? Complicated?

A territory I had absolutely no idea how to navigate.

Ugh.

ME

All safe and sound. Thank you for an amazing night.

And morning.

I needed backup.

I pulled up my Contacts and then my Favorites folder and hit Bryn's name, holding the phone to my ear, hearing her answer, "Good morning—"

"I need help."

"Is this like 911 help? Or in-need-of-a-mimosa kind of help?"

I leaned back into the cushions. "Maybe somewhere in between."

"You spent the night at Lockhart's. Did something happen?"

"It went great, Bryn. I'm talking, it couldn't have gone better. Except ... he brought up Dear Foodie. But not in passing. Like, he really talked about her. That she has quite the influence on the food scene, and it's fucking crazy that she's been able to keep her identity a secret, and everyone wants to know who she is, and no one can figure it out." I slid out my elastic, letting my hair fall to both sides of my face.

"Do you think he knows it's you?"

"No." As soon as the word left my mouth, I backtracked and voiced, "I mean, it's possible, but I didn't get the feeling he knew. He was too nonchalant about it. He wasn't goading me. He was speaking freely about someone he—I don't know—admires in a sense? I don't even know if that's the right way to describe it. But he made my recipe for dinner—the Greek meatballs. And side note: his tasted better than mine."

"Good Lord."

"Yep."

"Okay, let's put this into perspective, shall we? The men I've dated in the past, I swear, if I had shown up to their house with flaming red hair, they wouldn't have noticed. And if I'd questioned them whether I looked different, they'd have probably asked if I got a new outfit. In other words, they weren't observant at all. Maybe Lockhart is the same?"

I rubbed my forehead. "I don't know ..."

"You hide yourself so well, Sadie. You disguise your voice. You don't show any part of your face. The only things people see are your arms and wrists and hands, and it's not like you have fingers that are distinct or super memorable."

I massaged between my eyebrows, where an ache was forming. "True."

My phone beeped, and I pulled it away from my ear to look at the screen.

LOCKHART
What do you have going on tonight?

ME
Girl dinner, LOL. You?

"I think you're safe, which is what you're worried about, right?" She paused. "You don't want him to know about Dear Foodie?"

"There's that, yes. But what happens if I eventually want him to know who I am?" I exhaled. "It's like he already knows her. But we're two different people who are, in some fucked-up way, the same. How do I even make that introduction? *Oh, by the way, you've been using my recipes to cook your family dinner. I'm glad you enjoyed them. Let's skip past the logistics of this nutty job I have and talk about—I don't know—the weather?*"

My phone beeped again.

LOCKHART
What's girl dinner?

I'm going out with my brother.

ME
A charcuterie board of whatever is in my fridge and pantry. Tell me you're jealous, LOL.

Ooh. Where are you guys going?

"You've never had to tell any of your dates about that side of you," she said.

I leaned forward, switching her to speakerphone while I held the phone on top of my knees. "And I've never had to have them sign an NDA, which is a hard requirement."

"Oh boy."

"Yep—again."

LOCKHART

Horned. Have you been back there since I stole you away from your reservation?

ME

Yesss! And I loved it. So much.

"I can see where the anxiety is coming from," Bryn said. "You really are a problem, girlfriend." She laughed.

"I know."

"I don't want to say *how do we fix this* because there's nothing to fix. You are who you are, and you're a total badass boss bitch. But this other side of you does create a few layers that will have to be worked around."

"And I have no idea how to do that."

LOCKHART

Sounds like I'll be impressed then.

ME

You'll be blown away. It's one of the best restaurants I've been to in a while.

I hovered my thumbs over the screen, tempted to mention Dear Foodie's review since I was sure he'd read it.

But I couldn't.

I was positive that would only send some bad karma into the universe.

ME

> Have the best time and save room for the
> butter cake. It's to DIE for. 😊

I watched the bubble appear under his name, showing me that he was typing, and then it quickly disappeared. It happened again, but no text came through.

My concentration on Lockhart was interrupted when Bryn said, "We'll figure this out, Sadie."

Another bubble popped up, this one only lasting a few seconds before it was gone.

"I hope so," I exhaled.

LOCKHART

> I'll be impressed then ...

> But last night's dessert is going to be hard to
> beat. I think piña colada cupcakes may be my
> new favorite. Licking that frosting off you?
> Fuck, I'm getting hard just thinking about it.

ME

> Agreed. xo

THIRTEEN

Hart

"I'm going to try my hardest not to be a grump, but it's what"—Sadie paused—"only a little past eight, and I'm just taking my first sip of coffee, so I have a long way to go before I'm caffeinated."

The sound of her always did two things to me.

The first was put this foolish fucking expression on my face.

The second was that she immediately made my dick hard.

"You don't have to say much at all," I told her. "I just wanted to wish you a good morning and hear your voice."

"Aw. You're sweet."

I finally turned at the light. "I don't know if that's true. I'm ready to get in our jet and fly to where I need to be before I rip someone's face off. The traffic is bullshit today."

"You have no idea how happy I am that I work from home. I could not deal with that bumper-to-bumper chaos every day."

I thrummed the steering wheel with my thumbs as the cars

in front of me began to get backed up again. "If I didn't have a meeting in ten minutes, my ass would be working from home too."

"Oh, I forgot to text you before I went to bed and ask how Horned was. Did you and your brother have a good dinner?"

Fuck my life.

Horned was the whole reason I was even going into the office today.

But what I couldn't get out of my head was the text conversation I'd had with her about it. She loved it there; she'd talked it up, using the highest praise to describe her meal, like there was no better food to be found in the whole state.

First Dear Foodie. Then Eden. Now Sadie.

All opinions I could confirm since Beck and I had eaten there.

And all that did was reinforce my decision—a decision Beck and I were going to pitch to Walker today.

"It was just like you said it was. In fact, I'll use your exact words—blown away and one of the best restaurants I've been to in a while."

And Walker wasn't going to want to hear that. I was already mentally preparing for the war that was going to take place in our conference room.

"Did you get the butter cake?" she asked.

"Sure did," I exhaled, wishing I had another piece right now. "Honestly, I could have eaten ten of them—it was that good."

Which had fucking killed Beck and me to admit because it was better than our cheesecake, our signature dessert at Charred. Another thing Walker was going to lose his shit over.

Our family had a lot to talk about today.

"Yay, I'm so happy you loved it."

I was tempted to explain why me loving it was a complicated scenario. But Sadie didn't know why I'd gone to Horned —either time. We hadn't discussed The Weston Group, and the only siblings I'd called out by first name were the unfamous ones. Our family business and my famous brothers were topics women loved to bring up to me once they found out my last name.

Maybe Sadie knew and was waiting for the right time to mention it. Maybe it didn't matter to her, and she had no interest in talking about it at all. Or maybe she didn't know, and sometime soon, I would reveal that part of me, the same way she would eventually invite me to her place.

But for once, it was a goddamn relief to not have a woman drill me on the mysterious, world-renowned Walker Weston; the wild Beck Weston, a multi–Stanley Cup winner; or the hundreds of restaurants we owned.

That was only part of my life. The more important part? That was what Sadie was really getting to know.

"Tell me, what are you doing tomorrow night?" I inquired.

"*Mmm.* Work? Yeah, lots of work, I think."

I was relieved as hell to see the high-rise of our corporate office up ahead, knowing I'd only have to put up with this bull-shit traffic for a few more minutes before I had to tackle a whole other battle.

"I don't like that answer, Sadie."

"Neither do I. How about you change it?"

I skimmed my teeth over my lip. "Dinner."

"*Yesss.*"

"I'll text you later."

"You'd better."

I chuckled as I hung up and pulled into the parking garage of our corporate office, getting out at the valet stand, and while the attendant parked my car, I took the elevator to the top floor. Since the ride was fairly long, I slipped out my phone from my pocket, avoiding any app that had to do with work, and opened Instagram—the best stress-free way to pass time.

The first post on my feed was from Dear Foodie with the caption, *Soy in love.* There were two photos. The first was of three pieces of nigiri on a plate and a perfectly positioned pair of chopsticks with a wad of wasabi on the end. The second was of a lychee martini, holding the mouth of the glass with her pink nails. She'd tagged the location; I knew it well. It was the restaurant where I'd run into Sadie and taken her out in the alley behind the building.

If Dear Foodie loved that place, I could only hope she felt the same way about Toro.

I gave the post a like just as the door opened to the executive floor, my assistant standing nearby since the security monitors had notified her of my arrival.

I nodded. "Good morning, CC."

Cecilia preferred the nickname, and my family and I had been using it since her first day, which was seven years ago.

"Everyone's already in the conference room." She waved me toward the hallway, and that was when I caught sight of her nails.

"You have pink too? What, does every woman in this world only use that color?"

"Pink?" She followed my line of sight to the hand she was holding in the air. "Oh! Dear Foodie inspired this manicure. What can I say?" She snorted.

I shook my head and checked my watch. "I'm not late."

"No, your siblings were just early. Can I get you coffee? Bagel? Anything?"

"Coffee, as strong as you can make it. Thank you."

I passed her and went through the double doors and down the hallway until I reached the end. The door to the conference room was already ajar, so I walked in, and the room turned silent as everyone looked at me.

"Suddenly, you're all overachievers?"

Eden smirked. "I came in early to get work done. You know, I'd be able to work normal hours if you guys actually left me alone during the day and let me do my job."

"I didn't sleep," Walker admitted. "Might as well be here than tossing and turning in my bed."

Colson groaned. "None of you are allowed to complain about sleep until you have a four-year-old who would rather sleep in your bed than hers, who positions herself sideways and mostly on top of you and insists on having no less than ten purple unicorns surrounding her. Then, you're allowed to bitch all you want."

"Fuck that. I have every right to bitch," Walker stammered. "Besides, I have plenty of four-year-olds, their names are Charred and Toro and their hundreds of kitchens that I manage, and they do a hell of a job at keeping me awake."

Kill me now.

Today was going to go over like a goddamn lead balloon.

I took a seat across from Beck and nodded toward him. "Do you want to do the honors?"

Beck was wearing an LA Whales hoodie, the team he played for, and he pushed up the sleeves before he clasped his hands on the table. "We need to talk about Horned."

"Jesus fucking Christ," Walker groaned. "I can't escape that restaurant, no matter how hard I try."

"What we're about to tell you is going to make things even worse," Beck said, clearing his throat. "Hart and I went there last night for dinner." He paused and looked at me before returning his gaze to Walker. "It fucking pains me to say this, but it was one of the best meals I've had in a very long time."

Walker looked like he was on the verge of tearing his hair out.

"And we want to buy it," I added.

Walker shot up straight in his chair. "You ... *what?*"

I nodded. "We think it'll be the perfect addition to our brand."

Walker glanced from me to Beck and back. "Why?" He stood, setting his palms on the table, and leaned forward, sending him even closer, as he was across from me. "Because what we have already isn't enough?"

"What we have is plenty," I explained. "But this is nothing like what we have. This is ..." My hand went to the top of my head, holding it. "Shit, I don't even know what this is. It's eclectic and original, and to put it bluntly, it's perfect."

"Are you trying to give me a heart attack?" Walker asked us.

"No, and that's why we think we should keep the executive chef," I said. "She doesn't want to manage the logistics of a business, and that's the reason she brought on the Gordons—she only wants to be in the kitchen. So, we let her do that. We pay her an extremely generous salary, she focuses on the food and menu, and we run the show. When we open new locations, she'll travel to train and then return to her hub in Laguna Beach."

"Really, she's no different than any of the other chefs we have on our payroll. The only *but* is that we need to buy the business from her. We throw her a couple mil and call it a day."

Walker's gaze shifted between Beck and me again. "The two of you are fucking serious."

"Dead serious," Beck replied.

Walker released a loud breath. "And you," he voiced to Eden, "are you on board with this?"

She held her chin with her pink fucking nails and said,

"You know how I feel about the meal I ate there. I don't see how this could be a bad investment."

Walker dragged his stare to Colson. "Your turn to weigh in."

Colson shrugged. "I haven't eaten there, so I don't have an opinion about the restaurant. But if those three"—he pointed at Eden, then Beck, and me—"think it's worthy, I know they wouldn't steer us wrong. I support whatever you all decide."

Walker's head dropped, his fingers turning white as he pushed on the table. When he glanced up, he said, "I need a fucking drink," before he walked out of the conference room.

The outside of my mouth was still wet from Sadie's pussy. My lips had been positioned against hers over the last fifteen or so minutes—a break from pre-dinner cocktails because there was something I wanted to drink more than my old-fashioned, and that was her cunt. My tongue swiped her clit so many times that I gave her two orgasms. I could still feel her on my fingers. The way she had tightened around them. The way she had soaked my skin. And I could still taste her on my tongue.

God, she was fucking perfection.

And now, as I looked down at the floor in my kitchen, only feet from where I'd eaten her on my island, she was there, on her knees, with my dick in her mouth.

Her lips were wide, her cheeks full, as she bobbed down my shaft as far as she could, using both hands to cover me—one palm swiveling around the remainder of my cock that she wasn't able to fit in and the other cupping my balls.

She knew what the fuck she was doing, and she was using every bit of power she had to draw the cum out of me.

"That's it," I hissed. My fingers were on the top of her head, squeezing her hair. Not to urge her on. Not to increase her pace. But because I just needed to grip something—that was how good she was making me feel. "Hell yes, Sadie!"

I didn't have to tell her to go harder; she was already doing that.

I didn't even have to tell her to go faster; it was as though she could read how close I was getting to the edge and sensed what I needed.

"Oh my God," I moaned.

Damn, this woman could give a fucking blow job.

A mouth that was relentless.

Hands that ruthlessly stroked me.

My head fell back as the bursts started to move through my sac. "You're going to make me fucking come."

As soon as those words left my mouth, she began to really suck, focusing on my tip while her fingers took care of the rest.

Grinding me.

Pumping me.

Forcing my orgasm to peak.

My head straightened, and we locked eyes.

"If you don't want a mouthful, then you'd better stop right now."

She deserved the warning.

But where I thought she might pull back and jerk me off into her hand, she kept her lips around my head, her tongue circling, her eyes large as they gazed straight into mine.

She wanted me to unload in her mouth.

She was going to get that wish.

"Shit yeah!" It only took a few more dips, and I was there. Full of fucking tingles. The wave of pleasure spread through me, combining all together and ejecting straight out. "Sadie, ah!" I could feel it squirt. I could feel the cum on her tongue as she dragged it around me. "Fuck! Fuck! Yes!" The last bit drained out of me, the sensation of the build now gone, and what was left was the after—the jittery feeling that ran through my body as it slowly dissolved. "Damn it, that was sick."

Her speed died down, her eyes never leaving mine, even after she came to a stop. She licked her lips as she stood, running her thumb across the bottom and then the top, smiling like she knew the control she'd just had over me.

"I've been dying to do that," she admitted.

I chuckled. "You're really fucking good at it."

I tucked my dick back into my boxer briefs and zipped the fly of my jeans, along with fastening the button and my belt. Before she could return to the old-fashioned I'd made her, I pulled her against me.

"We're covered in each other." She rubbed her thumb over the bottom of my mouth, and I licked the pad of it and then my lips. "You can't get enough of me, Lockhart."

"No, I can't, and I won't ever."

She smiled as I ran my palms down her back and cupped her ass, taking a quick glance at the stovetop.

"Whatever you're making for dinner smells incredible." I rubbed my nose over hers.

She laughed. "The only reason I haven't told you is because I love to surprise you."

Which she'd been able to do because she'd shown up with a Dutch oven that she put straight into the oven and some Tupperware that went into the fridge. I'd seen nothing of what she'd made.

But what I'd found interesting was when we talked about the plans for this evening, she'd expressed her desire to cook at my place. Something I certainly didn't have an issue with. I just didn't want her to think we always had to stay in since I'd made the comment once that I didn't want to be too far from a bed.

"I want to make something clear because I don't know if it

is." My hands moved to her face. "We never have to stay in. We can go out whenever you want."

She studied my eyes. "Where is this coming from?"

"I texted you once that I didn't want us to be too far from a bed." I let out some air with a grin. "Regardless of what just happened in my kitchen and at the sushi restaurant"—I laughed—"I promise I can control myself and take you out and make it through an entire meal."

She wrapped her arms around my neck. "What if I don't want to be too far from a bed?"

"That just made me like you even more." I pressed my nose to hers. "But I'm serious."

"I know." She leaned back a few inches and kissed me. "Tonight, I wanted to cook for you, but that won't always be the case. I'll get this antsy urge to go out, and you will too. I like that we love to do both."

"Same."

Her eyes suddenly turned wide. "Oh shit." She pulled her arm loose and looked at her watch. "Dinner is ready." She released me and went over to the oven, grabbing the mitts I'd set out and slipping them on.

I observed her from this side of the island with a view of her ass that I could stare at forever. "Can I help you?"

"Nope. I've got this." She took out the pot from inside the oven and set it on the stovetop. She then grabbed a fork from the drawer and glanced at me. "I'm really learning my way around your kitchen." After she winked, she took off the lid of the Dutch oven and dug through whatever was inside. "We're good. It's ready. Let's eat."

She grabbed two plates from the cabinet and a serving spoon from the drawer, leaving it all by the stove while she went to the fridge to get the Tupperware. She lined everything up and began to plate.

"Watermelon and feta salad." I eyed each scoop. "And potato salad."

"What's in the potato salad is what makes it special."

As soon as she set the main entrée on the plate, I said, "Short ribs." I nodded in approval. "Nice."

She looked at me from over her shoulder. "Sounds like an interesting pairing, I know. But you have to trust the process."

"I trust you. I'm not worried about anything." I took the plates from her hands and carried them into the dining room that had already been set while she brought in our cocktails. I immediately tried the short ribs. I couldn't wait; they smelled amazing. And I moaned, "Sadie," when the meat hit my tongue.

She smiled. "Now try it with some potato salad. There are dried cranberries in there, and when you combine it with the mayo and the rich, savory meat, it's divine."

She was right.

I whistled and added, "Shit, you weren't joking."

"The watermelon is just a refreshing addition to balance the heavy meal. The basil gives it an earthy punch, and the feta —well, I just love cheese."

"That makes two of us." The salad was as good as everything else. "This is outstanding. All of it. Thank you."

"No, thank you."

I watched her cut her meat into small pieces, wiping her lips after every bite before she licked them.

"You love food, and you're an excellent cook—I'm telling you, Sadie, I think I've found my future wife."

She laughed again. "It runs in my blood. I can't help myself."

I nodded. "I know that feeling."

She set down her fork and took a drink. "This is probably going to come across as very random, but I wanted to ask you something about Eden. You've mentioned her a few times to me, and when you were describing the dating patterns of your family, you said one doesn't date by choice." She paused. "Were you referring to her or one of your brothers?"

I hesitated. "Her."

She nibbled at the end of a watermelon chunk. "It's just not her thing?"

This wasn't information I was willing to share.

With anyone.

Even if I cared about them, like I did with Sadie.

"Single is her thing." And that was all I would say on the matter.

She nodded. "I get it."

But she didn't.

"How old is she?" she asked.

"Twenty-seven."

"So interesting."

I took down the rest of my old-fashioned and replied, "You'll meet her soon, and you'll love her. She'll come across as a little closed off at first. She's not the type to give you that warm and fuzzy greeting—that's the way she describes it, not me." I chuckled. "But once you get through that outer layer"—the emotion surrounding Eden was in my chest, it always was whenever I talked about her, but I refused to show it—"she's one of the best people you'll ever have in your life."

"I'm looking forward to that." She turned her face, giving me her profile. "But do you really think I'll meet her soon?"

"If I was a betting man—and I think you know I am—I'd say you're going to meet all my siblings soon."

That fucking smile.

I couldn't get enough of it.

FOURTEEN

Sadie

I didn't love digital to-do lists; there wasn't enough satisfaction in crossing off each item accomplished. I would check the box, and the task would disappear as though it never existed. But it had existed, in a hard way, and it could have possibly taken me hours to complete. I wanted to see all that hard work; I didn't want the reminder to just vanish. That was why I preferred writing my responsibilities on sticky notes. I had them in a rainbow of colors. And when I didn't get enough satisfaction in drawing a line through the duty, I would sometimes scribble multiple lines, and when that didn't give me enough relief, I'd use a Sharpie and black out every hint of it.

My trash was overflowing with crumpled-up sticky notes that barely had any color left—there was so much black marker covering them.

That was how my week was going.

And there was still an array of rainbow notes hanging on

every surface of my office, and when one task was finalized, ten more popped up.

Filming.

Editing.

Posting.

Commenting.

The life of an influencer.

But in between, there had been a break, where I spent an evening at a new Italian restaurant that had opened only a few months ago in the Gaslamp Quarter of San Diego. It had no more than ten tables inside; the family had relocated from Lucca, Italy, so the menu focused on flavors from their region in Tuscany.

As I sat at my desk, finishing up my glowing review—a vast improvement from last week's disastrous experience at a new French restaurant—my phone lit up with my boss's name on the screen.

The article would be done in less than an hour and wasn't due until tomorrow. I wasn't late on my deadline, and I hadn't been since the Horned incident.

There had to be another reason for his call.

I swiped my finger across the screen. "Hello?"

"Good morning."

I checked the time on my monitor. "Good morning—although it's not really morning, I suppose."

"Technically, it's afternoon, but it's morning to you. I assume you're still on your first cup of coffee?"

We'd worked together for so long now that he knew the way I operated.

"I'm about to start my second cup." I laughed.

"I won't keep you. There're just a few things we need to discuss. The first—your review of Horned."

I leaned back in my chair, rocking, even though the motion seemed to only make me nervous. "Okay ..."

"Since it was posted, viewership of *Seen* is up by twelve percent with a steady and consistent rise every day."

Not at all what I had expected to hear.

My head shook as I responded, "Wow."

"So, I wanted to call and personally congratulate you, Sadie. Our social media accounts are flooded with comments about you, our readers are desperate for more of your voice, and the executives at *Seen* couldn't be happier."

My boss wasn't one to give compliments. He told me the things I did wrong, never the things I did right, despite knowing I was a huge asset to the publication.

Therefore, the more he spoke, the more shocking this conversation was.

"You have no idea how thrilled I am to hear that," I admitted.

"We feel the same, and you're going to see some of our appreciation in your next paycheck. We've given you a raise."

"I was not expecting that. Thank you."

"The other reason I'm calling is that we've been given some opening dates for new restaurants in the area, and I wanted you to make note of them. One, in particular, we're really keeping an eye on."

I grabbed a pen and a green pad of sticky notes—the color that was the closest to me. "And that is?"

"Toro."

"Oh, yes, I know all about it." I tapped my pen. "The new concept Walker Weston branded. I believe Denver was his first location, Banff was his second, and now he's testing the LA market."

"That's what I understand too."

"I'm assuming you want me to go?"

"With the amount of buzz it's already getting, what I'd like to do is build up the momentum of your review the same way we did with Horned. Tease our audience. Get them salivating. And then hit them with your honest feedback."

I jotted down a few notes. "Is there a definite date it's opening? I've read mixed things online. Some say construction and permits are holding things up."

"I received an email from The Weston Group announcing the official date and inviting our team for the soft opening, so I suspect those issues have been worked out. I don't anticipate you'll come to the opening—and understandably so—but I wanted to extend the invite."

"I appreciate that, but I'm going to pass for obvious reasons." I paused. "Is there anything else you wanted to talk to me about?"

"That sums it up."

I put my pen down. "Until next time?"

He chuckled. "Until next time."

I hung up, and as I was placing my phone on the holder, a text came across the screen.

One that made me smile.

LOCKHART

I waited as long as I could in hopes that I wouldn't wake you, but, fuck, I miss you.

Instead of texting back, I decided to do something even better. I hit his name in my Contacts and brought the phone up to my ear.

"You're giving me your voice," Lockhart said as he answered.

"I thought that would be more personal than a stream of emojis." I picked my pen back up and put the non-ink end in my mouth.

"How are you, gorgeous?"

I sighed as I glanced around my office, the neon sticky notes catching my attention, my chest tightening as I realized just how many there were. "I'm currently swallowed in work."

"It's been too long since I've tasted you."

I exhaled again, this time deeper. "I hate it. Make it stop."

He moaned out a deep breath. "Tonight, I'm with the guys. How about tomorrow?"

"Tomorrow I can do since I'm with Bryn tonight."

"Are you going to let me take you out?"

I laughed. "*Maaaybe.*"

"Whatever you decide, I'm good with."

I didn't know if I should take him to my favorite Thai restaurant or the seafood one I'd fallen in love with a few weeks ago. Or if we should stay in and bask in his incredible cooking and finally take a dip in that big, wonderful Jacuzzi tub that was out back of his house.

So many decisions.

"I'll see you tomorrow," I said.

"You sure will."

***

"There's something so sexy about this restaurant," Bryn said as she sat across from me, turning the stem of her wineglass between two of her fingers so the dark red cabernet splashed along the sides. "And the food? Sigh, it's so good."

We'd decided on a steak house for dinner. One that was high-end and loved by most.

"You're not going to believe me when I say this, but I've only been to this location twice."

Her brows rose. "What? You live, like, five minutes from here."

"I know." I pulled off a corner of the sourdough loaf that was still warm and had the right amount of crispness, and I swiped it across the butter that was whipped and dusted with cinnamon and brown sugar. "There're just so many restaurants from Santa Barbara to San Diego that I need to cover, it's rare for me to come back to a place unless I really love it, like that sushi restaurant we always end up at. I dream about that nigiri."

"When food is your job, everything changes. You're eating for mortgage money, baby."

I slowly nodded with the biggest smile, my eyes closing as the sweetness of the sugar hit my tongue. "Truth."

A food runner approached and set a plate between Bryn and me and said, "Tuna tartare over a bed of avocado, ginger, and tempura flakes with a wasabi aioli drizzled on top and a splash of ponzu. There are fried wonton crisps on the side for dipping. Enjoy."

"Thank you," I said to him.

"I'm drooling," Bryn replied when he left our table. "Do you want a pic before I dig in?"

I laughed. "You know me too well." I slipped out my phone and pulled up the Camera app, holding my cell over the plate, snapping several photos from different angles. "All set."

She took one of the wontons and scooped it into the tuna like it was a dip. "Oh my God, yes." She spoke behind her hand.

"So, it's as good as it looks?"

She moaned, "Better."

As I was putting my phone back, a text came across the screen.

LOCKHART

I can't stop thinking about you.

"Only one thing in this world can make you smile that big, and that's Lockhart."

I held up a finger, letting her know I needed a second, and started to type.

ME

Stop ... you're going to make me think I've found my future husband.

"I'm that obvious?"

She snorted. "Come on. It's me. And it's him. Obvious is an understatement."

I put my phone back inside my purse and shivered as I brought the old-fashioned up to my mouth. "That man makes me tingle in all the places." I took a drink, holding in the whiskey, letting it burn my tongue. "He doesn't just say the right words, he does all the right things too. The way he looks at me, the way he touches me—I've never had that before." The candle flickering on the side of our table wasn't setting the mood; Lockhart was doing that inside my head. "I don't think I've ever felt this way."

"You haven't. I'd know." She reached across the plate and put her hand on my wrist. "I need to meet this man. Like, immediately. Seeing him at the restaurant that night wasn't enough. I didn't even get a chance to talk to him."

"It's going to happen very soon." I laughed. "Which is the same thing he said to me about his siblings."

"*Ooh*, you're going to meet the family?"

When she released me, I grabbed a wonton and spooned some tuna on top. "He didn't say anything about his parents, just his brothers and sister, but that's still family."

She wiped her mouth with a napkin. "And he still hasn't been to your place?"

I shook my head, my cheeks puffing out as I filled them

with air. "He hasn't asked or pushed it in any way. Maybe I'll just ride this for as long as I can, and then when the timing feels right—I don't know—I'll lay my alter ego on him."

"It's going to be fine."

I groaned out a long breath. "My least favorite word in the entire universe, Bryn. Fine is never fine."

She lifted her wine. "Babe, I promise."

FIFTEEN

Hart

SADIE

> Stop ... you're going to make me think I've found my future husband.

If I wasn't with Eden and Beck, having drinks at the bar at Charred, I'd ask Sadie where she was so I could show up to the restaurant and make her come in the ladies' room, returning her to her dinner with Bryn like I hadn't just put my mouth all over her pussy.

But when I made plans with my siblings, I didn't cancel them.

Still, I couldn't fucking help myself; I needed her to know how much I ached for her.

ME

> I want you.

I set the phone on the bar and looked at Eden, who was mid-conversation with us, discussing Walker's reaction when we'd pitched him the Horned buyout.

"He's stressed," she said, dipping the straw into her vodka soda. "I called him a few hours after our meeting to check on him, and you know what he was doing?"

"I'm afraid to ask," I replied.

"He was in the kitchen—at his house, not at the restaurant, which is something he never does in the morning, banging around, pans crashing, the fire alarm going off. I could barely hear anything he was saying."

"Jesus," Beck groaned. "He was really going through it."

"He was two drinks deep, and it wasn't even ten," she added. "He didn't end up going into Charred that night."

"That's not like him at all," I said.

SADIE

You know you make me wet every time you say that to me.

ME

How wet?

SADIE

As if you were rubbing my clit—that wet.

ME

You're fucking killing me, Sadie.

"Are you telling us this so we drop the idea of the buyout?" I asked her.

"No." Eden's hand paused on top of the straw. "I'm saying this because I think we need to let Toro open first. I think we need to let all those kinks get worked out, and then, once Walker can take a breath, we can slowly transition into the buyout of Horned. But doing Toro and Horned at the same time is going to send Walker over an edge that he might not return from."

I looked at Beck. "That's doable, isn't it?"

He nodded. "I'll reach out to our attorney, Troy Wolf, at The Dalton Group and have him draft up a contract. At least then, when we go to the chef of Horned, we'll have the paperwork ready. She's not in a rush to sell—I know that—and once the Gordons find out we've made an offer, I'm sure there's going to be some negotiating and dancing back and forth." He took a sip of his bourbon. "They're going to show how big their dick is, and we're going to show that ours is larger. We'll win in the end."

SADIE
Yeah? How badly?

ME
There was one thing I didn't do to you when you gave me your body. I want that.

I want that right fucking now.

Eden sighed. "A love triangle. My least favorite trope."

"There's not going to be any love, Eden. It's probably going to get ugly, and it's going to get expensive." Beck raised his glass. "We can afford it."

"I fucking despise the Gordons," I ranted. "Horned will be ours—there's no question about that."

SADIE
My ass?

ME
Yes.

SADIE
I've never done that before.

159

I assumed ... which means I'll have to be extremely gentle with you.

"Are we really going to scale Horned to the size of Charred? Like we want to do with Toro?" Eden asked. "So, we're going to have three major restaurant labels *and* clubs?"

I attempted a chuckle even though my fucking dick was hard and I found nothing funny at the moment. "When you put it that way, for some reason, it does sound like a lot. More so than when we pitched it to Walker that morning."

"We're going to need more staff," she replied.

"We already do," Beck countered.

"And we're going to need a lot more buildings," she continued.

"Jenner Dalton, the Spades' attorney, can help with the commercial spaces," Beck offered. "He's brilliant at finding the lots where they build their hotels and an expert at zoning and working with city officials. Considering how large Toro and Horned are going to get, we should probably set up a meeting with him and discuss the areas we're considering."

SADIE

What if I hate it?

ME

What if I make you fall in love with it? To the point where you'll be begging for anal.

SADIE

I love your arrogance.

ME

Tell me more.

SADIE

> I just can't believe you're that confident. That you KNOW I'll fall in love with it.

"And you're going to do all of that after Toro opens," Eden confirmed. "Remember, we need to get through the family and friends' night and then the soft opening and then the first month before Walker can relax."

Beck smiled, swiveling in his chair. "You really drive a hard bargain."

"I'm always looking out for my brothers. It's what I do. And when I know one of you needs something, I make it happen. This is what Walker needs, and I know you want everything yesterday, but a few more months isn't going to kill you." She looked at me. "Or you."

ME

> I think I've proven how confident I am.

I leaned back in my barstool and took a scan across the main lounge, noticing how full the dining room was tonight. The bar wasn't nearly as packed, giving us some space from our guests—breathing room that I knew Beck appreciated. More often than not, he was approached in public for pictures and autographs, and when he came to our restaurant, he tried to keep it about family. But unless he wore a hat, which he didn't have on tonight, he was easily recognized.

As my stare dragged back toward the bar, something near the center of the room caught my attention. Something that made me smile so fucking hard and rub my hand over my pant leg as the sweat instantly set in.

Not something.

Someone.

A gorgeous, black-haired woman with a grin that made me

throb. Her face was lit up as she held her phone in front of her —I assumed she was typing a reply to my text.

Out of all places, baby, you came to mine.

> If that's what you want, then that's what you'll have. I trust you. With every part of my body.

One of our waiters stopped at her table and delivered a plate, setting it between the two women. Sadie held her phone above it, appearing to take several photos before she placed her cell on the table. She then filled her grip with a knife and began cutting what looked like the fresh burrata.

I called over the nearest server and said to him, "Table twenty-one. There are two women sitting there. I want you to find out what they're drinking, and I want you to send them a round. On me."

"Got it," the server replied.

As I looked back at my sister, she was also holding her phone in front of her face, her expression not one I liked.

"Is everything okay?" I asked.

"Fuck," she replied.

"Fuck?" I questioned.

She slowly turned the phone toward me.

There was a Celebrity Alert on her screen—some bullshit gossip site that was, sadly and unfortunately, accurate a lot of the time. They sent out notifications when they were tipped off about celebrity news.

In this instance, the words I was reading and the pictures I was viewing were some that hit personally.

"Fuck," I mirrored her statement and glanced at Beck.

Once Beck finished reading the alert, he scanned the bar, looking at the faces that surrounded us before his gaze returned to mine. "If they notice me in here, they're going to start asking questions about the Celebrity Alert—the one I'm sure they're reading like every other goddamn person in this world—and I'll get swarmed. I've got to get out of here before that happens."

I patted his shoulder, trying not to show how fucking pissed off I was at the tip that had been aired. "That's probably a good idea."

SIXTEEN

Sadie

I left my phone on the table in case Lockhart wrote back to my last text—when I'd told him I trusted him with every part of my body—and I took a bite of the burrata that had just been delivered.

Bryn was in the midst of telling me about the new guy at work who had asked her out for a third time. He sounded fabulous from everything she'd told me about him, so when she'd mentioned him in the past, along with tonight, I encouraged her to go on the date. But she refused, adamant that office romances led to nothing but awkwardness when they didn't work out—and they never worked out, according to her.

I was trying to prove that there were exceptions, and I was in the middle of a *you must go out with him* lecture when she lifted her finger in the air, halting me, and said, "We need to pause for Beck Weston."

Beck Weston?

"We need to do what?" I asked.

Her jaw dropped as she stared at her watch. "You know, Beck Weston, my pretend boyfriend, whose face is currently staring back at me. Sigh." A sly smile came over her lips.

"Bryn, I'm lost. Why is his face staring back at you on your watch? Unless you saved it as the background pic ... and in that case, did you really? And do you need an intervention?"

She grabbed her cell, shifting her focus there. "I wouldn't put it past me to save his photo, but, no, a Celebrity Alert just came through about him." Her smile grew as she read whatever was on the screen. "Ugh, I'm obsessed. That man is just so hot. No, *hot* isn't even the right word. That's for a normal level of hotness. His handsomeness is beyond that scale." There was a fiery gaze in her eyes as she continued to stare at her screen.

I felt the same way about Lockhart, so I understood exactly what she was saying and how she felt.

When several seconds passed and she still hadn't looked up, I said, "Beck is quite the heartthrob, huh?"

"No, he's a vag-throb."

I laughed.

"I was at his game the other night with the office crew—you know the group of people I'm talking about—and he was stretching on the ice during the warm-up." She put both palms on the table and leaned toward me. "I'm not talking downward dog, Sadie. I'm talking full on, spread out, hands holding his weight, basically doing a push-up, while his legs swiveled in, like, a frog kick. It's probably hard to envision, but basically, he was humping the ice. Literally grinding as if I were beneath him and he was giving it to me very slow and extra hard."

I couldn't stop laughing. "And you died, I'm assuming?"

"DIED." She fanned her face with her fingers. "I don't think he realized the audience he had when he was doing that move. Or if he did, that man was working it for us. I mean, I suppose he could have been opening his hips and stretching his groin and truly only focused on that, but there's no way my brain couldn't go there when I was watching *that*." Her head shook. "There was one thing on my mind and one thing only. And that thing"—she half moaned, half whistled—"I will take it anytime Beck Weston wants to give it to me."

"Now I'm really dying." The laughter continued. "How was the game?"

"What game? The only thing I saw was him. I can't tell you how he played—how his team or the other team did or even who won. I have absolutely no idea."

I smiled. "That's true love."

"No, babe, that's true lust."

I held up my glass and drank to my best friend. "Let's see what this Celebrity Alert is all about."

Once I put the tumbler down, I picked up my phone and tapped the notification, which took me to their app. At the top was the headline, *Beck Weston, Horned or Hungry?* Beneath was a photo of Beck at a table in a dark corner of Horned, where he was dining with another man whose back was to the camera. The angle of the photo told me a patron or an employee of Horned had taken the shot.

I briefly skimmed the article that explained Beck, one of the owners and investors in The Weston Group, was seen at Horned with his brother, Hart. The question was then raised if they were there to enjoy a meal or, given the amount of food they'd ordered for a party of two, had come to see if it was a business they wanted to acquire for their brand.

Underneath the last paragraph of the article were several more photos of Beck. Ones of him as he was leaving his table, showing a better angle of his face. I didn't know why I was flipping through them—I knew what he looked like, as Bryn's obsession had started years ago—but something made me swipe past the first two shots of Beck, immediately stopping on the third. In this one, Beck was out of angle, and the focus was on his brother, Hart, a few paces behind with his head pointed down, hiding most of his face.

I knew all about The Weston Group, the family of five siblings who owned hundreds of restaurants around the world —two different lines of cuisine and dance clubs. But I only knew what Beck and Walker looked like; the others were more of a mystery, working behind the scenes of their business.

I was curious about Hart, and since there were more photos, I continued to flip, finding myself completely frozen on the sixth picture.

The one where his head was no longer pointed down.

The one where he was finally looking up.

The one where he was staring right at the camera.

What the fuck?

I spread the picture between my fingers, zooming in, enlarging the pixels to make sure what I was seeing was real.

"Oh my God," fell out of my mouth.

"He's the hottest thing alive—am I right?"

"No. Not that."

The broadness in Hart's shoulders. His stance. Posture. The way the first two buttons of his shirt were undone—how they were always undone whenever he wore button-downs.

The darkness of his gelled hair.

His scruffy cheeks.

Those piercing green eyes.

It was ...

Lockhart.

Lockhart Wright.

Not Hart.

And not Hart Weston.

But ... was it?

I didn't understand.

I ...

I scrolled back up, rereading bits of the article until I found what I was looking for.

Hart. That was the name that had been published—I was seeing that with my own eyes.

But why were they calling him that?

When his name was Lockhart?

Hart Weston, Hart Weston, I repeated in my head.

Not ...

Lockhart.

Holy shit, they'd just shortened his name. Was that what he went by? He'd just given me the long version instead? Why hadn't he corrected me? Or was it a misprint? And why hadn't he mentioned he was a Weston? Why had he said his last name was Wright?

Wait.

Did he say his last name was Wright?

Or did he just call himself Mr. Right when I referenced Mr. Wrong and my brain spun that into Wright—as in his last name?

My mind was reeling, scanning every moment we'd been together and every conversation we'd had.

The *W* behind his desk—it had made sense when I saw it, but it really stood for Weston.

That meant the Eden I'd found on Instagram—was that even his sister? Or someone else?

He'd told me he was a foodie. He'd proven that to me over and over, and now I knew why.

He'd also said he wasn't the strongest cook in his family— and that was because Walker held that title.

His car, his house, his mention of a private jet—all signs

that he had a lot of money. But the Westons didn't just have a lot of money. They were billionaires, owning the largest brand of restaurants in the world.

I'd never suspected he was that rich.

I'd never suspected he was part of a family I knew all about.

And I'd certainly never suspected that Lockhart, the man I was falling for, was Hart fucking Weston, a part of a family who had as much influence on the food scene as me.

A family who was in the process of building Toro LA—a restaurant I was supposed to review in the upcoming weeks ...

I slowly glanced up from my phone, feeling everything inside me tighten—my stomach, chest, throat. "Bryn ... I'm about to—"

"These are for you," our server suddenly said, appearing out of nowhere—or maybe I just hadn't noticed him approach—and he set two drinks in front of us.

A wine for Bryn and an old-fashioned for me.

"We didn't order another round, did we?" Bryn asked.

I couldn't remember what we'd done.

Nor could I remember a single detail of this evening prior to the Celebrity Alert coming in.

"This round is courtesy of him," the server said, pointing toward the bar.

I followed his finger, my stare moving across the dining room and into the bar, where it landed on Lockhart.

Or Hart.

I didn't even know what to call him at this point.

But—*oh God*—he was here.

At the same restaurant.

And only a room away.

The air hitched in my lungs as he gave me that sexy, sensual grin that I knew too well. That normally caused every part of my body to tingle. But right now, there weren't tingles.

There was everything else—feelings, emotions, anxiety, all combining into a giant wave that was peaking.

"Mr. Hart Weston," the server added, "the owner—"

"Of Charred," I whispered.

And as soon as the words left my mouth, Lockhart got up from his chair and began to walk over to our table.

SEVENTEEN

Hart

The heat from Sadie's gaze followed me the entire way over to her table. It didn't even seem like she blinked— that was how focused she was. And with each step that brought me closer to her, the thoughts in my head built into larger ones. The last thing I wanted her to think was that I'd followed her to Charred or that running into her was anything more than a coincidence. But given that I was one of the owners here—a conversation I still hadn't had with her—I wondered if that was the reason she had come and she knew that I was part of The Weston Group. Or she knew nothing about my work, and crossing paths was merely by chance, my sighting of her random.

"Sadie," I said when I was only a pace away, stopping at the side of her chair, leaning down to kiss her cheek. "It's good to see you."

"Hi ... Lock*hart*."

As I idled for a moment, taking in her incredible scent, I let my lips linger on her skin. Was there ever a scenario where Sadie didn't look incredibly beautiful? I hadn't found one yet.

I whispered, "I'm surprised to see you here."

She caught my eyes as I pulled back. "Same."

"When I go out with my family, nine times out of ten, we end up here." I pointed behind me at the bar, but didn't look in that direction. "I was just in there, having drinks with my brother and sister."

"Our server mentioned you were the owner ... I didn't know." She paused. "Makes sense you'd choose to come here, especially with how good it is."

So, she didn't know, and this was nothing more than a coincidence.

I wondered if she was upset that I hadn't mentioned the restaurant—or any of the restaurants—during all my talk of being a foodie.

What I did know was that something about this situation felt off, and I couldn't pinpoint what it was.

"Oh my God, I'm being so rude," Sadie said. "Bryn, this is Lockhart." She gave Bryn her eyes. "Lockhart, this is my best friend, Bryn."

I extended my hand toward her best friend. "It's nice to meet you, Bryn. I've heard a lot about you."

"Lockhart," Bryn said, her eyes widening as she shook my fingers. "I think you know I've heard loads and loads about you." She smiled. "Funny enough, I was just telling Sadie how badly I wanted to meet you." She surrounded my hand with her free one. "It's so lovely to finally get the opportunity."

I flicked my bottom lip by running my teeth across it. "Loads and loads, huh?"

She laughed. "You're the man my girl can't stop raving about."

"Bryn ..." Sadie moaned.

"What? It's true." Bryn winked at her.

I chuckled. "However Sadie feels about me, I feel even deeper for her."

Bryn nodded, her grin growing. "Oh, I like you."

Our hands dropped, and I asked, "Are you enjoying yourselves at Charred?"

"We've only had the tuna and the burrata," Bryn replied. "They were outstanding."

"She's right," Sadie said. "I really loved both."

It was her eyes—that was what felt off. The way they were looking at me, the way they were trying to see right through me. And it was her tone too. Normally, it was full of flirtation and lightness, and those were gone. In their place wasn't a heaviness; she just sounded like a friend rather than verbally taunting me to shred the clothes from her body.

I was sure this had to do with my ownership of The Weston Group—something I now had to discuss with her. Not here, but tomorrow night during our date.

I glanced toward the kitchen, where Walker was making his way over. "Before I leave you two so you can get back to girls' night, I want to make sure you have something special to go with your dinner. My brother, Walker, happens to be in the kitchen tonight. I assigned him that task. Let's see what he came up with."

"Walker made us something?" Sadie asked.

"He sure did." As Walker stopped in front of the table, dressed in his chef's whites, my hand went to his shoulder. "Walker, this is Sadie"—I paused as they shook hands—"and this is her best friend, Bryn."

"Nice to meet you both," Walker said.

"To say I'm a fan would be an understatement," Sadie said. "I hope that's okay to admit?" She paused, clearly embarrassed. "I'm just a massive ... foodie. And anyone who loves food as

much as me knows you by name. I even have your cookbooks."
She grinned. "It's an honor to meet you, Walker."

"I appreciate that," Walker replied to her. "I've heard a lot about you. My brother speaks highly of you."

Sadie smiled in response.

"What I have here are some diver scallops." Walker held the plate down so the ladies could see what was on it. "I ordered them for my dinner this evening, and my distributor sent a few extra." He moved the tuna and burrata apart and set the scallops between the women.

"I hope we didn't take your dinner away from you?" Bryn asked.

"No, no, these are the extra." Walker smiled at her.

Sadie lifted her glass, and before she took a drink, she said, "There aren't any scallops on the menu."

"They're not, you're right." He pointed at the plate. "I'm not a fan of small scallops. They're often chewy and flavorless. That's why I don't serve them at any of Charred's locations." He tapped the air. "If I had access to this size, I would serve them daily, but diver scallops are extremely hard to find, and when I can get them, it's never guaranteed how many. That's why I usually keep them for myself, or I have my family over and let them indulge." He nodded toward me.

"One of my favorite meals you make," I admitted to my brother.

Sadie slid her fork through the center of one, cutting it again into fourths, and brought a small piece up to her mouth, groaning the second her lips surrounded the fork. "Walker—I can't ..." She spoke behind her hand. "I can't even find the words for how delicious this is. These are the best I've ever had."

"Thank you," Walker voiced.

Sadie lifted another piece and inspected it. "Butter? Is that your secret? And lots of it?"

"I coat both sides in melted butter that's cooled, dip them in flour, and cook them in stock. I make my own—a mix of chicken with lots of vegetables. I use oil in the pan, make sure the pan is extremely hot. I cook them for no more than ninety seconds on each side. That's the trick to the perfect scallop."

"A recipe you should add to your next cookbook," Sadie suggested.

Walker laughed. "And give away one of the most brilliant scallop secrets? Never. That's reserved for my heirs and now you."

Sadie had another bite. "I could eat a hundred more."

"I'm glad you're enjoying them." Walker put his hand back on my shoulder. "I'm going to head to the kitchen. It was great to meet you both." He squeezed me, and he was gone.

"What a treat, Lockhart. Thank you." Sadie reached for my hand and held it.

"Of course." I grinned. "Have a good evening at Charred." My gaze intensified. "I'll see you tomorrow night." I then glanced over at Bryn. "Once again, great to meet you."

"You too." Bryn smiled.

I kissed Sadie's bare shoulder, my mouth then going to her neck, where I whispered, "I told you I could keep my hands off you in a restaurant," before my lips grazed her cheek and I walked away.

EIGHTEEN

Sadie

I watched Lockhart walk away from our table, and the moment I was sure he was out of hearing range, my hand slapped against my chest, and I leaned as close to Bryn as I could get without actually being on the table. "I'm having a full-blown panic attack."

"Why?" She finished chewing a scallop. "What's wrong? He's so fabulous. I—"

"You realize what all that was, don't you? And what just happened? And what it means?"

She set down her fork. "Admittedly, I was a bit lost. The waiter said Hart Weston was the owner of Charred, and when the owner walked over, you introduced me to Lockhart, and then I met his brother Walker, who I assume is the chef? But why did the waiter call him Hart? And why did he call him the owner?"

I took a deep breath, my heart beating so fast that I couldn't get in enough air. "I've only known Lockhart as Lockhart. I

176

didn't know he was Hart." I let that simmer—not just in her brain, but in mine too. "Oh my God, Bryn. He's fucking Hart."

"I'm still confused."

I mashed my lips together, blown away that I was about to admit, "I also didn't know his last name was Weston. This whole time, I thought it was Wright."

Her eyes bugged out of her head. "Wait. Weston? As in the famous Weston family?"

I nodded. "Lockhart, Hart—whatever he goes by—is one of the owners of The Weston Group, and so is his brother Walker, who you just met. Which means Hart and Walker and their three other siblings own every single Charred in the world, along with Toro, the seafood and raw bar they're opening, and Musik, their line of clubs."

She rubbed the side of her face. "I'm slowly processing this."

I glanced at each side of us to make sure we were still safe to speak freely. "Walker is one of the top chefs in the world, Bryn. The man is a celebrity. And I know you don't know this because you're not into food, like me, and you're not into this world at all, but he has cookbooks that have lived on bestseller lists and a line of cookware that I've been paid to influence on my social media accounts."

Her cheeks inflated with air. "This is getting heavier by the second."

I rubbed my hand over the bottom of my dress, trying to wipe away the sweat. "What that also means—which I don't think you've factored in yet—is that Lockhart and Beck are brothers."

Her fingers went into the air. "Hold on. You mean to tell me that your boyfriend and my pretend boyfriend ... are brothers?"

"Yes." I lifted my phone off the table and pulled up the

Celebrity Alert, facing the screen toward her to show her the pictures. I slowly flipped through them—something she probably hadn't done when she read the alert on her phone. "Lockhart told me he was going to Horned a few nights ago to eat dinner with his brother. I had no idea he was talking about Beck." As I landed on the last photo, the one where Lockhart was staring at the camera, I added, "When I saw this shot of him, that's when it all clicked. If I can even call it that. It's more like that's when things exploded inside me. And then, seconds later, the waiter delivered the drinks and said Hart was here and had sent us a round"—I shook my head—"and I freaked out again."

She blinked several times. "I need to take this slow to make sure I understand it all. Let's go step by step." She held out a finger, like she was going to use them to count. "One, Lockhart and Beck are brothers?"

I sighed. "Yes."

"Two, you didn't know that Lockhart was a Weston?"

I put my phone down, my hand holding my forehead before my entire mind exploded through my skull. "Yes. This whole time, I thought he had a different last name—that part is a long story."

"Three, you had no idea what Lockhart did for a living? I think, at some point, you mentioned to me that he worked in the hospitality industry, but that's all you knew?"

"Right."

"Whoa."

I waved the air. "Keep going."

"Four, since he's a Weston, that means he owns half the restaurants in the world—exaggeration, kinda. But somewhat true?"

I tried to swallow. "Yes."

"And you're"—she cleared her throat, signaling she was using that gesture instead of voicing the word she wanted— "which makes things even more complicated because"—she cleared it again—"makes a living in this industry and has the most epic following and influence and to find out her—your— whatever boyfriend is part of this world, too, is overwhelming, to say the least?"

"I'm about to lose it for every one of those reasons." I tried to calm my heart rate, and it was pointless—there was no calming anything in my body. "I wanted to tell him I was"—I cleared my throat—"before I knew who he was. But now? How can I tell him I'm *her*? I'm supposed to review his new restaurant in a few weeks, Bryn. And now ... I don't think I can do that."

I stared at the plate in front of me that had a collection of drips that had run off the scallops I'd eaten and gradually glanced up. "I'm *that*. He's *this*. The two can't blend. We're like oil and vinegar in this industry." Emotion was rushing through me. And the speed in which it moved was more than I could handle. My stomach was a churning mess. My chest was so tight that my appetite was gone. "When you're on opposite teams, you have to—"

"Don't even tell me you're about to say you have to call things off with him." She grabbed my hand that was clutching my old-fashioned before another word could even think of escaping my lips. "Please, for the love of God, don't nod your head or say yes." She gave me a stern expression. "I don't know if you know this, but you were too far gone into the *holy shit, he's a Weston* land to even notice, but the way that man looks at you is unlike anything I've ever seen. It's like you're his goddess. Like he worships you. Do you know how rare that is?" She gave me a small smile. "And when he kissed your shoulder and whispered in your ear"—she squeezed me—"I almost died. I'm talking, I almost had to fan myself off because you two were so hot together."

I grabbed my drink with my other hand since her grip was so tight that I couldn't move it and chugged down several mouthfuls of the liquor.

"And when he said whatever feelings you have for him, his are deeper"—she licked her lips and leaned in to get even closer to me—"I was like, *Marry my best friend right now.*"

"I know," I whispered. "But, Bryn ... this is fucked. There's no other way to say it."

"We'll figure it out. We'll work around the problem. But don't end things, Sadie. Not over this."

LOCKHART

Hey, beautiful. How was dinner?

ME

I was going to text you once I got into bed. I've been soaking in the tub since I got back from your restaurant. It was absolutely delicious. I could brag about every mouthful.

LOCKHART

In the tub? I like that vision.

ME

LOL. You would.

LOCKHART

I want to talk about this tomorrow, but I should have told you I was one of the owners of Charred. I didn't want you to find out that way. It's a conversation that didn't really come up, and at the same time, I've avoided it. I'll explain things when I see you.

I tried to compartmentalize my feelings as I stared at his last message. I couldn't be upset with him that I'd misunderstood the entire Wright conversation and assumed a last name that he didn't have. I also couldn't be upset that he'd never brought up that he was a Weston when I was doing the exact same thing to him. I was more shocked that the topic of his job hadn't come up between us.

Although ... maybe it had?

During one of the occasions I'd been at his house, I vaguely remembered asking what his family did, given that they worked together, and he hadn't answered.

But with my knowledge of food and restaurants and owners in the LA space, I was surprised I hadn't figured it out. I was just so positive Wright was his last name.

The truth was, what he did for a living didn't matter to me.

I was falling for the man. For the way he treated me. For the way he looked at me. For the chemistry I'd never felt with anyone else before. For the way he made my body feel every time he touched it.

I didn't care how he made his money.

But now, it mattered.

Now, it affected everything.

Now, it was all different.

ME

Tomorrow night? Your house?

LOCKHART

I would like that very much.

I let out a long breath, my eyes closing, my chest pounding as I thought about how to reply.

ME

Me too.

I dropped my phone on the mat next to the bath, and I dunked myself under the water.

NINETEEN

Hart

"Yuo always said you never wanted to be the face of our company," Beck voiced as I held the phone to my ear. "My, my, brother, hasn't that changed overnight?"

I flattened my hand on top of my head, staring at the tumbler of bourbon on my kitchen island. It was my second glass, and I needed about ten more. "Don't get me started. I'd like to sue every motherfucker who owns, works, and sends in tips to Celebrity Alert."

"Has your social media blown up?"

"Fuck no. That shit is on private. But the follow requests have flooded in by the hundreds, and every single one got denied." I held the bourbon against my chest and put my back against the counter, staring outside at the Hills.

"Those pictures that were posted in the alert left quite the impression."

"How? I was walking away from our table. I didn't have my shirt off. I didn't pose. I didn't smile. Nor did I even know the pictures were being taken, so I didn't give them a goddamn thing."

"You didn't have to do any of that. But what you gave them, which was your face and your clothes-covered body, was plenty for shit to start spiraling."

"I haven't been in hiding, Beck. It's well known that you have siblings who are your partners. I was on the internet well before that alert went out. But I don't understand—why now? Why are things exploding like this after only a few photos? When all you have to do is google my name and see photos of me?"

"Because that alert put a spotlight on you, and the women of the internet caught sight. I'm not saying you were invisible before, people in the hospitality industry know your name and your face, but the public? No. And that's all it takes sometimes —one glimpse, and suddenly, everyone wants to ride you."

The anger was bubbling in my chest. Out of all the times I had gone out with my brother—and during offseason, that was on a weekly basis—I'd never been photographed. That was his life—it came with the territory of being in the NHL—but it wasn't part of my life, and I didn't want it to be.

I ground my teeth together. "I don't like this, Beck."

"It's too late for that. Everyone wants to know who my brother is."

"I'm the arrogant one. That's who the fuck I am. And that's all they need to know."

"Just wait. It gets worse."

My head fell back. "Don't tell me that ..."

"You know when a golden retriever tries to kiss you, and you block your face, and all they do is wiggle their snout in between your arms, digging out a spot to get in? That's what happens when you get outed and try to keep your life private. They dig, brother, and they'll keep digging until they find you."

I huffed. "I'm not that interesting."

"The reel I saw on Instagram this morning disagrees. Hart, the ladies are loving you. You should see all the collages that were posted and all the comments beneath."

"The what? Jesus." I walked toward the sliding glass doors, hoping that getting closer to the scenery would force me to relax. Because this news? I wanted nothing to do with it. "There's only one lady I want, and she's on her way over." I took a sip. "Don't you have a workout to get to or a stretching session you need to be at? What the hell are you doing on Instagram anyway?"

He laughed. "I wanted to see if anyone was talking about our buyout rumor. Sometimes, Instagram is the best source—it's where rumors either spread or go to die."

"And?"

"Oh, it's fucking spreading."

My eyes closed. "Shit. Is there really a lot of talk out there?"

"Are you asking if there's talk about you or Horned?"

I filled my lungs, letting the air out slowly. "Beck, you're fucking killing me. You know I'm not asking about me."

"I just love giving you shit." I could hear the smile in his voice. "Word is spreading fast, which is why I already contacted our attorney, Troy, to have him draft up a contract. I also reached out to Jenner Dalton, the Spades' attorney, whom I mentioned last night. I'd like us to start identifying areas we want to open in, so that part is behind us and Jenner can find us land where we can build or existing spaces we can convert."

"What about Walker? Eden thinks if we start anything before Toro opens, it's going to send him over the edge."

"Toro's opening is already going to put him there. I don't see how adding more to our plate is going to make him more stressed. The dude is already at capacity. Besides, he's not doing all the lifting. The four of us have our roles, and we're good at what we do. Not to mention, with that Celebrity Alert going out, I don't think we can wait. It's either we move forward or the Gordons beat us to the punch."

"They're not going to fucking beat us," I growled.

"I hear you, but there's only one way to ensure that. That's why I got the ball rolling."

I walked back into the kitchen, checking the time on my watch. "Have you heard from Walker since the Celebrity Alert went out? I expected a text from him this morning or at least one sometime today and got nothing."

"Same. I think he's stewing over the world now knowing we're interested in buying Horned. I'm preparing for an explosion."

I chuckled. "I shouldn't laugh. Whatever that explosion looks like, it isn't going to be pretty." I pulled the phone away from my face as the alert came through that Sadie was at my gate. I pressed the button that opened the gate and said, "I've got to go."

"I'll let you know when I hear back from the attorneys."

"Good," I said, and we both hung up.

I grabbed the other bourbon I'd poured along with mine and made my way to the front door. As I opened it, Sadie was walking across the driveway and up to the front entrance. With each step, her eyes became more focused on mine.

"It's been a long day," she said, waving her hands down the front of her, "and clothes just weren't happening."

"What if I told you I loved this look on you?"

Her black hair hung down her shoulders, meeting the sides of her zip sweatshirt that was open, revealing a pink sports bra underneath that showed a hint of her stomach before the start of her leggings. Those were capped off with high socks and sneakers.

"Do you? Really?" She stopped on the top step, and now that she was closer, I could see the emotion in her eyes.

Either today had been a hard one or she was torn up about what she had learned last night.

I handed her the drink. "One of my favorite things about you spending the night is when I wake up before you and get to watch you sleep. When your hair is all over the pillow and wild, and you have no makeup left on your face, and you're either naked or you put on something of mine. I never need you to dress up for me, Sadie. If you wore nothing but my button-downs or that"—I nodded toward her—"I'd be more than fucking happy."

She took a deep breath. "I'll cheers to that." She clinked her glass against mine and took a sip.

"Thank you for coming over." I moved out of the way, allowing her in, and as she stepped through the threshold, my free hand went to her waist. "I hope I didn't fuck things up between us." I pushed my head against the side of the door. "I have a lot of things to explain to you."

She nodded. "Me too. That's why I'm here."

Still holding her waist, I gradually leaned into her neck, watching her eyes close as I neared her skin. And when my lips got there, I waited for her to back up, to move away, to tell me to stop. But while I breathed in her fruity jasmine scent, none of those things happened.

I kissed a soft section of her flesh that was between the bottom of her ear and her throat, and I whispered, "Come with me," and I grabbed her hand and led her into the living room, sitting on one of the couches.

She slipped her feet out of her sneakers and faced me, and that was when I grabbed her heels and set them on my lap.

"Before you say anything, I need to tell you about the whole Wright thing and where my head has been at."

"The ... *what?*" I said.

She rolled her eyes. "Exactly." She pushed several pieces of hair off her face. "Do you recall our conversation at Horned when I said something to you about how all I'd been doing was meeting Mr. Wrong and you came back with the Mr. Right statement?"

"Yeah. I remember."

"I took your statement literally, thinking your last name was W-R-I-G-H-T and you were just using it in a fun, clever way. And then I saw the *W* over your desk in your home office, and that confirmed my thought. I never considered you were referencing R-I-G-H-T and that you were playing with me."

"It's funny, I thought that joke went over your head, but I didn't mean to ignore it and never clarify what I was actually referring to. I was only—"

"I know." She touched my arm. "It's my mix-up, not yours. But now I also have to ask you this: is Eden a blonde?"

"No." I laughed. "My parents both have dark hair. They produced no blondes. Her hair color is the same as mine. Why?"

She groaned, "That's a story for another day." She then let out a small giggle. "Mr. Lockhart Wright—what the hell was I even thinking?"

I laughed with her. "I don't know."

Once she quieted, she said, "Tell me all the things, Lockhart. Start at the beginning."

I shifted my body, pointing it more toward her. "I'm going to try to explain this the best way I can. I don't know if I'm going to make any sense, so bear with me."

I'd thought about how to address this, but those thoughts and plans were gone.

Sadie had asked me to start at the beginning, so I voiced, "Walker and Beck have been in the spotlight for a long time.

Walker made a name for himself in culinary school, and Beck has been a star since high school. I didn't want what they had—I never wanted that."

I balanced the tumbler on my thigh and wiped my lips. "I've been open with you about my past and how my dates ended after one night, but what I didn't tell you is that a majority of, if not all, those women knew who I was, going into it. They knew about our family business and our financial status and my famous siblings. But you, Sadie ... you were different." When my hand returned to the drink, I took a long pull of the bourbon. "You knew nothing, and I can't tell you how refreshing that was." I squeezed her foot. "To not have you look at me like I was made of dollar signs. To not have you bombard me with questions about Walker and Beck." I was rubbing across the tops of her toes and stopped. "Did I let that ride for too long? Probably. Should you have heard my last name before the server gave it to you last night? Yes." I resumed, but I moved my fingers under her toes and worked my way down. "For that, I'm sorry. I'm sorry for all of it."

She crossed her arms, still holding her drink. "Initially, the news was shocking, but maybe that had to do with the Celebrity Alert—I don't know. I had just read it on my phone minutes before the server came to our table with your cocktails, so I went from seeing your pictures and connecting you to being Beck's brother to having the server say you were the owner of Charred and that you were a Weston, not a Wright." Her hand went to her forehead and pushed against it. "It was an info dump, and it all happened basically at once."

"It was a lot, for sure."

When her hand left her forehead, her thumb went to her mouth, and she chewed at the corner of her pink nail. "I knew whatever you did in hospitality, you did it well. You had to—between your car and your mention of a jet and this house"—

she gazed around the living room—"but honestly, it didn't matter to me." She went quiet. "I do wish I hadn't found out from the alert and the server, but I'm not angry." Her lips pulled inward, and she inhaled a full breath. "I can't be angry with you for keeping that from me, Lockhart."

"You have every right to feel however you want to feel."

"What I'm saying is, I don't feel like you lied to me. The Wright thing wasn't malicious, it was a misunderstanding. You didn't intentionally mislead me. And as far as The Weston Group is concerned, you just didn't tell me. That's not lying either." I watched her throat move as she swallowed. "And I get it—I get all of it."

"If I'm being truthful, I didn't think you'd be this forgiving."

Her head bobbed, and she broke eye contact. "Sometimes ... things need to play out the way they're supposed to." Her gaze slowly returned to mine. "And things did. With us."

I massaged her arch. "I like the way you're viewing this."

"Lockhart ..." Her voice trailed off as she looked toward the wall of windows. "You wanted someone to fall for you—not your brothers, not your family, not anything you have material-istically." When she gave me her eyes again, she whispered, "You got that."

"You have no idea how happy it makes me to hear you say those words."

Her eyes closed for a moment, and when they reopened, the emotion was working its way out of them. "Now, had this been Bryn, you would have had a *pretend boyfriend* situation on your hands."

My brows lifted so fucking fast. "A what?"

"She's in love with Beck."

"She's part of a very long list of women."

"I'm sure." She captured my hand between both of her feet. "Things happen for a reason—I truly believe that. Look, you weren't into dating—you were a one-night-stand kind of man—and I wasn't really interested in dating anyone because I'd met far too many Mr. Wrongs." She winked. "We found each other at Horned—a place that fuels both of our passions—and things unfolded. I think it's the perfect starter." Her brows furrowed. "The only thing I don't get is anytime I've ever called you Lockhart—even a few seconds ago—you never corrected me. Why?"

"Lockhart is my real name, everyone just calls me Hart for short. Shit, my mother calls me Lockhart. But it goes back to what I was saying about my past. All the others have used Hart. But from the moment we met, our intro was nothing like any of the previous women—and that's because I told you to call me Lockhart. I liked that. I liked that you had a piece of me that no other woman had. That's why I never corrected you." I set the drink on the table beside me and reached across the back cushion, positioning my hand on the base of her neck. "Why I told you to call me Lockhart that night we met at Horned was because I was there undercover." I chuckled. "That sounds so official, but when new restaurants open in the area, Colson, Eden, or I go and check them out. Walker and Beck can't—they'd be immediately recognized. So, I was in that bar to assess our competition. I just didn't make it further than a cocktail."

She smiled. "Oops."

"In case a waiter or a patron or the bartender heard me tell you my name was Hart, I went with the name I'm not known for. Even though Walker and Beck are the two most well-known Westons, our family is extremely public with what we own, and—who knows—there was a chance someone could have connected me, and I couldn't take that chance." I brushed under her chin.

She gave me a large, almost-emoji-like grin. "I'd say quite a few people know who you are now."

I hissed out some air and shifted my hand to her shoulder. "Yeah, about that."

"You were all over the internet today."

I shook my head. "Make it stop," I groaned.

She laughed. "You said it yourself—you have a famous family. It's probably a miracle your face hadn't already blown up over the internet." She mashed the gloss across her lips. "It's such a pretty face too." She winked. "I can see why all the women are melting over you."

"Sadie, you're not helping the situation." I still chuckled despite my response. "I already lost my shit on the phone with Beck when he told me there were fucking reels made of me. I don't want that."

"I might have scanned some of the posts." She pushed her lips out, attempting to prevent herself from smiling. "Beck's not wrong. But there's more than just reels. You're on every social media site, and the posts are ... well, they're exactly what you'd expect from a bunch of horny women who find you irresistible."

I sighed. "Fuck me."

"Looks like I've got some major competition out there."

I could tell she was joking, but I still said, "You don't." I grabbed her hand. "I want this. You. Us. All of it." I waited. "I hope I've made that clear. And I hope none of this changes how you feel."

The emotion had completely drained from her eyes, but it was back. "You've been different for me too. From the beginning, nothing has felt like anything I've ever had." She stopped to breathe. "I like you, Lockhart. I really, really like you."

"Why do I feel like there's a *but* coming?"

Her face lowered, and she stared at the way I was holding her hand. "There's no *but*." She finally glanced up again, her chest rising and falling. "No *but* at all."

"We're in this."

This time, the emotion came through her lips as they pulled wide. "Yes. We most certainly are."

As I smiled, I stroked my thumb around hers until I felt the roughness of plastic. There was a Band-Aid wrapped around the back part of her thumb. "What did you do to yourself?"

"Oh. That." Her cheeks flushed. "I burned myself cooking."

I grinned. "What were you making?"

"Just ... I don't know ... sautéing some veggies."

"Shit." There was a series of vibrations in my pocket. "One second," I said, and I pulled out my phone, exhaling when I saw the message on my screen.

WALKER

We need to talk.

"Is everything okay?" she asked.

I tucked my phone away back in my pocket. "It's just Walker. He's pissed."

"At you?"

I gave her an exaggerated nod. "Oh, yeah."

"Why?"

"I'm assuming by now, he saw the Celebrity Alert, and that stirred up a shit ton of drama."

"Why would he be upset about the alert? Unless you're talking about the part that mentioned you guys buying Horned. Wait, is that really why you and Beck were there that night?" She held up her hand. "I'm sorry. I didn't mean to drill you. None of this is my business, and you do not have to talk to me about any of it. I shouldn't have even said that—"

"Yes. To all of it." I released her hand and was back to holding both feet, pushing under her toes, and her eyes told me how good it felt. "I'm admitting that to you because I trust you.

And I hope that bit of knowledge I just confessed proves my trust." I held still. "I never talk about work to anyone outside of the family. I can't. But I just did with you, and I see that happening more. Because what I also see with you, Sadie, is a long future. A future that has no end date."

She stared at me silently, and then she maneuvered onto her knees and crawled the short distance up my body, straddling my waist, her arms wrapping around my neck. "I want that too." She lowered herself, aiming her pussy on my cock before she kissed me and whispered, "And I want this."

TWENTY

Sadie

I hadn't climbed onto Lockhart's lap because he'd confessed that he withheld his family's business and then trusted me with top-secret business information and the guilt was eating me alive. I'd climbed onto his lap because the man filled me with a sexual energy that I hadn't known was possible.

But I'd be lying if I said the guilt wasn't present. That when he had been honest about his reasoning, I'd had every chance to come clean, and I couldn't do it, and that made me feel like the worst person alive. The words just weren't there. I'd tried to spew them from my lips, and they wouldn't budge. I just wanted to get this boulder off my chest and share that part of my life, and something wouldn't let me.

That same something also reinforced that he was the man for me, especially after he shared his feelings. I couldn't let him go despite what Dear Foodie wanted or what was best for her future—those things didn't matter.

What mattered was the way I felt about him.

But instead of opening the door of honesty, I'd let the tingles inside me win. I let them send me to my knees, and I'd crawled over his legs and sat on his lap and wrapped my body around his.

And while I brushed myself over his growing hard-on, I said in the softest tone, "And I want this."

His hands moved to my face, holding me with his strength. A power that I now craved when I wasn't in his presence. "My dick—that's what you want, Sadie?"

I kissed his thumb that was near my lips, the wetness between my legs thickening as soon as he'd spoken. "Yes."

He moaned, "Where do you want it?"

That was a loaded question, considering we'd talked about things I'd never done and how I was going to do them with him.

I didn't know if that was what he was asking or if he was inquiring about what part of his home I wanted as scenery. In the past, we'd christened his kitchen island and the floor in front of it and his bedroom. There were still so many rooms left.

In case he was asking about the latter, I glanced outside—where the sun had already set, the sky lit with deep magenta and ancient gold hues—and the fresh air began to nag at me.

Tease me.

My skin prickled with desire, just like it had when he fingered me in his car.

"I haven't been in your hot tub yet," I said.

When my stare returned to him, his lips were parted, the hunger in his eyes exploding. "You want me to fuck you in that water?"

"Or the pool."

His gaze dipped to my mouth, and while he studied that area, his thumb ran across both of my lips. "There's one problem with the water. I don't think a condom will stay on me. It'll be so wet that it'll slip off."

The tingles were turning to throbs.

Everywhere.

In my chest, in my pussy, racing a wide course from one to the other.

"That's okay," I told him.

"Then tell me where you want me."

I shook my head, and his hands didn't move.

"No, I mean, it's okay, you don't have to wear one."

His stare intensified, his teeth scraping over his bottom lip. "What are you saying to me, Sadie?"

"I have an IUD. I'm clean. We're together." I smiled. "Unless you tell me a reason why I should worry, I don't think we need a condom."

"There's no reason on my end."

I leaned into his neck, smelling that sexy, warm, woodsy scent. "Take me outside, Lockhart. Hot tub, pool—whatever."

"Surprise you," he growled, and he put his head back as I kissed across his throat. "You know, that's what you've done to me tonight."

My hands flattened against his chest, feeling the hardness of his pecs, the etching as deep as stone. "You weren't expecting this outcome?"

"To be fucking you without a condom—something I never do? Hell no."

I sang, "Surprise, surprise."

He chuckled. "You have too much on." He released my face and pulled the sweatshirt down my arms, leaving it on the couch beside us. With his hands free, he reached for the bottom of my sports bra and pulled the elastic material over my head.

"Do you need help with—" My voice cut off as he stood, lifting me with him.

He turned us around, my back now to the couch, and he set me on it. While he stayed in front of me, he grabbed the waist of my leggings and peeled them down my legs, bringing my socks along.

"I can't even get myself naked this fast."

He grinned, and—*oh God*—it was such a beautiful sight. "We'll call it a secret talent that I have."

As he lifted his T-shirt over his head, I pulled at the buckle of his belt and undid the button and zipper of his jeans, letting them fall down his legs. He stepped out of them, and the only thing left on his body was his boxer briefs, so I tugged on those, watching them drop, and I leaned back to take him in.

That raging hard-on, the rows of abs, his chest that I'd already felt tonight, the bulge of his shoulders, and the veins that ran down his arms—there wasn't a body more perfect than his.

I just wanted to touch it.

I just wanted to kiss it.

I just wanted to feel it against me.

"Are you out of steam?" he asked.

I shook my head. "Not even close. I'm just appreciating the view."

He pumped his cock, and my clit began to ache.

"It doesn't matter how many times I see you like this, it will never be enough."

His palm ran over the head of his dick. "Every inch of me is yours." He nodded toward me. "Just like every inch of your gorgeous body is all mine." He lifted me off the couch, and when my legs circled his waist, he said, "You have no idea how much I fucking dream about you." His mouth moved close to mine. "And now that nothing will be separating us, I'm going to know just how hot your cunt feels. And just how wet you can get."

"Stop making me wait."

"She has demands ..."

"I can't help it. I want you."

"Kiss me. Show me how badly you want me."

As my lips met his, I could feel us moving through the living room, heard the sound of the sliding glass door opening and felt the outside air as it hit my skin. When we went down a few steps, the temperature of the water told me which one he'd chosen.

"You picked cold." I smiled without shivering.

"Because I'm going to have you so worked up that you're going to be sweating in a minute. You don't need the water to do that for you."

"*Mmm*. Good decision."

He dunked us up to our necks, pushing my back against the center of the wall. It was an infinity style, so it gave the impression as though there were no ends to the pool, that I was just dangling along the side of the canyon.

"How many people see us right now?" I inquired.

His hands rubbed up and down my back. "I suppose anyone looking out their back window with a view of my pool can see us. But I didn't turn the pool lights on for that reason. With a dark interior finish, they won't be able to see into the water, they'll only see our heads. Until it gets pitch-dark outside, and then they won't be able to see anything without binoculars."

"And you're okay with that?" I was testing him.

"I am as long as they can't see your body. And they won't be able to, not unless I let you out of my arms—and I have no plans to do that."

I tightened my grip around his shoulders. "Lockhart doesn't share—not even visually."

"No." His hands surrounded my ass. "What's mine is mine. And you, Sadie, are so fucking mine."

TWENTY-ONE

Hart

The feel of Sadie's ass in my hands. The taste of her skin on my lips. The scent of her every time I took a breath.

Life didn't get any better.

Except it did.

Because only minutes ago, she'd told me I didn't have to wear a condom, and that meant the second I lifted her a little higher against the wall of the pool and set her on the tip of my dick, I would feel her.

In a way I hadn't felt her before.

"Do you know what I love?" I asked.

She slid her hands up my neck. "Tell me."

"You've given me your body. And I can do anything I want to it. Which means you never know what to anticipate. Everything I do comes as a surprise."

She brushed her hands through my scruff. "And it all makes me breathless."

God, she was fucking gorgeous.

"My mouth does that to you?"

"Yes."

"How about my fingers?" I slid them in between her cheeks, tapping the higher hole. As I rounded the rim, I felt her intake some air.

"Yes."

"What about my tongue?"

I moved it to her ear, gently licking the outer edge before going behind it to her hairline, down her neck, and across her collarbone. She tilted her head back to give me more room, and I used every inch she offered, dragging it to where the water met her chest and back up to her lips.

"Does it make you breathless when it's on your clit? Or when I slide it down your clit to lick the rest of your pussy?"

"My God, yes."

"I want to give you my mouth, Sadie." I lifted her a little higher, aiming my tip so all I would have to do was jerk forward and I'd be inside her. "I will sometime this evening, but right now, I need to feel how tight you are." With her legs around me, I was locked in place. "And I want to feel you come on my dick."

Her lips were wet and glistening—it wasn't from the pool; it was from her tongue—and I just wanted to fucking devour them.

She slid her hands into the back of my hair. "Are you going to come in me?"

A question that made me throb.

And that made me even harder.

"Only if you want me to."

"I do. I want to feel—"

That admission was all it took for me to thrust in, burying my cock until it couldn't go any further. "Yes," I hissed. "I've been fucking waiting for this feeling and—shit, it's good."

"Lockhart!"

That wasn't a scream of pain; it was a scream of pleasure.

"Jesus Christ," I moaned. "How can anything feel this good?"

How could I describe this sensation to her? I could tell her she was dripping. I could tell her she was warm. I could tell her she was tight.

But unless she was experiencing this, she'd never understand. Not when a piece of latex was normally between us, preventing most of this sensitivity, and I was finally getting to have these feelings.

With her.

Each rock of my hips sent a wave of water across her tits, and I leaned my face down and took one of her nipples into my mouth. It was so hard, getting even harder as I flicked it with my tongue.

"Oh," she cried as my teeth grazed the end of it.

I moved to the other side, blowing against it at first before pulling the bud with my lips.

"I ... can't take it. This is ... too good," she breathed.

My thoughts exactly.

But I was about to add to it.

With my hand still on her ass, I found that forbidden spot again, and I rubbed it with my finger. All along the outside, building the anticipation. I didn't need to add wetness—we were in a pool of it. I just didn't want to go right in and shock the hell out of her.

So, I took my time, taunting her, building her trust, moaning, "I can't get enough of your cunt."

And I couldn't.

Even though my fingers were busy, my fucking cock was loving every second it was inside her.

"You don't have to," she expressed. "You can have me whenever you want me."

"*Mmm.*" I increased my speed, twisting my hips while I was fully in her. What that did was hit her sides and tap her G-spot, in turn making her even tighter, the friction elevating her passion, which caused her to narrow around me.

Not just a little.

She was fucking squeezing me.

And shouting, "Yes! Harder!"

"Be careful what you ask for, Sadie. My finger is right outside your ass."

"That doesn't scare me."

I held her face with my other hand, using my body weight to keep her against the wall. "Why?"

"Because I know you wouldn't give me anything that doesn't feel amazing."

An answer that was so goddamn hot.

I waited until I gave her a few more thrusts, when she was even needier for my dick, when she was gasping even louder, before I carefully gave her just the tip of my finger.

"Ah!" she exhaled.

But she didn't pull back.

She didn't wince.

What she did—what surprised the fuck out of me—was moan as I went in a little deeper.

"You want more?"

As she looked at me, she bit her lip and nodded. "*Yesss.*"

My naughty girl.

She was going to get more than what she asked for.

She was going to come.

I could already feel how close she was—not just from what I felt while I fucked her, but from her voice, her breathing, her nails as they found my shoulders and dug right in.

203

"If I give you more, it's going to make you come." I kept my finger halfway in, letting her get used to it because I knew the second I gave her all of it and bobbed it in and out of her ass, I'd lose her to pleasure.

She was going to get that.

Just not yet.

"Will I feel you?"

"Feel me what, Sadie?"

She panted several times. "Will I feel you come inside me?"

Because I was going to fill her fucking pussy with streams of my cum. And that was what she wanted to feel.

"When I make you come a second time, you will," I promised.

She smiled. "I want the second time to be from your mouth." She tapped my lips. "In this pool, right now, I want us to come together. I want to feel it before I'm so lost in orgasms and so spent that I don't even know what's happening."

I'd seen her in that space.

I put her there almost every time we fucked, so I understood what she was saying.

"And you know what makes me come the hardest?" Her lips were directly in front of mine, and I could taste the sweetness on her breath. "When I hear you get close and I feel it start to happen, the fear of you stopping and pulling out and losing my chance, it forces me to get off faster, and"—her head tilted back, like the idea was even a lot for her to think about—"I love it."

"Then that's what you're going to get." I slid my finger the rest of the way in. "Right now."

Her eyes widened as she processed what was happening—the difference between what she had expected and how it actually felt. And as my hand reared and returned, those eyes went back to their normal size.

Her lips parted, and she let out a long, pent-up groan, "Oh!"

"I told you. Just wait, it'll get better."

I made sure the short, rough hairs above my dick were pressed against her clit, and as I increased my speed and the way I rotated my hips, my thrusts turning even more powerful, my finger stroked her ass.

"That's it." I let out some hot air. "You're going to come just the way I want you to."

She wanted to feel fucking amazing, and I was going to make sure that happened.

So, I didn't hold back.

"Lockhart!"

That was the sign that she was there, that the edge was only a few slams away, that what would make her get there even faster was to know I was on my way too.

It took almost nothing for that to happen. I was already there—hell, I'd been there almost all along.

"Yes, Sadie. Agh, fuck!" What I'd saved for this moment was a burst of energy, a plunge that went deep, that went hard, that drove in extra sharp. "You want to feel my cum?"

"Yes!"

I kept my finger in, but not my dick; that was pounding her, urging my cum to lift through my balls and squirt out my tip. "Ah! I'm there. I'm so fucking there!"

That was what she needed to hear.

Because once the sound of my orgasm hit her ears, I felt her fall apart.

"Oh my God," she cried. "Don't stop!"

She was still going to get more of me—I wasn't drained yet.

But I wouldn't tell her that.

I needed her to fear the end so everything inside her would amplify.

"My God." I gave her ass a small bump from my finger, just enough to make it pulse. "Damn it, you're fucking milking me."

It took several more dunks, each one ramming her with more intensity, before the rest of my cum was drawn out.

She wanted it.

She begged for it.

And she yelled, "I can feel it!"

The shudders were dominating her body, and they were doing the same to mine. I held on with my free hand, working past the build and the fall, not stilling until I was empty.

Breathless, she clamped us together with her arms and legs and positioned her mouth in front of mine. "Now, that was a surprise."

"You mean by how much you liked it?"

She nipped her lip. "Yes."

I put my nose against hers so she could feel my words. "You're going to say that again after I come in your ass."

TWENTY-TWO

Sadie

Just got home from Lockhart's. We talked it all out, and everything is good. I know you wanted to know, and I know you're saying, pheeeew, the same way I am right now.

BRYN

Wait, you told him about YOU?

ME

No. We just talked about his side of things. The whole Weston-Wright thing and why he didn't tell me he was one of the owners of the company.

BRYN

Girl, you let the man bare his soul and you said nothing about DF?

ME

I couldn't. I wanted to. I tried. And I completely locked up. The words just weren't there, Bryn.

I think once I get past the opening of Toro, I'll feel better, and I'll be able to share some of this with him. At least, that's what I keep telling myself.

BRYN

But what if your review of Toro isn't good? Then what? Will you actually be able to admit to Lockhart that you tore his restaurant apart? Seems to me that coming clean then would be even harder than coming clean now?

ME

Let's just pray it's a 5-star experience and the conversation will be easy on the both of us.

BRYN

But what if it's not?

ME

Well then, I'm fucked.

BRYN

Let's say it's 3 stars. Would you be honest about it in your review? Or would you lie for your boyfriend?

ME

I can't lie. I've built an entire career on honesty. I don't know how to do it any other way.

BRYN

JFC.

ME

I know …

I pushed one of the lighting tripods aside to make room at the kitchen counter, giving me just enough space to eat lunch.

It had already been a very long morning spent filming a homemade macaroni and cheese video. The company that created the cheese grater I used was the sponsor of the segment, and once it finished baking, I'd mixed it all up and put it in Tupperware—hiding most of the signs that Dear Foodie had made it—and brought it down to my doorman for him to take home and enjoy. If I ate a heaping bowl of pasta, especially one made with four different kinds of cheeses and thick, curly noodles—a meal I craved, made with extra comfort and love—I'd be full and asleep in less than twenty minutes. And I didn't have time for sleep, not when I had two more videos to film today, an article to write, and several static posts I needed to shoot and schedule.

While I nibbled on my lunch of two hard-boiled eggs and cut-up veggies and hummus, I attempted to get through some of the comments on the video that had gone live this morning—one that I'd shot a few days ago. There were thousands of comments to weed through on each social media site. I started with Instagram—the friendliest of the bunch—and read what my followers had written, responding to the more important questions.

Best spin on a salmon bowl I've ever seen. Can I hire you to be my private chef, Dear Foodie???

I'm a nail tech in LA. Hit me up. I would love to paint your paws.

Do you use Kewpie Mayo or, like, Hellmann's?

Why do you make everything look so delicious? Goodbye, protein diet. Hello, carbs.

Ew. Who cooks with a Band-Aid? Do you know how unsanitary that is? The least you could have done was wear a glove.

Who gives a fuck if she has on a Band-Aid? Leave her alone. She's human.

Human and everything I want in a woman. She can wrap those fingers around me any day.

A text came across my screen, saving my eyes from the wildness of my followers, and I clicked on it.

> **LOCKHART**
> I just tasted you.

> **ME**
> How?

> **LOCKHART**
> One of the best things about eating your pussy after I shower for work is that you're on my face for the rest of the day.

> **ME**
> You're telling me you're at work … and you can still taste me? Like, you're going through meeting after meeting, conversations with your family—all the things—and I'm there, on your mouth, like it's no big deal?

> **LOCKHART**
> That's exactly what I'm telling you.

> **ME**
> Oh God.

> You know you're making me wet again, don't you? And I realize I just had you, what, five-ish hours ago, but this is what you do to me. You keep me constantly turned on.

I had just hit Send when my phone started to ring, my boss's name on the screen.

I knew what he was calling about. I just didn't have the stomach for that conversation today.

Except I didn't have a choice.

I swiped my finger across the screen and said, "Hi."

"Sadie, good afternoon. Do you have a minute to chat?"

LOCKHART

Do you want to know what you do to me?

ME

Yes.

"Of course." I found a small pad of paper and a pen near where my camera was set up on the counter, and I grabbed it. "What's up?"

"When we last spoke, we talked about the opening of Toro, and I mentioned that with the amount of buzz it's getting, I want to build up the momentum of your review, like we did with Horned. My plan is to really get our audience salivating."

"Yes, I remember, and I like your plan a lot."

"Good. Because it's time to initiate it."

I tried to fill my lungs, my eyes closing as I said, "Okay."

"Here's my idea, Sadie: we're going to divide the buildup into three stages, dragging it out even longer than we did with Horned to amplify things even more. Stage one will be a review of Charred. Stage two, a review of Musik. And stage three—the final stage—is your review of Toro."

My eyes flicked open. "Hold on a second." My heart was pounding so hard and so fast that I swore he'd be able to hear it in my voice. "You want a total of three reviews? For all three of The Weston Group locations in LA?"

"Sounds like you think that's a bad idea."

Was it? Or was I just freaking out because I was dating a Weston?

I was too skewed to tell at this point.

I needed to put my brain in a pre-Lockhart setting.

But I could barely even remember what that life had felt like—that was how much he dominated my thoughts now.

"I just"—I let out some air—"think that's a lot."

"And I think it's going to bring in so many viewers that our site is going to crash."

LOCKHART

> You make me so fucking hard. I'm about to lock my door and jerk off to the sight of you in my pool last night. And the shower we took after. And the way I woke you this morning with my mouth on your pussy.

I shook my head, trying to find the air I'd just released, my lungs so tight that I didn't think I could get any in. "Are you talking full reviews of Charred and Musik or little glimpses of my experience there?"

"I like the idea of a glimpse, but it must include your opinion. Consider it a shortened review with photos. Less fluff for those, more meat. We'll post the review of Charred next week, the following week will be a review of Musik, and the week after will be your full review of Toro."

"What about the two restaurants that are on my schedule for the next two weeks? Do you still want me to go to them? And write the reviews? Or are we pausing those and only focusing on The Weston Group?"

LOCKHART

> Tell me I get to see you tonight?

"Yes, I would still like you to go to the others," my boss said. "For those weeks, we'll be sharing two of your posts—one from The Weston Group outing and the other from where you are scheduled to eat." He paused. "I understand that, during those weeks, you'll be working for *Seen* for two evenings when we

212

normally only have you for one. And I know that means double the work. You will be heavily compensated for this, Sadie."

I wasn't worried about that, nor was I worried about the amount of work he was putting on me.

I could handle it.

Charred wasn't a huge issue either. I'd recently been. I took plenty of photos. The meal had been superior—from the bread to the espresso martini I had during dessert, a vast improvement from the one I'd had at the Manhattan location of Charred—which meant I could use what I already had and didn't have to go back.

My review would be stellar, so at least when it came to that restaurant, I could breathe a sigh of relief.

But at Musik and Toro, I didn't know if my experiences would be the same.

"I'll get it all done," I assured him. "No worries."

"Like I said, I'm going to run two of your articles per week. Charred and Musik will run mid-week. If you could get me the write-ups after this weekend for Charred and next weekend for Musik, that would be best."

"I'm on it."

Even though my stomach said otherwise.

"Sadie?"

My pen tapped the blank paper. "Yeah?"

"I told you the viewership of *Seen* was up twelve percent after your article on Horned. When we run the articles on The Weston Group, with their reputation and following and with the way we're building anticipation, our numbers are going to increase even more."

The spit I swallowed felt like acid going down my throat. "I know."

"What I'm saying is, this isn't going to be huge. This is going to be massive—for *Seen* and for you. The foodies of LA and all throughout the state are going to react, and this will end up affecting every location of Charred across the globe and the other locations of Toro as well as the ones that are slated to open this year."

My stomach was now churning. "It most certainly will."

"This will probably be the largest feature you'll ever write for *Seen*. Remember that—when you're writing and when you're taking photographs. This is the one, Sadie, the one that really matters."

If he was expecting a response, I didn't have one to give him.

"We'll talk soon," he said, and he hung up.

My screen didn't go dark. It showed the last message from Lockhart.

I wanted to comment on how hot it was to have the image of him jerking off to me in my head. I wanted to tell him I wished I could stop by his office and pay him a visit so he wouldn't have to do anything himself, that I'd be there to take care of him.

But I couldn't.

I ... felt too sick to type those words.

ME

Tonight = yesss.

I put my phone down, my gaze dropping to my plate of eggs and veggies and hummus, and I brought it over to the corner of my kitchen, where the trash receptacle sat. I held it over the opening, waiting to see if my stomach changed its mind.

It didn't.

So, I dumped the paper plate inside, and I walked into my office.

TWENTY-THREE

Hart

ME

I fucking love when you say yes to me.

And knowing I'm going to see you tonight makes the ass chewing I'm about to get a little more tolerable.

SADIE

Walker?

ME

How'd you guess? LOL. He's on his way in.

SADIE

Would a night in help with the sting? Or do you want to go out?

Or do you want me to surprise you?

"Are you busy?" Eden asked as she popped her head into my office, her dark strands framing her face.

ME

Surprise me.

"Not anymore." I set my phone down and watched her take a seat in front of my desk. "Is everything all right?"

She crossed her legs and her arms, pulling at the fabric of her black suit. "Beck isn't coming in for the meeting?"

I shook my head. "He's got hockey shit to deal with."

"Which means you're tackling Walker all on your own."

"I'm a big boy, I can handle it. Besides, it wouldn't be the first time I've had to go head-to-head with my brother." I stared at her silently, knowing that complex, layered, complicated mind of hers was churning. "Why don't you tell me why you really came in?"

SADIE

Oh, now, this is going to be fun.

She let out a small laugh. "There's no hiding anything from you."

"Me? No. But we have the kind of relationship where you can come in and put it all out there, and we don't have to beat around the bush, which is what you just did." I nodded toward her. "Tell me what you're thinking."

Her arms dropped from her chest, and she gripped the armrests. "When Brady's in town, I've decided that I'll go to the game with you guys, but I'm not going to go out after."

I had expected this.

But I still didn't fucking like it.

My brows furrowed. "Why?"

"I just ... don't want to."

> What's it feel like to know you can do anything you want with me? I give that kind of power to no one. But you.

I exhaled. "You're telling me this so when everyone gives you shit when you inform them you're bailing, I'll have your back and tell them to lay off—am I right?"

She nodded.

"I always have your back—you know that," I said.

"But the collective sigh I'll hear from everyone—that's what I don't want." She ran her tongue over her teeth. "You know, the thought of how thick they'll lay it on and all the shit they'll give me makes me almost not want to even go to the game."

"They do it because they love you, Eden, and they want to hang out with you."

She was pulling her hair off her face, her black nails gaining my attention, halting halfway past her forehead. "I don't want to hear it, Hart."

"All right. Then leave before you have to make the announcement. The second the game is over, dart out. Everyone will be so focused that they won't even notice until they turn around and you're gone. That way, you don't hear any collective sighs, no one will be able to lay it on thick, and you won't regret attending the game."

She slowly nodded, a smile appearing. "I like that plan."

"But for the record, I fucking hate that you're not coming out with us."

She waved her finger at me. "Stop."

"I want to ask you to think about it and consider changing your mind ... but I won't."

She rolled her eyes. "Except you just did."

"I planted the seed. I didn't come out and ask you."

"It's the same thing."

I chuckled.

SADIE

It's exhilarating. I suddenly feel all this pressure to plan something perfect.

ME

Don't. I could sit in front of my fireplace with you and a bottle of red wine and a loaf of sourdough and a plate of cheese and be the happiest man alive.

But really, I don't even need the food. I just need you.

"What are you up to tonight?" Eden asked. "Looks like you're busy doing something." She paused. "Is that Sadie you're texting?"

I glanced from the screen of my phone to my sister. "Yeah, we're making plans now."

"Will I be meeting her at the game?"

I set my cell on my desk. "I'm going to ask her to come."

"I hope she does."

"What about you? Cooking tonight?" I asked. "Ordering in? Picking up from Charred?"

"I planned on picking up from Charred until I saw the recipe Dear Foodie posted this morning of her homemade macaroni and cheese. Did you see it?"

I shook my head. "Let me look."

I pulled up Instagram, and Dear Foodie's post was the first one displayed in my feed. I clicked on her video, which enlarged it on my screen. The voice was computerized—something I couldn't deal with initially, but I'd been following her for so long that I was used to it. She had all the ingredients set up in small bowls on her counter, and in front of those were blocks of cheese. Her pink nails were moving so goddamn fast as she grated a sharp cheddar.

When she finished and picked up the Gruyère, I noticed the Band-Aid. It was wrapped around the back of her thumb—the same spot Sadie had hers.

What was it with these women and hurting themselves in the fucking kitchen?

"Save me the leftovers," I ordered. "I need some of that. It looks delicious."

"Right?" She was gazing at her phone as she spoke. "Four different types of cheeses, more cheese sprinkled on top that gets baked and melted and a little crispy along the sides. Thick, springy, ribbed noodles. I'll have to spend hours at the gym tomorrow."

"Your weight is something you don't have to worry about. You can afford to eat the entire pan, Eden."

SADIE

Remember the whole "I found my future wife and husband" thing we once said to one another? I'm feeling THAT. In a hardcore way.

ME

It's mutual, baby.

"No need to meet me in the conference room. We can chat right here," Walker said from the doorway of my office.

My attention snapped in his direction.

He came in and looked at Eden, rubbing her shoulder. "Are you sticking around for the spectacle?"

She smiled at me. "I don't know. Hart, do you need backup?"

I chuckled. "Fuck no. Go get some work done. I'll come see you before I head home."

"Good luck," she said before she left my office.

Walker took her chair, wearing his chef's whites, and as he sat, a hint of something sweet-smelling wafted off him.

I moved my phone off to the side. "What have you been cooking?"

"Baking. Testing new desserts for Charred since I saw the photos of the fucking butter cake and listened to you and Beck moan about it."

I decided it would be best not to laugh even though I wanted to. "Any contenders?"

"I've been playing around with a nontraditional banana pudding and a bread pudding."

I moaned, "Talk to me about the bread pudding."

"It's made of homemade cinnamon raisin challah bread with a drizzled-on bourbon glaze, a garnish of cinnamon-infused whipped cream, and a scoop of caramel ice cream."

"Jesus Christ." I patted my chest. "That right there is your winner."

"You need to try the banana pudding."

I shook my head. "I really don't. I'm not interested in anything banana-flavored or that has a pudding consistency—pudding is for fucking kids."

He scratched his scruff. "But it's not the main act. It's just a scoop that sits on the side of a fresh slice of banana bread, and you dip the bread into the pudding instead of ice cream or whipped cream."

"Okay ... now we're talking."

He chuckled. "Trying to warm me up, Hart? Because you know I'm on the verge of losing my fucking shit."

I smiled. "Hit me with it, Walker. I'm ready to hear everything you've got."

He leaned back in the chair, setting his hands on top of his chest. "Which one of you thought it was a fucking genius idea to go to Horned, sit in the main fucking dining room, and order half the menu?"

He didn't pause because he expected an answer. He paused because his mind was blown that Beck and I had done that.

"Had it just been you, I don't think you would have raised any attention, and I wouldn't be in here, having this conversation. But bringing that knucklehead with you, you might as well have called the fucking paparazzi and reported that you were there."

His head fell back, and he whistled out a mouthful of heated air. "I don't like how it looks—two partners of The Weston Group eating at our biggest rival. But that's only half of it." His gaze reconnected with mine. "The other half is that somehow, someway, the Celebrity Alert bastards got wind that we're interested in buying Horned." His brows rose. "Someone didn't just pull that news out of their ass, Hart. They either got tipped off by one of our employees, our attorney, or someone overheard you and Beck talking at the restaurant—which I'm leaning toward because I know you two had a driver that evening. And I know that means you had quite a few cocktails. And I know that when cocktails are involved, you two can become loose-lipped."

He moved forward, setting his arms on his knees, crossing his hands between them. "So, now, the whole fucking world, including the Gordons, knows that we want to buy Horned. Do you know what happens when vultures get a whiff of a fresh carcass? They go after it, which means whatever price we were going to offer for Horned, we might as well double it."

I leaned on my desk and stared at my brother. "Our offer is getting drawn up as we speak, and I'm not adding a penny to it. Once it's submitted, she'll have forty-eight hours to accept the deal—and she will."

He had a look of disgust on his face as he shook his head. "You're way too sure of yourself."

"Not of myself. Of our business. Our brand. And our reputation." I licked my lips. "When that contract hits her email, she's going to be honored that a company like ours wants her. And she's going to sign so fucking fast that the vultures won't even have a chance to fly."

TWENTY-FOUR

Sadie

I set my overnight bag on the floor in my kitchen since there wasn't enough room for it on the counter and began to fill a cooler with things from my fridge—an olive tapenade, hummus, some diced-up vegetables, a plum jam. While I continued to dig through the shelves, looking for good additions for the picnic I'd planned, I pulled out my phone from my back pocket, hit the button to call Bryn, and held it to my ear.

"Is it girls' night?" she asked after the second ring. "Or is that tomorrow night? Or the night after? God, Sadie, I'm losing it, I swear. My brain is a pile of mush."

I laughed. "It's okay. I don't know what day it is either."

"I put on two different shoes this morning—that's what I'm currently dealing with. And the best part is, one was a pointy toe and the other wasn't—like, how did I *not* notice that?"

I looked down at my feet while I set a container of grapes in the cooler to make sure I at least had done that right. "Is it work? Is that where the brain mush is coming from? Or something else? And if it's something else, I'm going to spank you for not talking to me about it."

"Work." She sighed. "And more work on top of that."

"I get it," I said gently. "Tomorrow night, which is girls' night, I'm going to make sure you forget all about it. Oh, and by the way, next Saturday, don't make any plans."

"Why? What's cooking on Saturday?"

"We're going to Musik—the club that Lockhart and his family own."

"Let me confirm that date. One sec." I heard her typing in the background, as if she was looking up her schedule on her desktop at work. "Saturday is good, but if something comes up and say you need to move it to Friday, I can't, just FYI. Thursday would be out too. I've got a two-nighter in Manhattan, but I'll be back in time for Saturday night."

"If you're flying back that day, will you be too tired to go to Musik?"

"Too tired?" She snorted. "I'll sleep when I'm dead—just like you."

I groaned, "Amen."

"What's the deal with Musik? Are we going with your boy and his family or something? Please say yes because that means there's a chance I'll get to meet Beck, and I will literally drop dead if that happens."

"If things with Lockhart keep going at this pace—and I hope they do—I'm sure you're going to be meeting Beck very soon, I'd imagine, and I really don't want you to die when it happens. I need my best friend." I added a bottle of champagne into the cooler. "As for Saturday, you're stuck with just me. *Seen* is doing a feature on the Westons three weeks in a row. Mini reviews on Charred and Musik, followed by a full write-up on Toro when it opens."

She let out a long breath. "Oh boy."

"Yep." I sighed. "I have to submit my review of Charred in a couple of days."

"Are you going back, or are you just going to base your opinion off our dinner the other night?"

"Our dinner." I paused midair, staring at the small bag of figs in my hand. "I don't think the photos I took will give anything away. I assume lots of people get the tuna and the burrata as appetizers. It's not like we got anything out of the ordinary." I thought about my response and added, "Right?"

"Besides the scallops."

I placed the figs on top of the blue cheese–stuffed olives. "I won't show those."

"Then you're fine." She cleared her throat. "What about your review? What are you going to say?"

"It'll be glowing—I mean, we did have an excellent dinner."

"We sure did. I loved it."

I squatted to rearrange some of the things inside the cooler but ended up holding on to the sides of it instead. "Things feel so perfect. Yet, at the same time, like everything is on the verge of a nuclear disaster."

"Babe"—her voice softened—"a few more weeks, and then this will all somehow, someway, be behind us. I say us because we're in it together."

"And I love you for that."

As I repositioned some of the containers, I saw the shrimp spring rolls I had filmed earlier today that was scheduled to post on my social media next week. I took them out of the cooler and set them back in the fridge.

"But, yes, a few more weeks. After Toro's opening, I'm telling him. I have to." Satisfied with the assortment, I zipped up the cooler and glanced around my busy, film-ready kitchen. "And the thought of that should give me some relief." I squeezed my eyes shut, remembering when I had started this career, which, back then, was nothing more than a hope. I'd filmed on a hot plate, dreaming of the days I'd have a setup like this. "But it doesn't. Bryn, I'm terrified of coming clean."

As the breeze hit my face, Lockhart's hand was there, tucking the wild pieces of my hair behind my ear. But it was pointless. Unless I tied back my strands with the elastic that was on my wrist, the ocean air was going to keep them flying.

I didn't mind.

That was why I'd brought him to Laguna Beach—for the wind, the waves, and the scenery we couldn't get at his house or any of the restaurants I could have taken him to in town. And even though there were beaches closer to LA, there was something about this one that I felt was prettier than those.

I snuggled into his chest, the softness of his cotton button-down cozy against me as we sat beside each other, staring at the water, the bases of our champagne flutes buried in the sand. "When I was driving you to Laguna, I bet you thought I was taking you to Horned for dinner ... didn't you?"

He hadn't asked any questions when I picked him up or during the drive here. He let tonight unfold just the way I'd wanted it to.

As I turned my body to look up at him, he was already gazing down at me, the greenness of his eyes more vibrant in this light.

"I couldn't imagine why else we were coming this way. The beach was a surprise and a hell of a good one."

"I wouldn't bring you to Horned unless you asked me to. It wouldn't feel right."

I looked forward again, and he set his lips on top of my head.

"I'm not going to lie—I fucking hated how much you loved that restaurant."

"I even rubbed it in about the butter cake—ugh, I'm so sorry."

"Not your fault. You didn't know. And even if you did, you're allowed to love other restaurants." He picked up a strawberry from the container beside me. "That one just happens to be a sore spot in my family."

I assumed that when he had read Dear Foodie's review of Horned, that had really stung. And now that I was learning a lot more about Walker, I bet he'd lost his shit over it.

So, he hadn't just heard it from me.

Lockhart had heard it from both versions of me.

Oh God, it was going to be impossibly hard to tell him who I was.

"You should know that your opinion reinforced my decision to buy that restaurant," he continued.

"Is that happening?" I stopped before I said another word.

A girlfriend would ask him that question, I told myself. But my brain was having a hard time differentiating what Dear Foodie wanted to know about LA's food scene and what Sadie would inquire as a caring partner.

God, this was getting more complicated by the second.

"We'll be submitting the offer in a couple of days," he replied. "The paperwork is still with our attorney."

"Do you think it'll end up being yours?"

He chuckled. "When I want something—when my family wants something, we get it. Not just because we have the money to buy it, but because we know how to work things in our favor." He tilted my face up to look at him. "I think you've experienced some of that ... when it came to you and how badly I wanted you."

I smiled. "You certainly know how to work it." I winked.

227

He kissed me.

And as my hair flew around both of our faces, he deepened that kiss.

"You're lucky we're in public right now and we're sharing the beach with others." He kept his mouth close, letting me feel the words against my lips as he murmured them.

"I do have a back seat, you know."

He laughed. "Don't entice me." He lifted my hand and held my fingers near his face, my skin getting small, brief hints of his scruff. "Tell me something—are you free next Saturday?"

Next Saturday, next Saturday.

Why did that date sound familiar?

And then it clicked.

"I have plans with Bryn. Why?" I popped a grape into my mouth.

"One of my friends, Brady, is coming in for the weekend. We're all going to Beck's game and then heading out from there. I want you to come."

"Shit, I wish I could. That does sound like fun."

"Bring Bryn. We have plenty of room in the suite."

I knew Bryn would want me to accept Lockhart's offer, but that was the only night I could go to Musik before the article was due. The problem with going to the game was that Bryn and I would get roped into going out with them after—besides, I'd want to go out with them—and I couldn't let that happen when I had work responsibilities.

Even though this was such a tempting offer, this was one of those situations where I had to choose work over pleasure, and I hated to do it, but it was necessary.

"I would love that so much, and so would Bryn, but it's a work thing"—I didn't know why I'd said that and instantly wished I hadn't—"and I can't get out of it."

"Working on a Saturday night?" He kissed across the back

of my hand, his lips as soft as the pressure he used. "I guess social media never shuts off."

"Unfortunately, it doesn't."

The guilt. It wasn't just nipping away at me. It was gnawing.

"Is it normal for you to work on a Saturday?"

I guzzled half the champagne and set the plastic flute back in the sand. "Not usually." I held my breath while I said, "Why do you ask?"

"I have some places I want to travel to, and I want to take you with me. I'm trying to determine how flexible your schedule is to see if I can drag you away for a week."

A week of travel.

With Lockhart.

This man couldn't possibly get any dreamier.

"I would just need to know ahead of time so I can plan my work accordingly. But it's most definitely possible."

"What if I wanted us to travel, say, once a month? Would that be an option?"

I turned toward him. "Once a month?"

He lifted a blue cheese–stuffed olive out of the container and placed it between my lips. "I would like that, yes."

As I chewed, I forced myself to look away, slanting my face toward the ocean. "I work for myself for the most part—I don't know if I told you that—so I create my own schedule. I do, however, have a lot of obligations that require me to be online at least a few times a day, so as long as I could plan ahead and take an hour or so to get caught up every morning"—I nodded—"I could make it happen."

His arm stretched across my chest, his hand resting on my lower stomach. "We have a full-time social media guru on our staff. She comes into the office a few times a month for marketing meetings and works from home for the rest of the time, traveling to our different locations, collaborating with our global staff to get content for our corporate pages. It's a world I understand, but one I'm not a part of. Shit, I haven't even posted on Instagram in years."

"What do you use your personal account for?"

"Mostly to keep a close eye on the food scene in LA and other major metro markets. And to check out Dear Foodie's daily content. I don't know of a food influencer who's bigger than her." Still holding my hand, he turned it, positioning my thumb on top. "It's funny, she had a Band-Aid in the same spot as you in one of her recent videos." He kissed where I'd burned my skin, the Band-Aid now gone and no longer needed, as the mark was about half healed.

But as his lips landed on me over and over again, my stomach dropped onto the sand, rolled down to the shoreline, and washed away with the waves. While his mouth worked its way to my wrist, I made sure he couldn't see any part of my face, hiding the panic that covered every inch of it.

"You need to be careful in the kitchen, Sadie. That's probably going to leave a scar."

TWENTY-FIVE

Hart

"I want you to review each of these markets and let me know your thoughts," Jenner Dalton said as he sat at the head of his conference room table, where my family and I were listening to him present.

Jenner was one of the partners of the firm Beck and I had hired to discuss the future locations of our restaurants.

"My team pulled reports on buying patterns, including food, and this is how we came up with each of these cities. We then cross-referenced the cities with your current locations, along with your competitors—specifically the Gordons—to make sure there weren't restaurants there. We also took into consideration the accessibility of seafood versus meat and the popularity of each in these cities, and we made a recommendation of whether we think Toro or Horned should be built there."

I flipped through the thick packet his assistant had handed

to us at the start of the meeting, the cities highlighted on every page. The most popular restaurants in those areas were broken down, showing how much revenue they brought in and his suggestion of what we should open there.

This data was fucking genius.

"As you get deeper into the information we put together," Jenner continued, "you'll see three to five real estate options for every city we picked. If you don't like any of the ones we offered—or the cities we chose for that matter—my team will go back to the drawing board."

"This is excellent, Jenner." I glanced at Beck, and he was nodding at me in agreement. "We thought we'd have to give you suggestions on where we were interested in opening. I don't think any of us thought you were going to do that work for us."

Jenner laughed. "You've worked with The Dalton Group before. You know we don't fuck around when it comes to business. If I'm going to find you land, I'm going to tell you why I think you should buy it. Same goes for the cities—I use numbers, and I use my gut, and neither ever steers me wrong."

"And that's why we're in this office and why we didn't want to work with anyone but you," Beck said. "I think we need some time to review this, but I see endless opportunities on these pages."

"I work on your timeline," Jenner admitted. "Just keep in mind, these are buildings that are available as of this morning. That doesn't mean they'll be for sale tomorrow. You know how the commercial market is—space could sit for months or hours. I have no control over that. My control comes in when you want to make an offer."

"I think we'll end up narrowing it down to five or six cities," Eden chimed in, rocking in her chair as she held the packet in front of her. "I'll then jump on our plane and go view each of the properties you chose. From there, we can make some decisions."

"You don't have to go alone," Walker told her, gripping Eden's shoulder. "Any of us will go with you."

Eden acknowledged him with a nod.

"Let me know how I can be of further assistance." Jenner pulled his tablet off the table and held it in his arms. "Don't hesitate to ask for anything. I'm here to make sure your family finds exactly what you're looking for, and my team won't stop until you're pleased."

"We're already pleased with your work," Colson offered.

Since the Daltons were such good friends with the Spade family—our buddies who owned the international hotel chain, where we'd built many locations of Charred in their lobbies—I knew that when Jenner said that, he meant it. The Dalton Group wasn't just a law firm that offered advice and reviewed contracts as they sat behind their desks. They were full service, and today was a perfect example of that.

"Thank you, Jenner." I shook his hand.

He glanced around at each of us. "I'll wait to hear back from you." He stood from his chair. "Unless you have questions or anything else you'd like to discuss with me, I'm going to send in Troy to chat about the contract for Horned."

I waited for one of my siblings to speak up, and when they didn't, I said, "I don't think we have any questions. You can go ahead and send in Troy."

While Jenner worked his way around, shaking everyone's hand, I took out my phone and checked the notifications.

SADIE

It's much more fun waking up at your house than waking up at mine. Alone. And without you.

ME

Sounds like you missed me this morning …

SADIE

I did. Sob.

ME

Spend the night at my place tonight. I need you.

SADIE

You just read my mind. See you tonight.

ME

I can't fucking wait to pull you into my arms.

I flipped through the rest of my notifications, and a message from my assistant, CC, really caught my attention.

CC

I assume you haven't read Seen's article? If not, when you get out of your meeting at The Dalton Group, look at it. Immediately.

As Jenner was stepping out of the conference room, closing the door behind him, I quickly pulled up *Seen*'s website. There was a picture of our signature porcini-rubbed rib eye at the top of the page with the headline, *Charred, A Night That Ended with a Standing Ovation.*

Jesus fucking Christ. What is this? And why didn't I know about it?

I drew in as much air as I could hold and tapped the headline. A new page loaded, which showed multiple photos of Charred's food, along with a review.

All written and posted by Dear Foodie.

I quickly skimmed the first of two paragraphs, a smile dragging across my goddamn lips as I said, "I need all of you to pull up *Seen*'s website. Right now." As I watched my siblings take out their phones, I added, "Did any of you know that *Seen* was reviewing Charred this week?"

"*Seen* reviewed Charred?" Walker barked.

"Apparently—and I had no idea," I told him, knowing that was probably going to earn me an earful.

Walker didn't like surprises. He relied on me to find out these kinds of things before they happened, especially if the result was going to end up in print.

With everyone listening, I read from my screen, "*From an appetizer list that would satisfy lovers of seafood or meat and even vegetarians, I chose the tuna tartare and the fresh burrata and tomato salad. My hope was that the cheese would balance the salt and tanginess of the fish, and the fish would even out the richness of the cheese plate. What I hadn't expected was that the two were self-sufficient. They needed no help whatsoever; they didn't even need grated pepper—although that was offered.*

"*Chef Walker Weston has taken traditional offerings and woven extremely unique spins on both. These dishes were so packed with flavor they could stand as main courses, and you would be more than satisfied. That's quite a powerful introduction, I would say.*

"*Now, let's discuss the main course ...*"

As my voice trailed off, Walker instantly took over, reading the rest of the article out loud while I focused on the pictures. The first shot was a perfect angle of the tuna, showing the vibrant red of the fish, on top of a pop of ginger and avocado, with a nest of wontons on the side. But as I stared at the appetizer, switching between this one and the burrata, I couldn't help but notice a third plate off to the side.

I waited until Walker finished reading, and the excitement between him, Colson, and Eden began to die down before I said, "Walker, will you take a look at the photos?"

"I already did," he replied, his brows rising higher, the longer he gazed at me. "What's the problem with them?"

"There's no problem. I'm just curious about the plate that's next to the tuna and burrata." I turned my phone, attempting to see if a different view would help identify what I was looking at. "What the hell is on it?"

The room turned silent.

"A bread plate?" Eden offered. "Maybe?"

"I don't think so," I told her. "It's too large, and that doesn't look like a slice of bread."

Colson thumped his hand on the table. "Could it be an extra appetizer plate? A chunk of the bread sitting on it? A bite of a shrimp?"

I exhaled. "She didn't say she got shrimp."

"She's not required to list everything she ordered," Colson said.

"No, she's not, but she normally does," I told him. "There are times she orders ten things. So, why would she leave out shrimp if it's something she got?"

I analyzed the other photos, and the mystery plate wasn't present during the main course. The center of the table was filled with our one-pound baked potato, our lobster macaroni and cheese, and our sautéed wild mushroom medley. Which meant the server had cleared the appetizer plates, just the way they were supposed to between courses.

But that didn't explain the photo with the unidentifiable fucking plate.

"God, the way she blurred it out is making it so hard to tell," Eden said. She was turning her phone the same way I was.

"Why would she blur something out?" I pushed my chair back and set my phone on the edge of the table. "Normally, she crops the picture, she doesn't blur."

Beck pointed at his phone. "She couldn't crop it. It would have cut off the side of the tuna."

"Maybe she dropped something on the plate, and it wasn't photo-friendly?" Eden set her phone down. "Whatever it was, it wasn't aesthetically pleasing, so she made it too fuzzy to see. That's my guess."

I shook my head. "What would she drop? The blob looks white-ish. What do we have that's white?"

"Butter," Beck suggested.

"A giant wad of gum," Colson offered.

"Gum?" I asked.

Colson laughed. "My kid is notorious for doing that."

I ran my hand over the top of my head. "It's not fucking gum—I can tell you that right now."

"Then, what is it?" Walker pressed.

"Holy shit," Eden voiced. "Will you all stop talking about the white blob and pull up our reservation app and look at the numbers that are coming in? Every time I refresh, they go up by at least a hundred more reservations."

"A hundred!" Walker yelled. "You're telling me we're getting a hundred more reservations by the second?"

"Across all of our locations, and, yes, that's what I'm telling you," Eden said.

Walker pounded his fist on the table. "Dear Foodie, I fucking love you."

He did *now*.

But we still had to get through Toro's review, and I was doing everything in my power to make sure that review was going to happen.

I took a screenshot of the photo and saved it on my phone and replied, "I'm going to show this to our sous chef and see what she says. Whatever I have to do, I'm going to get to the bottom of the white blob."

"Who cares what it is?" Colson said. "The result is everything we could have hoped for. The plate doesn't matter."

I slowly shook my head, unable to take my eyes off it. "It matters to me."

TWENTY-SIX

Sadie

I was turning into Lockhart's driveway, only feet from his gate, when my phone rang, and my boss's name appeared across the screen of my dashboard.

Shit.

I quickly rolled down my window and hit the button on the call box to notify Lockhart that I was here. As I rolled the window back up, my finger hovered over the screen to accept the call.

The timing was horrible.

But if I sent my boss to voice mail, I wouldn't be able to call him back until the morning, when I left Lockhart's house, and I feared that would be too late.

I tapped the screen, connecting us, and the sounds of whatever he was doing in the background came through my speakers.

"Hi."

"Good evening, Sadie. I'm sorry for the late call. Today got away from me, and this is the first chance I've had to reach out."

I pulled into my usual parking spot, and as Lockhart appeared in the doorway of his house, I gave him a finger and pointed at my phone so he knew I was talking to someone and I'd be there in a second.

He nodded in response and closed the door.

"It's no problem. What's up?" I asked.

"I just wanted to update you with the results of the Charred article."

I knew the results.

My social media had skyrocketed from the moment the piece went live. What helped was that The Weston Group had an extremely large following, and they'd shared my review, which then sent their followers to me. Days later, I could still feel the effects. Engagement was at an all-time high. My following was increasing by the hour.

If this was happening for me, I could only guess the same was true for *Seen*.

I held the steering wheel as though it were a set of fingers. "Are you pleased with the outcome?"

"Pleased?" He huffed. "It's the highest-read article that's been published in *Seen*. Ever."

That should have been some of the best news of my career.

I should be dancing in my seat.

I should have this burning desire to go celebrate.

But all it did was make me ache.

I hit the back of my head against the cushion as the pain moved through my body. "So happy to hear that."

"You don't sound as happy as you should."

"No, I am," I replied, forcing my tone to change, hearing how flat it was. The last thing I wanted was for my boss to think I was ungrateful. "Sorry, it's just ... I've had a really long day too. I honestly couldn't be more thrilled about this. What an accomplishment for all of us."

"Indeed." He paused. "You're all set to go to Musik, yes?"

"I am, yes."

"Excellent. We're already hinting that there's more coming from The Weston Group—I don't want to let anyone down."

"You won't." I took a deep breath. "And I'm almost done with my other review that's due—you know, the Thai fusion restaurant in Huntington Beach that you wanted me to go to. I went last night and worked on my write-up this morning. I should have it over to you in a day or two."

"Perfect. And, Sadie ..."

Oh God.

Why did I sense something else was coming?

My eyes squeezed shut. "Yes?"

"I want to talk to you about one additional article that we haven't discussed. I suppose I was waiting to see how the Charred review did, and to no surprise, it exceeded my expectations."

"Okay ..."

"What are your thoughts on a comparison piece? Charred has locations across the world. I'm not saying you have to fly to Scotland or Alberta, where they have restaurants, but what if *Seen* flew you to some of their other locations in the States? You'd order the same things you got in LA, and you'd highlight whether the brand was consistent across the board or if somewhere other than LA was better."

My eyes flicked open, my heart pounding.

He was obsessed with the Westons.

Or did it just seem that way because I was in the middle of this nightmare?

And why did he want more written about them?

For views—that was why.

Seen was on fire. He didn't want the temperature to die down; he wanted to ride out this wave.

I couldn't blame him, but that didn't mean I wanted to be a part of it.

"But *Seen* is LA-based," I offered. "Why would I write about a location outside of the area?"

I needed an excuse.

An out.

Because ... I couldn't do this.

"The question is, does LA have the best Charred? Or does Laguna Beach? Or maybe Boston is better than the ones in our territory. Or maybe Park City, Utah, is far superior compared to Manhattan or Las Vegas. Do you see where I'm going with this?"

"Yes." I sighed. "I see."

"It doesn't seem like you think it's a good idea."

He wanted me to go on tour, tasting their other restaurants, opening my boyfriend up to another opportunity of possibly being shredded.

I wasn't the right person for a task like this. And I didn't think I ever would be.

I would fulfill the three Weston reviews I'd promised.

But that was it. I wouldn't do any more.

I just didn't know how to have that conversation with my boss.

So, I said, "Can I think about it?"

"Of course. It's a commitment—I understand that."

He understood nothing.

"Thank you," I said. "Is there anything else you want to talk to me about?"

"We've covered it all. I'll be in touch soon."

We hung up, and I stared at Lockhart's front door, my hand on the bag of food that I'd brought. I felt like I was sinking into the seat, the guilt piling on top of me, weighing down every part of me.

I couldn't stand this feeling.

And I didn't know how to make it stop, but I needed to.

I turned off the engine and grabbed the food, and I made my way to his door. Letting myself in, I headed straight for his kitchen.

"Baby, hi." He was walking in from the living room with two drinks in his hands, both his famous old-fashioneds.

I set my bag on the island and grabbed one of the glasses, and without toasting him or returning his greeting or even pulling him in for a hug, I downed every drop.

"Thirsty?" He smiled.

I wiped my lips, my chest scorching from the liquor, and I banged the center of it, urging the cocktail to go down faster.

"If I'd known you wanted to drink like that, I would have poured you a tequila shot." He took the empty tumbler from me.

"It's ... been a day." My body slumped—my face, my shoulders, my entire posture.

"Are you all right?"

I shook my head, and when I noticed the concern in his expression, I changed my gesture to a nod. "Work stuff. I'll be fine."

I wanted nothing more than to tell him about the conversation I'd just had with my boss.

To unload not just that, but everything.

To give Lockhart all the pieces of me.

I'm Dear Foodie. That was all I had to say. Once that was out, the rest would follow. It was that three-word sentence I just had to get past.

"I'm ..." My arms wrapped around his neck, and I gazed at his face.

He deserved the truth. Every single bit of it. I could do that. I could confess. I could put everything out there and see where it took me.

So, I started over, much more confident this time, and I voiced, "I'm ..." But I got stuck again. Like there was a wall between the tip of my tongue and my lips and nothing could get through it.

He studied my eyes. "You're what, Sadie?"

"I'm ..." I tried again. Again. And again. And the only thing that came out was, "Starving."

He chuckled. "Me too."

"But what I brought over is going to need about thirty to forty-five minutes in the oven. I did bring some homemade guacamole. We can snack on that in the meantime."

I hated myself. I hated that I didn't have the courage to tell him. I hated that I was waiting for the perfect moment, and I knew there was a chance that would never come, depending on how the review went with Toro. If it was bad, could I ever forgive myself? Could he? And if it was good, could I admit I'd been keeping this from him the whole time?

"How was your day?" I asked.

He sucked in some air before he pressed his lips against mine. "Things have been a little wild at the office."

"Yeah?"

"Since Dear Foodie's review of Charred, Walker has been off the wall. He's working day and night to make sure Toro opens without any hiccups. But so much of that is out of our control." He set down my glass and took a drink from his. "What if the staff has a shitty night? What if a patron asks a question our servers aren't trained well enough to answer? What if we cross-contaminate food and serve it to someone with an allergy? What if an appliance breaks? What if someone calls in sick? So many variables, and that's not even a tenth of them."

Why the hell had I pushed him for this answer? Hadn't I known deep down this was coming?

Especially with the review Dear Foodie had posted?

Of course it affected him. And of course it'd only added to the stress they had already been feeling.

"It's a lot, huh?" My voice was barely above a whisper.

"Since her review posted, we've gotten thousands of new dinner reservations—not just in LA, nationwide. But that means if Dear Foodie reviews Toro, it could really make or break us." He focused on my right eye and then shifted to my left. "We're feeling that pressure."

I nodded. "I get that."

He stared up at the ceiling for a second. "Walker said if her review isn't positive, it could put the restaurant under."

My stomach dropped, my lunch threatening to rise. "No way. I don't believe that—"

"She has that much power, Sadie. Her review of Charred brought up reservations by over twenty percent throughout the country. There isn't another influencer in this space who could replicate that result."

Just like my boss's compliment on what the article had done for *Seen*, I should have been flattered by what Lockhart was saying.

I should have been proud that all the years of hard work had paid off.

But I didn't feel that way, not even a little.

I felt ashamed, knowing so much was riding on my opinion. I felt embarrassed that I couldn't come clean. I felt distraught that once Lockhart found out the truth, nothing would ever be the same between us.

I pulled my hands back from his neck and positioned them on his face. "Listen to me. Everything is going to be perfect. You and your family are a team of rock stars. The build-out will get finished, and it's going to be spectacular. The staff will get trained. Walker will get the kitchen in the shape it needs to be. And the diners are going to flock to Toro. Not because Dear Foodie sends them in, but because your company has a reputation that's untouchable and you've worked your ass off for it." I gave him a soft kiss. "You have nothing to worry about. So, I don't want you to focus on the things that could go wrong or what she's going to say or any of that noise. I want you to focus on what you guys know how to do right, and that's opening restaurants that exceed everyone's expectations."

He rested his forehead against mine. "I appreciate you."

"I'm just speaking the truth."

I was—I believed that.

But I wasn't fully speaking the truth, and that killed me.

I pulled my face back, separating us. "How about I pop dinner into the oven, and you make us another drink—or, I guess I should say, make me another drink?" I tried to laugh, although I was sure it sounded forced.

"You got it." As I went to move away, his hand lowered to my ass, and he stopped me from leaving. "Are you sure you're okay? You feel ... tense."

When I swallowed, my throat felt extremely tight. "Just one of those days when anything and everything has kicked my butt. I'm sure you know what that's like."

He nodded. "I do."

As I pressed my lips to his, I realized where the tightness was coming from. It was the knot that was wedged in the back of my throat, and every second it sat lodged there, the emotion was threatening to spill from my eyes.

"I just want to make sure that whatever it is, it has nothing to do with us," he added.

I flattened my hands against his chest, and as I tried to breathe through the anxiety, I knew the only thing that could make this situation feel worse was if my experience at Toro turned out to be a fail.

"No, it's not you," I said to him. "I promise, this is all on me."

I gave him a light kiss, and then I turned toward the counter, pulled out the pan of enchiladas I'd prepared this afternoon, and set it in the oven without even bothering to preheat it. I set the correct temperature, and as I faced Lockhart, I realized he hadn't moved. He was still in the same spot, staring at me.

"Do you want another old-fashioned?" he asked. "Or do you want—" His voice halted as he reached into his pocket.

"Sorry, my phone is blowing up. I just need to make sure someone isn't dying or there isn't a fire ..." He looked at his screen. "The Weston and Spade group chat. I should have known." He shook his head. "Everyone is chiming in about the hockey game since Brady just got into town. They can all wait. It's date night." He smiled as he put his phone away. "Are you sure you and Bryn can't come to Beck's game? You know I would love to have you there. And Eden and Colson are dying to meet you."

Things couldn't get worse unless Toro was a flop. I believed that in my heart.

Until now.

"I wish I could. I want to be there. So badly." I was running out of air, my throat getting narrower as I held off the tears. I held my neck and added, "But I can't."

He nodded. "I'm going to make that drink. What are you feeling?"

The only words that would come out were, "Surprise me."

TWENTY-SEVEN

Hart

F our minutes. That was how long the LA Whales needed to keep Dallas from scoring, or the game would go into overtime. But the entire team, including Beck, was tired. In every move they made, I could see the three days they'd just spent on the road, playing back-to-back away games, catching up to them—in the way they were skating, in the way they were holding their defensive stances. Hell, I could even see it in their offense. They didn't have their normal speed or agility. If Dallas wasn't a weaker team—their athleticism incomparable to the Whales—the one-goal lead would be double, if not triple.

Beck had scored two out of the three goals tonight, and I knew—because I knew my brother better than anyone—he was going after a hat trick. The Whales were on a four-game winning streak, and Dallas had been shit-talking our team in the press and across social media. Our guys were fucking starving for this victory. I could feel it in the buzz of the locker room when I had gone in before the game.

At this point in the game, they had one thing to beat.

That was the clock.

"God, I'm on fucking edge right now," Brady said. He stood next to me behind the second row of seats in our suite, where I was gripping the hard plastic back of Colson's chair, watching the puck like it was my fucking job. "Do you think Beck has one more goal in him?"

"Look at him." I nodded toward the ice. "He's beat. But he won't let that stop him. He'll fight like hell to get the third."

"All that traveling wears a body down," Macon, the youngest Spade brother, said, sitting next to Colson. "When I go back and forth to Hawaii several times within the span of a few weeks, I feel like shit. I can't even process living on the road, like these guys do, for three-quarters of the year."

"It's more than just living on the road," Cooper, the middle Spade, announced. He had his arm on his girl's shoulders while they stood toward the side of the suite, Rowan smiling at him as he spoke. "It's working out and practicing, sleeping in strange beds, being off your normal schedule. It's making sure you get in enough food and nutrients to fuel your body. Being a professional athlete is no fucking joke."

"I couldn't do it," Rowan said. "And we basically live in a hotel—and I still couldn't do it."

"I hear you. I couldn't either," I said to her, reaching into my pocket to take out my vibrating cell.

SADIE

Miss you.

ME

What part of you is aching for me?

249

SADIE

My heart—first and foremost. My hands—
they're dying to touch you. My lips—they
want to kiss you. And that spot you love to
put your mouth on—it's throbbing. For you.

ME

I wish I could put my mouth there right now,
baby. I miss the taste of you.

SADIE

Is that the only part of you that misses me?

"That makes three of us who couldn't," Macon added. "I'm all for sports, but playing at that level requires a dedication I just don't have."

"You did it in high school," Brady said to him, referring to when Macon had played soccer. "Had you accepted the offers from the colleges that wanted you to play for them, you'd probably be in Europe right now and an international superstar."

Brooklyn, Macon's girlfriend, wrapped her arms around his neck. "I'm so glad you're not—in Europe, that is."

Macon kissed her and said to Brady, "What, and not help manage the family business? Come on. We both know I wasn't meant to live in Europe—unless it's in a hotel that I'm rebuilding. The hotel business is in my blood, it's all I know."

"I feel that about food ... in a hard way," Walker said quietly.

"Rhett, you played high school ball too," Macon said to the older Cole brother, who was business partners with the Spades.

Rhett, sitting in the front row, turned around and replied, "Yeah, football."

"No desire to play in college?" Colson asked him.

Rhett looked at Lainey, his girl who sat beside him, and said, "That's a long story. But, no, I majored in partying and minored in getting the most fucked up I could every night."

Lainey held his chin as she gazed at him.

"I majored and minored in the same," Ridge, his younger brother, said, laughing.

ME

No. Every part of me wants you. Fuck, I wish you were at this game.

SADIE

Me too.

I checked the game clock and looked at Eden, who was now chatting with Addison, Ridge's girl. I then waited for Eden to make eye contact with me, and when we locked stares, I gave her a nod, letting her know that it was a good time to escape. She wouldn't bother saying goodbye to Walker or Colson. She'd just slip out the door, unnoticed, and text me when she got home—that was the deal we'd made when we rode together on the way here.

ME

But you're having a good time with Bryn at this work thing, yeah?

SADIE

Always.

ME

And tomorrow night, you're mine?

SADIE

It depends.

ME

On what?

SADIE

How badly you want me.

ME

Are you going to make me beg, Sadie?

SADIE

Maybe. 😊

"Sixty seconds," Cooper called out, moving toward the front row, near Rhett.

I could feel each tick of the fucking clock in my chest.

When Beck and his teammates were tired, they unintentionally let their guards down. Aside from letting their opponent score, it was when the most injuries happened. Beck still had a long season to go, and I wanted him healthy for it.

"I can barely watch," Walker admitted as he stood beside me. "My nerves are shot for him."

I nodded. "Same." I took a quick glance behind me, and Eden was already gone. When my gaze returned to the clock, I voiced, "Thirty seconds."

"You've got this, Beck," Colson chanted.

Beck and both of his wings were positioned at the goal, sliding the puck between them, waiting for an opening, a way in, even if the angle was difficult. They just needed a small goddamn hole.

In the meantime, they had an audience full of people who could barely breathe, the ones in our suite included. And I could hear every reaction from the crowd—the quiet murmuring as we waited for the offense to make their move, the gasps each time the puck was passed. A sea of blue and white and silver—the Whales colors—all waiting to scream over the win.

"Fifteen seconds," Macon called out.

"I need a drink," Brady proclaimed as the clock stopped due to a penalty. "This is fucking stressful."

As he headed toward the bar on the side of the suite, I said, "Make me one too."

He returned a few seconds later and handed me tequila—not as a shot or even in a tall glass. This was the whole bottle.

"Drink up," he ordered, holding a bottle of whiskey that he clinked against my tequila.

I was taking in a mouthful when the announcer came through the speakers, letting us know one of the defensemen had gotten a two-minute penalty for roughing. That meant they'd be short a man, giving us the advantage.

The crowd fucking roared.

"Now, let's watch Beck score," Brady said.

The clock started back up, our entire suite counting down, "Nine, eight, seven."

I joined in, "Six, five, four, three, two—"

Beck, still in the middle of his two wings, reared his arms back before his stick connected with the edge of the puck, sending it soaring. It went a few yards across the ice before it lifted into the air, hooking around to the right, like a fucking boomerang. The goalie was staying low, thinking the puck was going to drop, and he wanted every hole covered on the bottom of the net.

But the puck didn't stay low.

It maintained its height due to the speed in which it was flying, plowing right through the top-right pocket of the net, the buzzer going off at the same time the goal lights illuminated.

Four to two.

Final score.

We'd won, and Beck had gotten himself that goddamn hat trick.

The crowd erupted, and so did everyone in our suite, screaming Beck's name as the whole team celebrated on the ice.

"Jesus," Cooper hollered, "now, that's one way to end an evening."

"That's not an end to this evening," I countered. "This is just the beginning, you guys."

I grabbed Walker's arm and shook it. And just as I released my brother, Brady clicked his bottle against mine again, and I joined him by guzzling another shot of tequila.

I winced as the hard liquor went down. "It's nice to have you home, my man."

Brady smiled. "It's nice to be home."

I gave the bottle to Colson so he could have some while the group got up from their seats and made their way toward the front of the suite.

"Listen up," I said. "We're going to head downstairs, where there are three SUVs waiting for us. Beck is going to meet us— he has a press conference he must attend and a meeting with his coach, and then he has to shower up. Is everyone ready to go?"

"Fuck yes," Brady growled.

"I can't wait to celebrate Beck tonight," Macon declared.

"Me too." I opened the door to the suite, ready to lead everyone to the bank of elevators.

I was only a few steps past the doorway when Walker gripped my shoulder and voiced, "I'm ready to get my drink on."

"You didn't do that during the game?"

"Those beers were an appetizer," he said. "Vodka is going to be my main course."

I chuckled. "Fair enough. You've earned that."

As we reached the elevators, Colson asked, "Where the hell is Eden?"

"She took off," I told him, glancing from him to Walker so

they could both hear me. "She slipped out before the game was over. She didn't want to party. You know, it's not her scene."

Walker shook his head. "That's so like her—and I fucking hate it. I want her here."

"I know," I agreed.

"Maybe one day, we'll be able to convince her to join us," Colson offered.

"Maybe."

But as my brothers and I gazed at each other, we knew that probably wouldn't ever be the case.

I stood between the two, holding the doors open while everyone filed in. When I was the only one left, I chose the one less full and hit the button for the ground floor.

"You haven't told me the plan for tonight," Brady said, his arm dangling around Lily's shoulders as the lift began to descend. "What do you have up your sleeve?"

"Please tell me it's not a strip club," Lily groaned.

I laughed at her statement and typed a quick reply to Sadie.

ME

For you, I would fucking beg. And the second you walked through my door, I would get on my knees. That's how badly I want you.

I slid the phone away and said to the couple, "There's only one place I'd take you."

Brady gave Lily a grin, and then he nodded at me. "Musik."

TWENTY-EIGHT

Sadie

Musik was a vibe. I'd felt that from the moment Bryn and I walked through the door. Although I didn't have many clubs to compare it to, as bars and restaurants were much more my scene, there was something about this place that clicked with me.

Maybe it was the actual music that played. I felt it—on every level.

Not just in my ears or my body, making me want to dance—although it was doing that too. But what this club did that no other one ever had was target every one of my senses. In the drink that I swallowed, loosening me up. In the decor that filled every space I gazed at, a fluidity that soothed and rocked my eyes. In the scent that I would describe as sex in a bottle, smelling it with every inhale. Pictures did zero justice to this place. It had to be experienced firsthand.

I'd booked us the VIP section, so Bryn and I could bounce between the main dance floor to the private area on the second story, overlooking the dancers, where we currently were. We'd positioned ourselves along the overhang, a glass half wall that kept us from falling below, and beneath our feet was a glass floor, allowing us to see everything from every angle.

And what that did was create an illusion that we were floating.

This was where we'd hung out for the last couple of hours, the club slowly getting busier, and now it was packed.

"I never thought I'd say this, given that I'm not a club girlie," I voiced to Bryn, my shoulder pressed against hers—we were standing so close—"but the more crowded it gets in here, the more fun it feels."

"I think that's usually how clubs work, no?" She took a sip of her drink. "Not that I have a lot of experience. I can't even remember the last time I was at a place like this—college maybe —but I assume the more people, the more ... *opportunities*." As she emphasized that word, she gave me an expression I recognized.

"Oh, yes, this has to be the mecca of one-night stands."

"Followed by a shit ton of regret." She snorted. "You're one of the few I know whose night of romping turned into something amazing."

I tilted my whole body toward my best friend. "And this is all his"—I quickly glanced around—"which is wild to me. A Weston—what are the chances? My God."

"No kidding." She pointed at the ceiling, her nails short and pink, like mine. "But it's one gorgeous club. Whoever designed and decorated it deserves an award."

She was right. Everywhere I looked was something beautiful—from the large oval domes that hung from the ceiling, caging the couples dancing within them, to the white scarves weaved above the cages in a pattern that looked like clouds. Everything from the cages down was mirrored and glass, painted or decorated in black or white. The only pop of color was their signature drink, a rich pink they were known for and was served at all their locations.

"Even this is pretty." I held up my tumbler, the glass thick and concave, somewhat resembling the curves of a woman's body.

"Right? And whatever it is, I can't get enough of it." She took a sip. "What do you think they put in here? Besides vodka, obviously."

I filled my mouth with some to refresh my palate. "Fresh lime, fresh orange, muddled cranberries, simple syrup and"—I took another drink—"a splash of Cointreau."

"So, you're telling me it's a fancy cosmo?"

"A cosmo-ish."

My phone vibrated from my purse, which was pressed against my hip so I could feel it, and I pulled it out and read the screen. There was a text from Lockhart about getting on his knees the second I walked through his door—that was how badly he wanted me.

My God, that man.

He got sexier and more delicious by the day.

ME

I want THAT.

How am I supposed to survive the night with all this teasing?

"When's the article on Musik due?" Bryn asked.

I slipped my phone away and folded my hands over the banister, taking a deep breath as the stress returned to my chest. "Immediately."

"What are you going to say about the club?"

I could feel her eyes on me.

"You mean, what's running through my head right now?" I

looked at her. "A lot. In addition to a lot-lot-lot." My head fell back, and my eyes closed as I whispered, "This is beyond messy, and it keeps getting messier," just loud enough for her to hear me.

"I don't envy you."

My eyes opened, and I set my drink on top of the banister, looping my arm around hers. "Musik is going to get a good review. Even though it's not our thing, that won't affect my opinion. If I were a club-goer, I'd come here. And despite not being one, I'm still really enjoying myself, and our drinks have been delicious."

"I figured. We've had too good of a time for you to rate this anything but stellar." As she gazed at me, her eyes widened. "It's Toro I'm freaking out about."

"Me too."

She was silent for a few seconds. "Subject change because I don't want to make you more anxious than you already are." She tucked a blonde curl behind her ear, revealing the hoops I'd bought her for Christmas. "I went on a date with Office Guy."

I squeezed her arm, even shaking it. "What? Why didn't you tell me? I want to spank you right now, woman!"

"Because it was exactly how I'd feared it would be—boring as hell. He's good on paper. But there was nothing about him that made me want to crawl across the dinner table and jump his bones. We lacked everything in that department. And that's why I was afraid of saying yes to him in the first place. And now he needs to go find himself a new job ... he wants date two, and I never want to see him again."

I gave her a compassionate smile. "I'm proud of you for at least trying."

She rolled her light-blue eyes. "It's never happening again, FYI. One and done—work-wise. But if you'd like to give me

Beck Weston on a platter to devour whenever and however I'd like, I would not turn that down."

I laughed. "I have no control over that situation. I haven't even met him yet."

"Well, make it happen already, will ya?" she squealed.

I unhooked our arms and wrapped one around her shoulders. "Let's get the Toro review behind me, and then let me come clean to Lockhart, *and then* I'll see what I can do."

There was a vibration in my purse, and I wiggled my hand inside and took out my phone.

LOCKHART

Doesn't look like you have to endure any more of this teasing.

ME

What? Why?

LOCKHART

Look behind you ...

Look behind me?

I turned around, and my stomach did a full flip ...

Lockhart was standing at the bar, his back against it, staring directly at me.

TWENTY-NINE

Hart

Sadie had told me she had a work thing. She told me that was why she and Bryn couldn't come to the game tonight. She'd told me more than once that she wished she could be with me this evening.

But if all that was true, then why was she standing in the VIP section of Musik, near the balcony that overlooked the dance floor, with our signature cocktail in her hand?

Why did I have no idea she was coming here?

My text, telling her to turn around, was showing that it was delivered, and as I was slipping my phone back into my pocket, her body began to swivel toward me.

Her eyes scanned the entire bar until they locked with mine.

This was a moment that proved two things.

The first was that Sadie's gaze sent a feeling into my stomach that told me, without question, this was the woman for me. Her presence hit me everywhere, and it wasn't just a desire

261

and a need I had for her. The feeling hit much harder than that. My hands had this burning desire to hold her, to slide up her face and cup her cheeks as I told her just how deep these feelings went.

And two, as she looked at me, her chest rising, her eyes bugging out, I knew I was the last person she'd expected to see tonight.

She said something to Bryn, and her best friend's eyes darted in my direction, both women gawking at me for what felt like far too long before Sadie made her way over. I allowed myself a dip down her body, taking in her tight leather pants and a red shirt that hugged her chest and stomach, leaving her shoulders bare. A pair of heels, making her several inches taller, looked incredible on her feet.

Fuck, she was sexy.

As she reached me, with our signature drink in her hand, she wrapped her other arm around my waist and leaned up on her toes. "Hi." She put her lips on mine and kept them there, as though she was breathing me in.

I did the same.

That scent.

The feel of her against me.

The taste of the cocktail—one I knew well because Walker and I had invented it—in her mouth.

I couldn't get enough.

I pulled back and licked my lips, getting a second round of the flavor. "Hi."

"What are you doing here?" She smiled in a teasing way.

What am I doing here?

I owned this place.

That question should be directed at her, but I started with, "I came after the game." My head tilted as I then added, "Tell me what you're doing here."

I wasn't sure what her expression was showing, but whatever was in that mind of hers made her look away from me.

"My work thing was nearby. Since it was long and daunting, Bryn and I decided to come here after. For a drink." When her face returned to me, a soft smile grew across it. "I'd never been. I was excited to check it out, given that it's yours."

"I would have brought you."

"Oh, I know."

This conversation felt off—maybe because it didn't make any goddamn sense.

She had known I would have brought her.

She had known the place belonged to my family.

Yet she had come without saying a word to me.

"We've been texting all night," I voiced. "You never mentioned that you were coming or that you were here. Why?"

Her chest rose and stayed high without deflating. "Are you angry?"

"Angry? No. I'm ... confused." I didn't know how to really get into this. I didn't want to fight. I wanted to understand. "I just assumed if you were here or at Charred, you'd say something about it. Now, I know when you last went to Charred, you didn't know it was mine. But the situation is different now."

"You're right. I should have." Her voice was getting quieter with each word. "I'm sorry."

"You don't need to apologize. Like I said, I'm not angry. I'm happy you're here." I was holding her lower back, and I moved my hands to her hips.

How could I tell her that I thought this was strange as fuck? That I found it odd that she and Bryn had been enjoying themselves in our club and I had no idea that was happening? That if I had been in an establishment she owned or near where she lived—if I knew where she lived—I would have mentioned it to her.

"Maybe next time, just tell me. At least so I can take care of your bill, waive your entrance fee, send you a bottle —something."

She took a drink and unhooked her arm, setting her hand on my shoulder. "Next time, I'm sure I'll be here with you. But, yes, I promise that if Bryn and I come back for girls' night, I'll tell you."

I wasn't going to harp on this. I'd told her how I felt, rephrasing it multiple ways, and digging for a better understanding would only make me more confused.

She'd heard me—that was what mattered most.

So, I kissed the bridge of her nose, and I just hoped she felt comfortable enough in the future to talk to me about things like this.

"Did you come alone?" she asked. "Or are you here with everyone you went to the game with?"

My lips left her face. "Everyone. The Spades and Coles— who we do business with—their wives and girlfriends, and my siblings. Minus Eden."

"She didn't come? Why?"

I shook my head. "Not her scene."

"I get that. I get that. It's definitely not everyone's thing." She gently tapped my chest. But out of nowhere, her eyes began to widen. "Wait a second. Does that mean Beck is here?"

"He'll be here later. He has some press shit to do."

She wiggled as she let out a bizarre-sounding hum. "Bryn is going to lose it when she finds out. You have no idea. This is her dream come true."

I chuckled. "Then tonight is her night."

"I'm not going to tell her. I'm going to keep it a surprise and let that nugget reveal itself when it happens."

I kissed her because that was cute.

And because I'd been missing her lips all evening.

And because something felt off, and I couldn't put my finger on it, and I wanted things to feel right.

"Do you want to meet everyone?" I nodded toward the bar where everyone was standing.

"I would love to."

When she gave me the same grin she'd just used when she spoke about Bryn meeting Beck, my stomach should have settled.

But it didn't.

I thought that when I got home, after having a shit ton of fun at Musik with my friends and family and Sadie, the restless feeling in my stomach would fade. I certainly thought a shower and some sleep would ease whatever was happening in my gut.

But when I opened my eyes the next morning and went to my home gym to work out, the feeling was still there. I made it a leg day—the hardest of all my workouts—and maxed out on every set. That did nothing. I ran four miles on the treadmill, and that did nothing either.

Whatever this was, it was fucking nagging at me relentlessly, like a woodpecker's beak pecking at a trunk of wood.

I couldn't get my head straight during my commute into the office, and when I got to my computer, I forced myself to go through my emails and attended an unnecessary and unrequired meeting, hoping something—anything—would take this feeling away.

But nothing would shake it.

So, when I returned to my office, I logged in to the system that tracked the reservations for Musik.

I hadn't wanted to go this route. It felt wrong to dig into this information—the little amount of insight I had access to. Because if I had to investigate, then I was solidifying that something was wrong.

And I didn't want it to be wrong. I wanted everything with Sadie to be right.

I typed in the required information, which was the date and the location of the club—since we had several—and the reservations began to load on my monitor.

A small percentage of people could walk into Musik and get immediate access to the VIP lounge. But that was reserved for celebrities and business executives and names that were preapproved.

Which raised the question, *How did Sadie get in?*

I toggled to the name category, putting them in ascending order by first name, and found Sadie near the bottom. I then clicked the details tab, and everything that was known about her reservation appeared.

A reservation she had made four days ago, where she had entered her full name and Bryn's, and done it online at around six in the evening. It showed her email address and the type of credit card she'd used to pay for her entrance fee.

Beneath that was a time stamp—the exact time she had checked into Musik.

9:06 p.m.

A time that set off several alarms in my head.

I hadn't arrived until close to eleven thirty, so that meant she had been there for almost two and a half hours before I saw her.

I picked up a pen and clicked the top with my thumb; the energy pouring out of me made me click it harder and faster.

The more I stared at my screen—studying her name, the time, calculating how long she'd been at Musik, as though the

266

simple math wasn't really that simple at all—the worse this felt.

"My work thing was nearby. Since it was long and daunting, Bryn and I decided to come here after. For a drink."

Her response, which continued to repeat in my head, made it seem as if she had randomly stopped in and only for a drink. But she'd had all intentions of coming, and that time span was long enough to have more than one drink.

So, she hadn't told me she was going to Musik. She hadn't told me she'd made the reservation four days ago. She hadn't told me she was there, and she hadn't mentioned that she'd been there for hours.

She'd lied—at least it seemed that way—about all of it.

I dropped the pen and slid my hands through the sides of my hair.

Why?

Why did she need to be so dishonest?

Why does all of this feel so fucking off?

Am I missing something?

SADIE

I hated waking up alone this morning, but I loved waking up to the thought that I'm going to see you tonight.

Oh, and good afternoon.

ME

Hey, you. I just had a meeting with my family, and they were saying how much they enjoyed meeting you.

SADIE

Aww, same.

What are your thoughts on this evening? Stay in? Go out? I'm down for anything.

I set the phone on top of my desk, finding the nearest pen, and while I continued to stare at the screen, I jammed my thumb on the clicker again.

Not that I'd expected her to bring up last night and our accidental run-in. I was sure it was a topic she wanted to avoid and hoped I'd moved on from it, but what the fuck?

Was I making too big of a deal about this?

Was I not seeing things clearly?

Did I need a voice of reason?

Shit.

I left my phone on my desk and carried the pen to Eden's office, knocking on her door, and when she said, "Come in," I cracked it ajar.

"Do you have a second to talk?"

She pulled her hands off her keyboard. "Of course."

I closed the door behind me and took a seat in the chair across from her desk.

I could feel her eyes on every inch of my face as she said, "Why do you look defeated?" She did another sweep. "I can't tell if you're hungover from last night or if you have sad puppy eyes, like you're missing Sadie. But even during our meeting earlier today, you looked this way, and it's past lunchtime, which would have wiped out your hangover because food solves all the hurt, so I'm going with my *sad puppy eyes* theory." She pulled at the sleeves of her gray blazer.

I rubbed my palms over the legs of my suit pants, staring past my sister, through the windows and at the view of LA. Once the clamminess was off my skin, I resumed the pen clicking with my thumb. "I'm neither."

"Then it's not a look of defeat. It's anger. *Hmm.*" She

rubbed her lips together. "All right, lay it on me. What's got you worked up?"

"I've got a puzzle for you to solve."

She leaned into the edge of her desk and folded her hands together. "My favorite." She smiled. "Give me every detail. Leave nothing out."

"It's about Sadie."

"Sadie?" Her brows rose their highest. "Now I'm even more intrigued."

ME

How about your place?

SADIE

How about your place?

I'll bring dinner. What are you in the mood for?

She'd met my family. She'd been to my house more than a handful of times. We'd been spending several nights a week together, most of those ending in a sleepover.

I no longer wore a condom when we fucked.

And she'd told me on more than one occasion that she thought she'd found her future husband.

But she still wouldn't invite me over.

Eden had told me a few minutes ago that Sadie would respond this way. But I had hoped that she wouldn't, that I'd finally get the invite.

I wanted to prove my sister wrong.

And, fuck, I couldn't.

ME

Surprise me.

The sound of my phone vibrating on my nightstand should have been what woke me. But I'd barely gotten any sleep, and I was already awake when the alerts began to come through. It didn't matter that Sadie had brought over dinner, that the evening was perfect and it felt as though nothing was wrong, that she lay next to me in bed, cuddling my chest all night, until about an hour ago, when she'd rolled in the other direction.

I still couldn't get these goddamn thoughts out of my head.

Every time they circled, when I recalled the conversation I'd had with Eden, sleep moved further away until it was eventually out of grasp.

I picked up my phone, first turning down the brightness so the screen wasn't like a sun shining throughout the dark room, and then I checked my notifications.

WALKER

I'm guessing Eden and Beck are probably the only ones awake right now, but when the rest of you get up, check out Seen's review of Musik and then go to Dear Foodie's Instagram. 2 for fucking 2, family. I couldn't be happier.

BECK

I just saw. Fuuuck, dude, Dear Foodie is loving her some Westons.

EDEN

I'll keep an eye on the VIP reservations for each of our locations and see how many come in now that she's praised us so highly. I'm assuming they're going to explode.

I spoke too soon. They're already exploding.

COLSON

Damn, I love that woman. I wonder if she's single ...

BECK

Now, wouldn't that be some shit? Colson and Dear Foodie. How do we make that happen? For the perks alone, LOL.

Before I replied, I pulled up *Seen*'s website. The article on Musik was listed first with a collage of photos.

For some reason, I wasn't interested in the review—at least not yet. There was something about the pictures that drew my attention.

One showed small, pink-painted fingernails, gripping our signature cocktail at the banister of our VIP section, over-looking the dance floor. I zoomed in, intensifying the view of her wrist, where a delicate gold bracelet sat—one I was sure I'd never seen before—and the top parts of her thumbs were bent back from the glass, a flexibility that not everyone had.

Why did that pose look so familiar?

Why—

"*Mmm.* Good morning."

I flattened my phone against my chest and glanced toward Sadie, her eyes heavy as she looked at me. I hadn't felt her stir or roll onto her back, like she was positioned now. I hadn't even felt her stare.

"Have you been up for a while?" she asked.

I returned my phone to my nightstand, a place that suddenly felt like the right spot for it. "Not long, no."

"How'd you sleep?"

I gently nodded. "All right." I fucking hated not being

honest, but I didn't want to tell her that she was the reason I'd been up all night. "You?"

"I always sleep perfectly when I'm next to you."

"You're sweet."

I lifted the hand she'd just placed on my arm, and as I was bringing it up to my lips to kiss across the back of it, I noticed her nails. I held them in front of my face for several seconds before switching my grip to her thumb, casually moving it back, testing how far it would go. When I was able to easily bend it the same way Dear Foodie's was in the photo, my chest began to pound.

Fuck me.

Is this merely a coincidence? Or is it another *sign?*

For now, I attempted to push those thoughts from my head, refocusing on her nails, even though my heart was still thumping away.

"Do you ever wear a color besides pink?" I asked.

"Not often. I'm just a pink girlie. What can I say?"

I was careful with the words I chose—all picked for a specific reason.

"My assistant was wearing the same color, and I made a comment to her about it. She told me Dear Foodie had inspired her manicure."

"That's funny."

My heart rate didn't go down, not even a little as I waited to assess her reaction as I asked, "Did Dear Foodie inspire your nails?"

Her stare slowly lowered to my mouth and stayed there. With her pulse banging against my fingers, she smiled so calmly. "Inspire them ... no."

I let a few seconds of silence pass. "She reviewed Musik—Dear Foodie, I mean. The article came out this morning. It was an excellent review. It's going to help business a lot." I nodded toward my phone but kept my eyes on her. "I was just reading the article when you woke up. Checking out the photos. Apparently, she liked the same spot you and Bryn were in—you know, the banister in the VIP area—since that's where most of the pictures were shot. And she was drinking our signature cocktail, just like you did." I paused. "Looks like you and Dear Foodie have similar taste."

Her stare eventually rose to mine, and in that second, I fucking knew.

I felt it in her pulse.

I heard it in her silence.

It was confirmed in my gut.

"It's the best spot in the club," she whispered, her voice so soft. "It lets you put eyes on everything."

I sighed. The realization ricocheting through me. "Except, there, you can't see what's behind you. Who's watching, who's picking up on things." I paused. "Like I watched you that night."

ME

Good evening. I'm going to send you a photo. Is there any way you can take a look at it and tell me what you think that white blob in the corner is that's been blurred out?

ALEXA, SOUS CHEF—CHARRED LA

That's the photo that was posted on Seen, right? And in Dear Foodie's review?

ME

Yes.

ALEXA, SOUS CHEF—CHARRED LA

I have a few theories, but I want to look at it again in the morning when I have fresh eyes and a clear head. You'll hear from me before lunch.

ME

I appreciate it.

THIRTY

Sadie

I couldn't do this anymore; I couldn't continue lying to Lockhart and keep Dear Foodie a secret. Every part of my body felt ill from it. I was having a hard time even looking him in the face.

This wasn't what I'd wanted.

And I couldn't stand another second of it.

That was why I reached out to my boss as soon as I got home from Lockhart's house and told him we needed a meeting. Immediately. This wasn't a conversation I could have over the phone. I needed to do it face-to-face so my boss understood how heavily this was weighing on me.

And what he would do with that information, what he would decide, I couldn't predict.

I couldn't remember the last time I'd been at the office. I kept my distance for a multitude of reasons—the biggest was that I didn't want any of the employees to ever figure out who I was.

When I had first been hired, my boss and I had made sure my true identity stayed buried from *Seen*. The direct deposit went into my business account. They had my tax ID, not my Social Security number. No one in finance or HR could trace Dear Foodie to Sadie Spencer.

And because I went into the office about once a year, I wasn't really worried about walking through its doors today or taking the elevator to the top floor and giving the receptionist my name. I didn't wear credentials around my neck, like all the other employees, nor did I mention to her that I was one.

She made a phone call—I assumed it was to my boss—and as she hung up, she asked me to follow her. She led me past a large section of cubicles, the magazine's accolades hanging on the walls that framed the area—maybe some of those due to my influence. Toward the back of the room, she halted outside the door of his corner office. She knocked twice, and when my boss called out, she opened the door and told me to go in.

I thanked her and made sure the door was shut tightly behind me, slowly turning to him and smiling. "Good morning."

"It's a bit early for you, isn't it?"

I laughed.

"I'd be lying if I said I wasn't shocked that you texted before nine and then requested an in-person meeting. I don't think in all the years we've worked together, you've ever done that."

I took a seat in front of his desk. "I haven't. You're right."

His curly hair had grown since the last time I had come here, and he now wore it back in a tight ponytail, the thin gray pieces lightening the sea of black strands.

"I'm assuming you're here because you want to talk about my request of having you travel to more of The Weston Group locations and reviewing them so we can do another Weston feature?"

I gradually nodded and crossed my legs, holding my knee like it was a handrail. "Yes, but not in the way you think."

He rested his forearms on his desk. "Okay ... I'm intrigued."

I took a deep breath, thinking of the words I'd rehearsed during my drive over here, wishing I'd remembered them since they were suddenly gone from my mind. "After my article on Toro, I don't want to review any more of The Weston Group restaurants. I'm just ... not comfortable doing it." I took in several more breaths, hoping they would loosen the tightening in my chest. "I promise to finish out my obligation, but I'm declining your offer regarding the new feature you want done on them."

"And why is that?" He blinked several times, turning his face as though he was posing, one side being better than the other. "I'm assuming there must be a reason?"

I didn't like the feeling that was in my body. The way I was so full of anxiety that I could even feel it in my fingertips.

I had to get this out—whether it sounded pretty or not, that didn't matter.

"I'm in a relationship with Hart Weston."

His eyebrows rose and didn't come back down, even after he said, "I see."

"Before you ask, Hart doesn't know that I'm Dear Foodie. I wouldn't break my NDA with *Seen*. I wanted to tell him—no less than a million times—but I haven't."

His exhale was loud and drawn out. "Tell me this: were you dating Hart Weston when you reviewed Charred?"

It killed me to nod and say, "Yes."

His brows dropped and pushed together. "And were you dating him when you reviewed Musik?"

"Yes, but"—I held up my hand before he could say

anything—"you need to know that I was a hundred percent honest in both of those reviews."

His head fell back, and he groaned, "Jesus Christ ..."

"Please believe that Dear Foodie wrote those reviews, not Sadie. Please." I slid forward in my chair, hovering over the edge. "You have nothing to worry about regarding either—please tell me you believe me." I waited and got no response. "This job means everything to me. It started my career. I wouldn't jeopardize that for anything ... or anybody."

His quietness was making me more nervous.

So much so that I felt the need to add, "I know you didn't ask this, but I have to tell you that when I first started dating him, I had no idea he was a Weston. We met in the bar of a restaurant. I didn't recognize him, and he didn't offer his last name or even the shortened version of his first name. He went by Lockhart, and ... things escalated from there. So, I didn't intentionally bond with a restauranteur—or anything that even looks like that."

He leaned back in his chair, his hands going to the bottom of his chest, where his fingers linked. "What about Toro? How honest are you going to be with *that* review?" He pushed his tongue into the inside of his top lip, making it jut out and round. "You told me Charred and Musik were authentic—"

"They were."

"I've been to both numerous times, and my reviews would be very similar to everything you said in yours, so I believe you. But Toro is entirely different."

"I ... know."

"Sadie, you have an extremely loyal following that expands far beyond Los Angeles, and you have influence that I'm not sure you even realize you possess. You're one of the top food influencers in the country, which is why *Seen* is so honored to still have you on our team. But it's going to be hard to convince me that your boyfriend isn't going to run through your mind when you eat at Toro and when you write the review of his restaurant." He sat up straight, his hands returning to his desk. "A review that could, quite possibly, catapult the launch of the Westons' new seafood venture. Or if your review isn't positive, it could wreck their plans for future locations they intended to open."

My hand went to my chest, pushing against my heart.

Every word he'd just said had been eating at me for weeks.

Seen expected honesty.

My followers did too. That was what my entire brand was based on. If they sensed any kind of disingenuousness coming from me, they'd call me out and unfollow me in a second.

"I might not have anything to worry about when it comes to Charred and Musik, but you never assured me that you'd take the same stance with Toro." His head tilted down, and he looked at me through his lashes. "Can I expect the truth from you? Or is Sadie going to rate Toro instead of Dear Foodie?"

I covered my face with my hands.

I just needed a second.

This was too hard.

This was too much.

I didn't want to be in this position. I didn't want to feel this way.

And I didn't want to keep feeling this way.

"Before you answer that," he said, "let's dig in even deeper. I'm assuming another reason you came here today is because you want permission to tell Hart who you are. Am I right?"

I uncovered my face and looked at him. "Yes."

He let out a long, pent-up breath and pushed up the sleeves of his thin sweater, showing dark leather bracelets on both wrists. "Sadie ..."

"I feel like I'm about to throw up," I said to Bryn as she answered my call, the elevator doors closing behind me, and fortunately, I was the only one in it, taking it down to the lobby of *Seen*.

"Why? What happened? Or are you sick and you're really about to puke?"

I wiped what felt like sweat off my forehead. "I'm just leaving *Seen*."

It took a moment for her to say, "Wait. As in you actually went into the office?"

"Mmhmm."

"Girl, that's hardcore. You haven't been there in, how long? Forever?"

I wasn't sure if I was holding in air or panting, but I let out a long exhale. "I had to talk to my boss in person. I couldn't have this conversation with him over the phone. It wouldn't have felt right." I watched the numbers light up on the monitor, letting me know I was getting closer to the lobby.

"About you reviewing more Weston restaurants, right?"

"And the NDA I have with *Seen*." My eyes closed for just a second, and I pushed myself off the wall I was leaning against and stood in front of the doorway.

"I know what these secrets are doing to you, babe. It's going to feel good to finally get them out."

"You don't even know the latest." I cleared my throat since the heaviness seemed to have formed a knot there. "I spent the night at Lockhart's last night, and everything was perfect. And then I woke up at the ass crack of dawn, and he was on his phone, and I knew he was reading the Musik review that had just posted on *Seen*'s website and across my social media. And I wanted to die, right?"

"Oh God, I'm getting clammy. Keep going."

"He started talking to me about Dear Foodie and her nails and whether they'd inspired my nail color. And that her photos were in the same place you and I were standing that night. And that we were both drinking the same cocktail, saying me and DF had similar taste."

"WHAT?" I could hear her breathing. "Does he know?"

"I don't know."

"Do you think he knows?"

I held my throat as a wave of heat blasted across me. "I mean, why would he say any of that? But at the same time, am I just looking into it too deeply? Am I hyper-focused and so close to the situation that I can't see it any differently?" I sighed. "I don't know."

"Well, I'm freaking out."

"You're not helping."

"Was I supposed to? I feel like you called to throw up—and I'm gagging with you. Like a few years ago, when we hit the tequila too hard and one of us was puking in the sink while the other was heaving in the toilet."

My cheeks puffed out as I moaned, "Bryn ..."

"Listen, it's a good thing you have DF-specific jewelry that you only wear during filming, or he would have—*shit*! Did he notice your bracelet in the bar? And he compared that with the pictures that were posted on *Seen* and on your social media? Is that how he connected you two?"

My stomach dropped.

I hadn't even thought of that.

Because, normally, I never ran into anyone I knew while I was filming content.

I was always so careful, but I hadn't anticipated seeing Lockhart that night. And when I did, it hadn't even dawned on me to take off my jewelry.

"I don't know. He didn't say anything about the bracelet or earrings or any of that." As the elevator opened, I stepped out and walked through the small lobby. "Regardless, I need to come clean. If I don't, I'm going to explode."

"What did your boss say about that? You know, with your whole NDA and everything?"

As I approached the lobby door, I reached for the handle and pulled it toward me. Just as I was about to walk through, I stopped myself before I ran into the large body that was walking in at the same time I was walking out.

"I'm sorry—" My voice cut off as I glanced up, my eyes connecting with his.

Lockhart.

Oh my God.

I heard myself gasp.

I felt myself almost drop the phone.

"Sadie, are you okay?" Bryn asked.

I couldn't answer her.

I had no words left. Whatever had been there ... was gone.

This was just like the night I'd met Lockhart at Horned, reaching for the door at the same time, except here we were, on opposite sides.

And I was sure the expression on my face had been much different on that day compared to what was showing now.

"Hello, Sadie." The shock in his eyes was as thick as it was in mine.

"Oh fuck! Is that Lockhart I just heard? Is he there? Sadie, answer me," Bryn screeched.

He stood in the doorway, a gift basket in his hand, his presence preventing me from leaving and mine stopping him from coming in.

And the longer we stood there in silence, I saw his eyes

change. What was in them and on his lips wasn't a look of shock. Something else had replaced it.

What I saw now was confidence.

Because he knew exactly who I was.

"Hi, Lockhart." My anxiety peaked so fast that my chest began to heave, ensuring it would be a long time before I could take a breath again.

"Tell me"—his stare intensified—"what are you doing at *Seen?*"

THIRTY-ONE

Hart

"**B**ryn, I've got to go," Sadie said into the phone that she was holding to her ear. She slipped the cell into her purse, gradually meeting my stare. "I, um ..." She swallowed. "I ..."

I'd asked her what she was doing in the lobby of *Seen*.

I didn't think she was going to admit the truth—not here. Not when Dear Foodie's identity was a secret and, if I had to guess, not many people in this building knew it was Sadie.

Shit, she hid that well. It had taken me all this time to figure it out with a little help from Eden, but the signs now were too obvious to ignore.

There was only one reason she would be coming out of this building, and it certainly wasn't because she managed their social media.

But I still said, "You what? You were having coffee with a friend who works here? They're hiring you for your social

284

media expertise? Or perhaps I'm avoiding the real reason ... the same way you are."

Emotion built in her eyes, and her head fell forward. "Lockhart ..."

"What, you didn't expect to see me here? We've had that conversation before, haven't we?"

She slowly glanced up, gripping the long strap of her purse.

"Say something, Sadie."

Her throat moved.

Her chin quivered.

Her eyes watered.

Her stare was darting everywhere, but it didn't stay on me.

She licked her lips and then licked them again.

But she didn't say a word.

"Do you want to know why I'm here?" I questioned. "I have a gift. For Dear Foodie. Although we sent an official invite to welcome her to Toro, I thought I'd double down and bring something for her and the team at *Seen*. You know, to sweeten them up a little."

The puzzle pieces had been floating around my brain, and while I stood here, staring at her, they began to slide into their appropriate places.

The way I had seen Sadie hold the martini glass when I ran into her at the sushi restaurant, wondering why those hands and position and nail color had looked so familiar. And a short while later, photos from that restaurant had appeared on her social media pages.

The Band-Aid on her finger—the same one that was on Dear Foodie's in her macaroni and cheese video.

The whole reason she hadn't gone to the hockey game and shown up at Musik, making the reservation days in advance. It wasn't because she was working in the area; it was because she was working *there*. She needed photos, she needed to experience the club, and she needed enough content to write about it. And the coincidences—the way she held our signature cocktail, the pictures of where she and Bryn were standing, the way her thumbs bent—hadn't been coincidences at all.

She wouldn't invite me to her place because she probably used her home to film, her kitchen as a studio—things she couldn't hide, things she couldn't have me see.

She worked in social media all right.

And she worked for *Seen*, the whole reason she was here today.

There was one final piece of evidence. Something I had to really dig for, something I hadn't remembered until now while details of the night at Musik slowly came back to me.

Her bracelet.

It had sparkled under the lights in the VIP lounge, and I recall noticing it, standing out just enough in my memory now that I could confirm it was the same one that had appeared in her review of Musik.

I adjusted my shoulder on the door, pressing the glass to keep it open. "I'm not sure I need to sweeten things up for Dear Foodie though, do I?" I continued. "Seems I've already done plenty of that. With my tongue." My lips locked together, and the anger that rose through me was like a goddamn lightning bolt, shocking my entire system.

How the hell could she have lied to me?

Didn't she care about me?

Didn't she want us?

"Lockhart—" She cut herself off as she wiped her eyes. "I ..."

I knew she wasn't going to admit to anything here.

Not with people in the lobby.

Not with more people going in through the door on the other side of the entrance since we were blocking this one.

My patience for listening to any more bullshit was nonexistent.

All I wanted was to get the fuck out of here.

I set the gift basket in her open arm. "Why don't you give this to her? Seems like you'll be able to reach her a lot faster than I can."

I moved my shoulder off the door and headed for my car.

"Lockhart!" Sadie yelled. A few seconds later, I heard, "Lockhart," again.

I had no intention of turning around or giving her another second of my time.

Fuck that.

How could she continue lying to me? Living a double life?

Were we a lie?

Jesus Christ, I felt sick.

I walked even faster and got into the driver's seat of my Audi. The second I revved the engine, getting ready to pull away, a text came across the dashboard.

ALEXA, SOUS CHEF—CHARRED LA

> I've thought long and hard about this, and the only conclusion I can come up with—and I know this makes no sense at all—is that the white blob is a scallop. Perhaps the ones Walker made the evening that your girlfriend was dining with us? I ran the idea by Walker, and he agrees. Which, again, makes no sense, but it's the only answer I have for you. I'm sorry I can't be more helpful.

Exactly what I suspected.

Motherfucker.

I pounded my fist on the steering wheel.

And then I pulled out my phone and typed a reply.

ME

Thanks, Chef. I appreciate you getting back to me.

THIRTY-TWO

Sadie

"It's me," I said into the speaker outside Lockhart's gate about an hour after I ran into him at *Seen*. "Will you please let me in? We need to talk."

There was no way I was going to let another day pass without telling him the truth. Based on how he had reacted at *Seen*, I could only imagine what was running through his head. I wanted him to hear my side, and what he did with that information, I couldn't predict.

I could only hope.

"Sadie ..."

My eyes squinted shut, and my jaw clenched at the sound of his voice, at the emotion that was embedded into each syllable, at the anger.

I rested my forehead against my steering wheel and pleaded, "Please. Please, Lockhart. Just open the gate. Let me tell you everything. And then, once you hear it all, if you want to kick me out, fine. If you never want to talk to me again, I'll fight like hell to make you change your mind, but"—I lifted my forehead and stared at the camera that was pointed right at me —"I will have to be fine with that too." The emotion was thick in my throat, and it was already threatening to spill. "But don't shut me out, not until you at least hear my side."

I knew that after today, there was a chance I'd never drive to his house again.

I'd never feel his arms around me.

I'd never see him.

It would break me.

Oh God, it would wreck me in ways I'd never felt before.

But hadn't I put myself here?

I could hear him breathing. I swore I could sense his mind going in a million different directions. And eventually, the sound of the gate unlatching and the metal clanging overshadowed those noises.

I carefully drove through, taking my usual spot in his driveway, and once I parked, I made my way up to his door. Normally, he was standing there, waiting for me when I arrived.

I didn't realize how much I'd loved that until I no longer had it.

And I didn't realize how much it would hurt to not have it until I stared at the closed door, my hand wrapping around the knob and opening it, a pang of emotion tearing my chest apart.

I found Lockhart in the kitchen, standing at the island with both hands pressed against the counter, leaning into the stone as though it were holding him up. A tumbler, of what I assumed was whiskey, sat between his hands.

I set the stack of papers in front of the glass. It was four pages that I had printed as soon as I got home from *Seen* and stapled in the corner before I rushed over here.

"Please sign that." I even brought my own pen and placed it on top of the pile.

He didn't look down. He didn't break eye contact with me. The only thing he did was lift a hand to pick up the drink and take a sip. "Are you Dear Foodie?"

There was no question in my mind that he had figured me out.

But hearing him say those words made it even more real.

I nodded toward the stack. "Sign that, Lockhart. Please."

He crossed his arms. "Why?"

"So I can tell you the truth." I waited. "So I can give you the answer you've been wanting to hear."

Because something told me that when we had been lying in bed and the review of Musik went live, he had known then. Maybe he had even known before.

He finally glanced down, and I watched him scan the words. "A fucking NDA? Are you kidding me, Sadie? This is what it's come to?"

"It's the only way we can have this conversation." My voice was soft and calm. "I'm sorry. It's not my rule. It's *Seen*'s rule." I paused. "You, out of all people, should understand how this works."

"It's bullshit. That's what it is." He lifted the pen off the counter, flipped to the last page, and signed his name at the bottom.

When he dropped the pen and looked at me, I said, "Yes, I'm Dear Foodie. And my mom, my dad, my sister, Bryn, and my boss at *Seen* are the only people in this world who know that." I was using my fingers to count, gripping each one as I said a name. "You make person number six." I let out a loud breath, holding my chest. "God, that felt good to say out loud to you." I grabbed his drink and shot back the remainder of what was inside, placing the empty on the counter. "You have no idea how long I wanted to tell you that, and I couldn't."

"Yeah ... you just lied to me instead."

The accusation hurt.

But it was the truth.

"It kills me to admit that, but I did." I held the counter with both hands. "In my defense—and I'm going to defend myself when it's warranted because I'm here to tell you my side—I contractually wasn't allowed to tell you. Yes, it was still lying, but all I was trying to do was spin things, like why I was really at Musik or how I told you I had to work nearby when I really didn't." Breathing was becoming harder and harder. "Those lies weren't spoken to hurt you. I never wanted to be dishonest. But I was required to twist the truth because my NDA prevented me from telling you who I was, and the lies were the result of a trickle-down effect"—I shook my head—"one that was horrific on my heart, on my gut, and—"

"On our relationship."

I nodded. "Yes, it was." I sighed. "And that's the reality of a binding agreement. It doesn't matter who it hurts, and it doesn't matter who I have to lie to."

He banged his fist on the counter. "Sadie, this is so fucked."

"Believe me, I know." I quickly glanced at the ceiling. "Do you know how hard it is not to say anything to my extended family? My aunts and uncles and cousins? Or any of my friends, aside from Bryn?" I felt my chest contract even tighter. "Or my boyfriend?"

I picked up the glass, gazing at the tiny bead of amber liquor that rolled around the bottom. "It doesn't matter how much I despise that aspect of my job. There's nothing I can do about it. I knew that when I signed their contract. And all these years later, I've never regretted it. Until now."

As my stomach churned, my eyes burning with tears, I

brought the tumbler into the living room, filled it with several fingers' worth, poured a second glass, and carried them into the kitchen, handing him one.

I positioned the liquor against my lips, but I didn't take a drink. I just breathed in the aroma.

I needed him to speak.

I needed to know where his head was at.

"Please, Lockhart, say something."

He hissed out some air. "I don't even know where to fucking start."

"Start anywhere."

His head hung, and he didn't lift it. He just looked at me through his lashes. "I understand you're under contract. I understand what kind of obligation you have to *Seen*. But I can't help but feel pissed off that I wasn't told until today. I shared things with you about our company, how we want to buy Horned—that's something I wouldn't have told you if I had known you were Dear Foodie." He let a few seconds tick by. "I think you carried this on for too long."

"I probably did, yes. But there are many parts to this that you don't know."

"Tell me." His fingers tightened into a ball. "Make me understand all of it. Because, Sadie ..." His voice drifted off, and he turned his head.

My heart shuddered.

He couldn't even look at me.

I had to make this right.

"When my boss asked me to review Charred and Musik, we were already dating. The weight that consumed me over that request, I can barely describe it. I felt sick." I let out a long breath. "I still do, especially knowing that Toro is coming next. But my boss's requests didn't stop there. He asked if I would travel to other Charred locations across the country and review them, comparing them to the LA location for an extended feature on The Weston Group. The viewership is so high right now. *Seen* is exploding. He doesn't want the heat to die."

I shifted, holding on to the counter, every part of me feeling weak. "But do you know the kind of pressure that put on me? The kind of heat *I* felt from that request? I have to be honest in the words I write for *Seen*, and I have been honest. But now my boss is afraid that I'm too biased to write Toro's review, and ..." My eyes were windows that allowed him to look in, and I knew he was seeing everything. "I'm afraid I am too." My hands moved to the top of my head. "What if I don't love Toro? What does that mean? For you? For me? For *Seen*? For The Weston Group?" I rubbed my lips together, patting my chest to push the air through. "So, I had the Charred review, the Musik review, and the Toro review—all eating at me. And then my boss wanted to send me out for *another* feature? No. I couldn't handle more. Not for the Westons—not when I'm in love with you."

There was an immediate change in him.

In the animosity in his eyes.

In the grimness of his lips.

Both lessening—even if it was slight.

But I still had a long way to go, and I still had so much more to explain.

"This morning, when I was in bed with you, I hit my breaking point. I couldn't take another second of the lies. So, I went to his office." I moved my hair off my shoulders and slipped out of my cardigan, setting it on the counter, my anxiousness making me sweat. "For one, to turn down his offer of traveling and tell him I couldn't review another Weston restaurant after Toro. And two, to discuss my NDA because I wanted to breach it for you."

I took several sips of whiskey. "I don't discuss my personal life with my boss. But today, I did. I told him how we had met. How I felt about you. And how I wanted to come clean to you." Every detail of that meeting was circling in my head. "He said he would give me one pass and one pass only, as long as that person signed an NDA with *Seen*. And I shouldn't waste that pass until I was absolutely positive I was in love." I wrapped my arms around my stomach, my face tilting as I gazed at him. "As soon as he said that to me, Lockhart ..."

I stopped to take a breath.

To observe his expression.

To process that once this was spoken, I could never take it back.

"There was no doubt in my mind who deserved that pass," I continued, offering him a soft smile. "I'm in love with you. I can see myself spending the rest of my life with you."

When he didn't say anything, I finished the rest of what I had poured and set the empty down.

"I left that meeting and called Bryn to tell her the pass was going to you. That I was going home to print out the NDA and I was going to drive to your house or your office, wherever you were, and have the conversation with you. And that's when I ran into you ..."

"Jesus Christ." He turned silent for several seconds. "I don't even know what the hell to say. I'm ..." His fingers dived into the sides of his hair. "My head is a mess."

"I'm sure it is." I moved around the island to where he was standing so there wasn't any stone separating us. "But I want you to know I'm sorry. For the things I did. For the things I said. For the lies I told you. If I could have been honest, I would have. I swear to God, I would have."

He wrapped his fingers around the booze, the liquor sloshing against the sides from his grip. "I couldn't figure out why you wouldn't invite me to your place, why you wouldn't want me there."

"I was hiding Dear Foodie—"

"I know." He ground his teeth over his bottom lip. "Or why I saw you at Musik, but you wouldn't go to the hockey game with me. I took that shit personally when I saw you'd made the reservation four days prior to going, and you were there for two and a half hours and said nothing to me about it."

I rubbed the wetness off my eyelashes. "All things I would have told you if I could. And I wanted to. I wanted to so badly, Lockhart."

He folded his arms over his chest. "I believe that. And I believe you. I just ..."

"You just ... hate me? You can't stand the sight of me?"

He rubbed his hands over his face, and when I finally got his eyes again, he said in the most harrowing voice, "I'm worried we were based on a lie."

"Never. Nothing that even remotely resembles one." The emotion was pouring in and out of me. Every time I took a breath, I swore it swished into my lips and swirled through my chest and went straight to my stomach and came up through my eyes. "I don't want you to think that. And I don't want you to think I chose my job over you. And I don't want you to think that any of this was a choice—it wasn't." I slid my palms over my bare arms. "When I went to my boss and begged him to let me break my NDA, that's when I made a choice." My fingers stilled. "Because I love you."

"Sadie ..."

"I do. I'm completely in love with you."

"Sadie—"

"And I want you to know the night we met at Horned, I was there as Dear Foodie, but that's not who you met. That's not who you took to your hotel room. And that's not whose body you had sex with. That was all me. This whole time, all you've ever experienced is me."

I closed the distance between us and held on to his shoulders. "Be mad at me—I deserve that. Be hurt—I deserve that too. Be disappointed. Tell me I handled everything wrong." I moved up to his face and held it while the tears poured down mine. "But don't tell me I-I ruined us-s. Don't tell me this-s is unforgivable. And p-please ... don't tell me that you don't l-love me."

I felt his exhales. They were coming out hard and fast.

"That's why this hurts so fucking bad."

My fingers fanned his cheeks. "You d-don't have to forget. You don't even h-have to forgive me—at least not n-now. But tell me w-we're somehow, someway, going to be okay-y. That we can eventually move on from th-this." The drips were running so fast from my eyes; I couldn't stop them from flowing past my chin. "That I w-won't have to live my life without y-you." I could taste the saltiness on my lips. "I don't want to live without you. I-I don't even want to spend a day without you—"

I was suddenly in his arms. My face on his chest. My breathing matching his.

"Lockhart ..." My tears were staining his shirt. But beneath the soft cotton was the warmth of his skin, and I needed that.

"We're going to be okay." His hug was so tight that it confirmed everything he'd just said.

I clung to him. My fingers. My arms. Even my face was somehow holding on to him. "You really mean that?"

"Yes." His lips pressed against the top of my head, and when he lifted them off, I tilted my chin up to look at him, and he began to wipe the wetness off my skin. "Because I love you, Sadie."

THIRTY-THREE

Hart

Nothing was perfect. I'd learned that in some of the most humbling ways over my career, and today was no exception.

The negotiations with the owner and chef of Horned, going back and forth multiple times, had been painful. Now we were waiting for her to sign off on our last and final offer or to tell us to fuck off.

But while Eden was at Colson's house, playing with Ellie, passing time until we got the news, and Beck was at an away game, and Walker was grinding it out in the kitchen of Charred LA, I was out to dinner with Sadie.

Our first official outing since she had confirmed she was Dear Foodie.

Our relationship was something else that wasn't perfect, but I loved it just the way it was.

Perfectly flawed, perfectly beautiful, and perfectly ours.

It had taken a day or so for us to find our footing again. For the anger to completely leave my body. To be in her presence and not dig into the topic even deeper.

I understood.

But that didn't mean I could completely let it go from my mind, that the situation wasn't at the forefront and I wasn't going to address it again.

Because being in love with Sadie and her alter ego presented a few challenges. I couldn't ever tell my family what she did for a living. All they would know was that she was in social media. But that also meant my family would never receive another review from her after Toro—a shout-out maybe on her personal page, like we had gotten with the espresso martini in New York, but never a full write-up. And I'd have to listen to Walker bitch and moan about that, and I'd never be able to tell him why or do anything about it.

And I'd have to curb my jealousy when she loved a competing restaurant, the way I had bitten my tongue when she loved Horned, although the situation was now different.

But for her? It was so fucking worth it.

She was everything I wanted.

Everything I needed.

And, God, she was gorgeous.

Her hair was curled and hung around her face, her eyes rimmed with a sultry black color, her lips glossy—a lipstick she had reapplied tonight since she'd given me head on the way here—and a top that was cut into a V, dipping just low enough that there was a hint of her tits.

She took a bite of her dolmas, and while she chewed, she spoke behind her hand and said, "Every time your phone lights up, I hold my breath. Does Troy have any idea when he's going to hear back from the owner? I'm dying here."

She even spoke Weston language.

Because she listened to every goddamn thing I told her.

299

I chuckled. "We gave the owner until the end of the day, so, technically, she has until midnight, and that's"—I glanced at my watch—"a little less than four hours away. We could have a long night ahead of us."

"I can't handle the suspense." She smiled. "I want this for you."

"Let me get your mind off it." I normally never had my phone on the dinner table. Tonight was the exception, and I picked it up, scrolling until I found the email I was looking for. "Jenner—our attorney handling the real estate part of this venture—found us some incredible properties. I met with my family this morning, and we agreed on these. I want you to look at them and tell me your thoughts." I handed her my phone, making sure no one was close by so I could talk freely. "The first two will be Horned restaurants—if we get it. One is in Portsmouth, New Hampshire, and the other is in Charleston, South Carolina. The third and fourth are for future Toros, which will be in Tampa, Florida, and Austin, Texas."

She pointed the screen at me, showing me the Tampa location. "I'm obsessed."

"Nice, isn't it?"

She tucked a piece of dark hair behind her ear. "The way it's sitting right on the Gulf. Ugh, I want to eat there immediately."

"What do you think of the others?" When she glanced up, I added, "You know this business, and I value your opinion. I want you to be honest with me." I wiped the sides of my mouth with my napkin. "We haven't made any offers yet, so there's still time to change our minds."

She pointed at the Austin location while she flipped it toward me. "Another perfect one. Right on the river, which instantly makes me think of fresh. There's something about eating sushi and fish on the water that hits differently than an inland location."

"Agreed."

"But the other two need work." She handed me my phone back and moved around in her seat. "Portsmouth and Charleston are eclectic cities. There's a quirkiness about them, and in the restaurants I've been to in each place—ironically, I've been to both—the quirkiness shines while you're dining there." She gazed up, her stunning blue eyes focused on the ceiling. "Think of vaulted, church-like ceilings in Charleston with lots of metal, a theme that screams of the Prohibition era, where the decor builds the anticipation of the food. What you picked screams nothing to me at all." Her gaze returned to mine.

I shook my head, impressed as hell. "Fuck, you're good."

"And in Portsmouth, I want to feel the New England charm, but I don't want to drown in it." She chewed the side of her light-pink thumbnail. "I don't want lobster decor. I want it in my food. I want to feel quaint, but I want to be engulfed in character. That location is way too blah."

I set my phone next to my plate and reached for her hand. "Will you come with me to look at the properties? I'm going to have Jenner pull new ones, and I would love for you to view them with me."

"Are you kidding?"

I brushed my fingers over my scruffy cheek. "Not at all."

"Lockhart Weston, you're speaking my love language."

"So, that's a yes?"

She smiled her hardest. "That's a hell yes."

I stroked the back of her hand. "I'll plan it in a few weeks. I need to get through Toro's opening, and then I can focus on our new ventures."

Her lips slid closed, no longer showing any teeth, but the grin remained. "We're going to skip right over that topic. 'Kay?"

"Yes, please." I chuckled.

"As for the traveling, just give me a week's notice so I can get all my filming and editing done ahead of time." Her teeth went to her lip in a playful way. "It feels so good to be able to say that to you."

"I—" The light from my phone caught my attention, and a notification from Troy was on the screen.

TROY

Check your email.

"The answer is waiting in my inbox," I told her. "I just heard from Troy."

Her eyes widened, and she rocked in her seat. "What is it? What did the owner say? Is it yours? Tell me!"

Her enthusiasm made me laugh, and I opened my inbox, scanning the first few sentences of the email, and slowly set my phone down.

"You're killing me, Lockhart. Straight-up killing me."

I shook my head, stretching my tongue up over my top lip. "Walker is going to fucking murder us."

She stilled. "Murder who?"

"Beck and me."

"Why?"

"Because we found out our competition had upped their offer, so we did the same to ours. And we might not have consulted him and made that decision on our own."

"And?" She shook her head. "So?"

"It was more than Walker wanted to spend."

"I don't get it." She flattened her hands on the table. "What are you telling me?"

"I'm telling you ..." All the built-up energy left my chest, and the corners of my lips tugged high as I said, "You're looking at the new owner of Horned."

"Oh my God!" She rose from her chair and came over to my side of the table, falling into my lap, wrapping her arms around me. With our lips aligned, she whispered, "I'm so happy for you."

"Thank you, baby."

"Now kiss me."

Her grin told me there was more, so I said, "Just kiss you?"

She stared into my deep green eyes. "And tell me you love me."

That made me smile so fucking hard.

THIRTY-FOUR

Sadie

You're at the office, right?

LOCKHART

Yeah. Why?

I'm going to stop by super quick. Are all your siblings there too?

LOCKHART

Everyone but Beck.

I know this will be the first time you're meeting Eden—don't worry, my sister is a vault. She won't say anything about DF to anyone. You're safe, I promise.

I've been worried.

LOCKHART
You have no reason to be.

ME
OK, good. See you in 20-ish.

LOCKHART
What are you wearing?

ME
Right now?

LOCKHART
Yes.

ME
Jeans. T-shirt thingy. Blazer. High heels.

LOCKHART
Put on the jacket. You know which one I'm talking about.

ME
You want me to wear THAT to your office?

LOCKHART
And you know what color panties and bra I want you to wear underneath.

ME
Lockhart ... it's your office.

LOCKHART
And?

ME
I'm not exactly good at being quiet.

LOCKHART
I'm not telling you that you have to be.

When I reached the top floor of Lockhart's building, I carried the large container of cupcakes out of the elevator and approached the receptionist. I gave her my name—the same process I'd done downstairs when I first walked into the building—and while she typed something into her computer, I took a look around the space.

Visiting The Weston Group's corporate headquarters hadn't been on my bingo card prior to dating Lockhart. But I was fascinated with the inner workings of a group as massive as theirs—how they operated, how they chose locations, and how they balanced so many different cuisines under the same umbrella. Lockhart had slowly been letting me into his professional world, and I was honored that he asked for my opinion on things.

The receptionist politely asked me to follow her down a long hallway of what appeared to be private offices. I hadn't envisioned what this space would look like. If it would be blank walls and bland carpet, the smell of wood cleaner in the air.

This was nothing like that.

The entire floor, from what I'd seen so far, had a design similar to Charred, with rich, bold colors and warm wallpapered walls and a wood floor that gave this long and endless hallway a cozy feel. It was masculine without being overwhelming and powerful, like there was a red carpet beneath your feet.

The receptionist stopped outside a closed door and knocked twice, and when called upon, she opened it just slightly and said, "Go ahead in, Ms. Spencer."

I thanked her, and as the door widened enough to let me in, I was surprised to find Lockhart wasn't alone.

"Hi, baby," he said from behind his desk. "Welcome."

"Hi!" I stepped inside.

"You already know everyone, except for Eden," Lockhart said.

Two other faces were staring back at me. Walker, who I'd originally met at Charred, and Colson, who I'd met at Musik.

"Nice to see you guys." I gave them a smile and a wave, and I approached Lockhart's sister, extending my hand. "It's so wonderful to meet you, Eden."

"And you." She offered a smile, but it wasn't nearly as large as mine, like she was holding part of it back.

I hadn't been surprised when Lockhart told me he'd gone to her for help, figuring out if I was Dear Foodie or not. But I had been surprised to hear she was a vault. Every woman had a weakness. Mine was Bryn. She knew everything. Maybe Eden's weakness was Lockhart. Or maybe she was a unicorn, and she truly didn't have one.

If that was the case, I was even more intrigued by her.

"I've heard endless things about you," I said. "I'm really looking forward to getting to know you." I winked at Lockhart. "Considering you are his favorite."

Her blue eyes shifted to Lockhart, a color so vibrant that it was unique and striking. "Your favorite? Now, I would have thought Beck held that title."

A quick glance told me Lockhart was putting his hands in the air, holding them by his face, but I was more focused on Eden. She was stunning, from her dark hair—a vast contrast to the blonde I had found on Instagram who I thought was her—to her sensual lips to her petiteness. Women would strive to look as beautiful as her.

But what was drawing me in was her demeanor. She had this magnetism about her that you almost couldn't look away from. And if you did, you were afraid you'd miss something. Something that would hint at what was going on inside her. Lockhart had told me she was closed off, and I could feel that.

Nothing seemed random about Eden—what came out of her mouth, how her body moved, the deepness of her stare. Everything was for a reason, and everything was calculated.

While she laughed at Colson, who was now teasing Lockhart, I moved around to the back side of his desk and set the Tupperware on top.

"What do you have there?" Lockhart asked after I gave him a peck.

"Tonight is a huge night for you guys, and even though I know the opening of Toro is going to be perfect and seamless and everything you want it to be, I wanted to bring you something to celebrate since I won't be there."

"You're not coming?" Colson asked.

I shook my head, feeling Eden's eyes on me. "But I'll be there in a few nights."

"If you're worried about getting a table, please don't," Walker said. "We've got you covered."

"Hart mentioned it has something to do with your bestie, right?" Eden announced. "She's your date, and she has to work tonight, which is why you can't make it?"

I quickly glanced at her, a smile gradually lifting on my face. "Yes. You're right. She has a work thing, and since Lockhart will be slammed, I have this weird thing about eating alone. Please don't hate me, you guys."

Dear Foodie didn't go to restaurants on opening nights because nothing ever went right for the restaurant or the staff. They needed a second to work things out, and even though two days wasn't enough time either, it was all *Seen* was willing to give me.

Lockhart and I hadn't discussed what I would say to his family or what excuse I would use if any of them asked why I wouldn't be there.

Eden had done this all on her own.

She had my back—something I'd never anticipated.

"Hate you? Hardly," Eden replied. "I think Lockhart would prefer you be there when it's less chaotic and things have cooled down a little. This way, he'll actually have time to spend with you. We all will."

Lockhart's arm went around my waist. "She's right."

As I looked at Eden again, she gave me a slight nod, and I gave her one back and said, "Anyway, I'm not Walker Weston in the kitchen, but I thought these would be fun."

I took off the lid. "They're champagne-flavored cupcakes." I handed one to each of them. The base was a light pink that was infused with champagne with a whipped buttercream frosting on top that I'd decorated with edible confetti, and stuck into the side of the icing was a plastic dropper. "The dropper has actual champagne in it."

"I'll take any and all alcohol at the moment," Colson said, pulling out the plastic and squirting the liquid into his mouth. "Oh, that's good."

Walker laughed at him and then connected eyes with me. "Cooking is my specialty. Baking is a beast I've battled my whole career. I bet these are better than I could make." He paused to take a bite and moaned. "What in the hell are these?" He stared at each side of the dessert. "Sadie, they're exceptional."

Walker, a wildly popular and highly respected chef, was complimenting my baking. I couldn't help but feel flattered, especially given that I'd thrown out the first batch, unsatisfied with how they had turned out.

"Thank you," I said, trying to hold back my excitement.

"He's right, they are," Colson groaned and reached inside the Tupperware. "I'm going to take another one of these."

I laughed. "Help yourself. I'm leaving the rest here, so take as many as you want."

Lockhart placed his on his desk. "I'm saving mine." He eyed me up and down.

As Eden stood from her chair, she wiggled down her black skirt before swiping her finger across the rim of the frosting and sucking it off. "I'm going to need this recipe."

"I've got you, girl," I said.

"Come on, guys. Let's leave them and get back to work," Eden voiced, giving me a wave prior to heading out into the hallway.

Colson and Walker said goodbye, and the door shut, leaving Lockhart and me alone.

With his arm still around me, I turned and faced him. "Just so you know, Eden and I are going to be besties—"

"Go lock that door," he growled, his eyes slowly dipping down my body. "Right now."

THIRTY-FIVE

Hart

Sadie was standing beside my desk, her jacket buttoned, the tie around the middle knotted, the outer garment hiding the bra and panties she was wearing beneath—both, I assumed, in my favorite color. Her eyes were sultry as she stared at me, processing the order I'd just given her to go lock my office door.

I couldn't wait another second to have her.

So, to speed up the process, I added, "And after you lock that door, come back here and sit on my desk. I want your legs spread, and I want your heels to stay on."

She traced her finger around the top of the champagne cupcake that I'd placed on my desk and sucked the frosting off her skin. "We're really going to do this in here?"

God, that was hot.

"Fuck yes," I replied.

"And you're not worried about—"

"Sadie, I'm the boss. I'm not worried about anything." I nodded toward the door. "Go lock it."

She smiled, shaking her head at me, but she made her way to the door and turned the latch above the handle, and as she returned to my desk, I wheeled my chair back, giving her plenty of room. She slid the keyboard away and positioned herself in the middle, along the edge.

"Take it off." I used my finger to paint the air down her body. "I want that jacket on the floor now."

"What about the windows?" She glanced toward the wall that was nothing but glass.

"Do you think I'd let someone see you naked?"

She grinned. "So, they're tinted?"

"Of course they are."

She pulled at the tie, loosening each side until it was undone, and slowly unbuttoned the jacket, letting it fall open before she slipped her arms out. She grabbed something from one of the pockets, hiding it in her hand, and let the coat fall to the floor.

"What do you have there?" I asked.

Her cheeks were becoming flushed. "I made a quick stop on my way here. You know, just in case ..."

"Just in case ... *of what?*"

She set a plastic tube beside her. A quick read of the label confirmed she was the sexiest woman alive.

"Sadie ... my fucking girl." I wheeled closer, in a range where I could smell her better, inhaling the scent I craved. "You wore red lace, just like I'd asked. And you brought me lube, just in case I wanted your ass." I paused. "Is that what you want me to do today? Fuck your ass? And finally make that virgin hole mine?" I rubbed the side of my scruff against her thigh.

Her chest rose high as she whispered, "I want you to surprise me."

But she wanted the option—that was why she had stopped to get the lube.

My exhale was loud. "What did I do to deserve you?"

"I'm in love with you. There isn't anything I wouldn't do for you."

"Like giving me this ..." My eyes dipped down her body, taking in the way the lace hugged her curves, how it covered her beautiful nipples and that smooth, delicious pussy. "That body, Sadie, my fucking God ..." My voice faded as I gradually made my way up, stalling on her navel, again on her collarbone, finally connecting our eyes. "I can't believe it's all mine."

I got in closer, sliding her legs apart even more and placing her heels on each armrest. I then picked up the cupcake, the plastic dropper sticking into the side of the frosting like a straw, and I pulled it out. When she had brought these in several minutes ago, she'd told us there was champagne inside.

I wanted to taste it.

But I wanted to taste it on her.

And because my patience was gone, I didn't bother tugging the lace down her hips and thighs and flinging it away after I got it past her feet. I tore a hole in the center of her panties instead, shredding them wide enough that I had all the access I needed.

"*Mmm.* I missed you." I kissed the top of her pussy, rubbing my nose against it. My lips. A tiny bit of my scruff.

Her hand dived into my hair, pulling at my strands. "*Yesss!*" she gasped when I pulled back, the cold of the office probably hitting the wetness I'd left behind.

"You're going to get more, don't worry."

I took the dropper of champagne and held it over her clit, squeezing the end so the bubbling liquid came dribbling out. I didn't let any go to waste. My lips were right there, at the bottom of her pussy, catching every drop.

"You have no idea how good this tastes." I was staring up at her with my tongue out, watching the heat build in her eyes, swallowing everything that ran down her.

Once it was empty, I picked up the cupcake, staying right where I was, and I swiped my finger across the frosting, scooping up a small amount and dragging the thickness over her pussy. Her breathing was speeding up, her exhales sounding like moans as I coated her in a thin layer.

"How does that feel?"

"Cold. Tingly from the champagne." She shivered. "Gritty and heavy."

With my tongue out, I licked up and down the sides, swallowing the sugary mixture, refreshing my tongue so I could clean the frosting off her. "It's so sweet."

"That's because it's buttercream." Her head was back, her mouth open, her sky-high red heels now balancing on the very edge of my desk.

"I was talking about your cunt."

She looked at me and smiled. "Oh."

When I began to lick harder and faster, the frosting completely gone, not even a swipe left on her skin, the only thing that remained was my need to give her an orgasm. That was when the screaming started. I could tell she was trying to keep her voice down, but she just couldn't.

I was giving her too much pleasure.

Because I knew how she liked to have her pussy licked.

I knew what would send her body into shudders.

And she was getting all of that—right now.

"Lockhart!"

Her wetness thickened around my skin as my finger

plunged in and out of her, and within a few more grazes of her clit, she lost it.

"Ah! Yes!"

Her body was in full-on quivers, her moans carrying straight to the walls of my office, her hips grinding over the wood beneath her ass, working her orgasm out. I kept my tongue on her, my finger deep inside, aimed at her G-spot, my movements only stopping when I was sure she was finished.

"Damn, that tongue," she panted.

I chuckled as I gently pulled it back—the tongue, that was—wiping the corners of my mouth. "It fucking loves to eat you."

"And I love when it eats me." She reached behind her back to unhook her bra, the lace joining her coat on the floor. "Now it's your turn to come." Her feet dropped from the desk, and as she stood, whatever was left of her panties fell to her ankles. "I want you naked, and I want you naked now."

"That demand just made my dick harder."

While she got to work on my belt and pants, I undid my tie and the buttons of my shirt and took off my suit jacket, standing to place it all across my keyboard. With her help, I was able to step out of my pants and boxer briefs, slipping out of my shoes and socks. By the time I sat back down, she was walking toward me, straddling my chair, moving her legs beneath the armrests and lowering herself onto my lap.

"I want you." She wasted no time, aiming my tip at her pussy and sinking down over my shaft. "Ah, yes, I want it."

"Fuck, Sadie." I held her waist as she stayed low, shifting toward me and back, having me hit each of her walls inside.

The tightness. The heat. The wetness.

It was a lethal combination, threatening to instantly make me come.

"You're taking this fucking dick like you can't live without it." I fisted her long strands, holding them, wrapping them around my wrist.

She gripped my biceps and then my chest, moving her hands against my shoulders, each time rising to my crown and lowering to my base. "I fucking want to come, Lockhart. I want you to come."

"Show me." I pulled back on her hair to expose her throat. "But when you get to that point—when you're seconds away from that edge—I want you to stop." I paused. "You can get as close as you want, but do not let that orgasm take ahold of you. Do you hear me?"

I licked her nipple, giving it a bit of my teeth. And as I was moving to the other side, she began to increase her speed.

"*Mmm.*" With each pump, she was narrowing around me. "Oh! Whoa!"

And that feeling only got more intense as I flicked her clit with my thumb. That was when every breath began to burst from her lips, when her screaming resumed, when her hips circled, gliding forward and back—a pattern that was picking up with each rotation.

"Sadie ..." Her name was a warning.

Even though I sensed she was getting to that place of no return, so was I, and I had to mentally bring myself back down.

But was she doing that?

Her face told me no—it was filled with far too much passion. Her nipples were hard. Her pussy dripping. Her moans were so loud that they vibrated in my ears.

"Sadie!"

She stilled. At least when it came to thrusting, but her body started to shake. "Oh my God!"

She'd edged herself there, and she was on her way down.

Which told me one thing.

"You're ready." I lifted her off my lap and set her on the

desk so she was facing me, widening her legs and standing between them. She was already so fucking wet, but I still squirted some of the lube over my shaft, and when that was all greased up, I put some on my fingers and rimmed them around her ass. "Do you trust me?"

"Yes."

I nodded at her response. "Trust me when I say I know what I'm doing and I'm going to try my hardest not to hurt you." I pulled her ass to the very lip of the desk and aimed my tip at that forbidden hole.

"I believe you."

"And I promise, if you just get through the beginning, it's going to feel good." I brushed my lips over hers. "You're going to come—mark my words."

She leaned back on her arms, keeping her elbows bent to hold her weight, and put her heels where they had been before. I held on to her knee and gripped the bottom of my shaft. We were both so lubricated that the tip slipped right in.

"Wow," she hissed.

The tightness, which I had known would be there since I'd fingered her here, was a fucking shock to my system. I tried to hold in my pleasure, knowing she wasn't feeling the same way, but it was impossibly hard. When something felt this good, you just wanted to fucking shout about it.

"Are you all right?" I asked.

She nodded.

"Sadie, I need to hear you say it before I give you any more."

Her teeth released her bottom lip to voice, "I'm all right."

I was gentle, slow, methodic as I sank my way in, reading her body to know how much it could accept, listening to her breathing to hear if the pain was too much.

But she didn't get to that point.

She took it.

Every goddamn inch.

Her eyes squinted shut as I reached the end, and I stayed there, stalled, letting her ass spread and get used to me.

"Breathe. It's only going to get better from here. You have all of me." I grazed her clit with a continuous motion, keeping her turned on, making sure she stayed wet. "Tell me when you're ready. I won't move until you say the word."

It was taking every bit of restraint I had not to come.

Not to pull back and slam in, drowning myself in this fucking feeling.

But I couldn't. I wouldn't.

I inhaled and exhaled through the pleasure, and I waited until I heard, "I'm ready."

I delayed my reaction in case she had second thoughts, and when enough time went by where I was sure she didn't, I slowly backtracked to my tip, and on my way in, her ass hugged me like a fucking suction cup.

"*Ohhh*," I roared.

A suction cup that was going to drain every ounce of cum from my dick.

But unlike me, she wasn't there yet.

"Within a few more strokes, you're going to be used to this, and something is going to change inside you—just wait."

Her clit needed more attention, so that was what I gave her, licking my finger to add spit to her skin. And I carefully glided in and out of her, making sure there was plenty of lube over the both of us.

I saw the change when it happened.

When the switch of pain turned off and her body accepted what I was giving to it, when it even got to the point where it wanted me, where she was suddenly enjoying having my dick in her ass.

"This is feeling good, isn't it?"

"I ... don't know how." She let out some air. "But it is." She held my wrist, keeping my hand on her pussy even though it had no intention of leaving her. "Lockhart!"

This was her first time. I wasn't going to drag it out and ruin her experience and make her so sore that she would hate me, along with the thought of this, and never want me in her ass again.

Because I had all intentions of being in this ass again.

As often as I could.

That was how incredible she felt.

An orgasm that was going to be positively mind-blowing.

And I was about to experience it.

Right fucking now.

"Lockhart!"

I slipped a finger into her pussy. I didn't want to just hear how close she was; I wanted to feel it too.

"Oh my God!" she yelled. "What is even happening?"

She was closing in.

Pulsing.

"That's it, Sadie." My thumb moved faster, massaging the top where my tongue had been, working that little bud. "Yes! I can feel it!"

Not just on my finger.

But on my dick, throbbing around me.

"You're going to come—"

"Yes!" she belted out.

The sound of her scream, the sight of her stomach shuddering, the feral look in her eyes—that was all it took for me.

The tingles shot through my balls, like a fucking bullet straight through my shaft, and I filled her. "Fuck yeah!"

Her nails were stabbing me, and I didn't stop. Her shouts

were piercing my eardrums. All that did was make me move faster, deeper, and with each plunge, her ass milked me more.

"Oh! Argh!"

She drew in a breath. "Lockhart!"

Stream after stream of cum shot from my tip, making me moan her name, along with words of satisfaction. The heaviness of my ejaculation added to the thick lube, helping me slide in and out even easier. But within a few drives, knowing she was past the build and already coming down, I gently pulled out. I moved one of her legs from around me and tucked her knees against her chest, turning her enough so that I could hold her. And when I wasn't happy with that position, I lifted her and placed her on my lap as I sat in the chair.

"There's a shower in there." I nodded toward the back side of my office and kissed the side of her cheek. "I'll take you in there in a second. Right now, I just want to hold you."

"I feel like I can't catch my breath." Her face was in my neck, her small breaths finally slowing. "I didn't expect that."

My chest constricted as I asked, "You mean the pain?"

It didn't happen immediately, but when the grin showed up on her face, it made me smile too.

"No. I didn't expect to love that. And I do."

THIRTY-SIX

Sadie

ME

> Just doing all the last-minute things. Leaving here in 10 to pick you up.

BRYN

> I'll be ready, babe!

I grabbed a purse from Dear Foodie's side of the closet, a wardrobe that never crossed into Sadie's—although tonight was an exception and there was far too much crossover for my liking —and as I opened the clutch to put my phone inside, it started ringing.

My boss's name was on the screen.

"Hello?" I said as I answered.

"I assume you're getting ready to leave or you're on your way?"

I caught a glimpse of myself in the mirror of my walk-in closet, turning to the left and then the right, assessing how this asymmetrical black dress hugged me. If I should wear the red heels or swap them out for a pair of silver ones. "I'm getting ready to leave, yes."

"Good. Let's chat for a minute."

There was a small island in the center of my closet where I kept my jewelry and sunglasses, and I set my arms on the quartz top. "Okay."

"You're a professional. You've been doing this for a long time. So, I don't need to remind you that you'll be there as an employee of *Seen*, not the girlfriend of Hart Weston."

"But you're going to ..."

"Yes."

My head dropped. "I deserve that—I get it." I paused. "Did you go to the opening two nights ago?"

"I did."

"And what did you think?" I shifted my stance, appreciating the little give the red heels had when the silver pair had none, knowing right then I wouldn't switch.

"I'm going to save my opinion until after you submit your review. Then I'll be happy to discuss it in great detail. I don't want to persuade you in any way."

"I understand."

"Sadie ..." His tone changed, and I could feel a lecture coming on. "I have Hart's signed NDA on file. I know why you told him about Dear Foodie and the circumstances that surrounded it, but now that he's aware that Dear Foodie will be there tonight, you'll be getting special treatment. That right there will alter your experience."

I sighed. "I know."

"So, already, things aren't on an even playing ground."

"There's nothing I can do about that. You know I wanted to wait until after Toro's review to tell him, but that didn't work out. So, now, I'm in this horrible position." I lifted my head and left my closet, the tight space making me feel more panicky. "And I'm a complete wreck over it. I've never been more excited and more distraught about eating at a restaurant in my whole life." I took a seat on the end of my bed.

"You know, I hate math. I can't fathom how something can have an exact answer. There are too many variables at play, too many things that can affect the outcome. But in writing, we can make room for those variables. We can color them in gray. We can finesse the words, creating a result that everyone can benefit from."

My heart stopped. "What are you saying?"

"Five stars is five stars. Just like one star is one star. There's no gray. No finessing. It's as exact as can be with zero room to wiggle. But your rating this evening isn't a number. There's no math involved. It's only words. Your words. And what those words mean to you could mean something entirely different to someone else."

My eyes closed, and I nodded. "I hear you. Loud and very clear."

"You know how I feel about honesty, but I'm also human, and there isn't anything I wouldn't do for my family. I gave you one pass, and he's who you picked. I'm not telling you to be dishonest. I'm telling you to use your words the best way you see fit."

I smiled. "I will."

"Have a good dinner, Sadie."

"Thank you," I said and hung up.

"You look absolutely stunning," Lockhart said as he stood at the side of our table, staring down at me with a smile I wanted to lick off his face. "God, I'm one lucky man."

"Well, I'm one lucky woman." I eyed him down—from the scruff on his cheeks to the starched white collar of his shirt to his dark brown leather shoes. "The way that suit looks on you? Whoa."

"Look at my girl blushing her hardest," Bryn joked.

I waved her off, laughing. "How's everything going? This place is"—I peeked around our table, where the energy was so hot that I could feel the buzz in my chest—"on fire."

"Eden thought it would cool off by tonight," he said. "But I think we're even busier than our opening night."

"Well, I'm completely in love with every square inch of this place," Bryn offered. "Charred owned my heart, and Toro has now stolen it—forever."

He smiled at her. "Bryn, it's an honor to hear that. Thank you."

He then glanced at me as I said, "Don't ask me how I feel about anything. My lips are sealed."

He laughed. "Fair."

Eden and Colson and Walker were making their way around the dining room—Beck was at an away game, or I was sure he would have been here tonight—and they slowed as they approached our table. As I looked at them, smiling, I could barely breathe, and that had nothing to do with the tightness of my dress.

This line that I was straddling was too thin, too unsteady, and too personal.

I wanted to be the professional that I was, but I loved this man, and I adored his family, and they deserved all the praise because I knew how hard they worked and what they had put into this restaurant.

So, the first thing I said when his siblings joined our table was, "I'm beyond proud of you guys." My head shook. "Look at this place. It's popping. I couldn't be more excited for you."

Since Bryn had met everyone but Eden, following my compliment, I quickly introduced the two.

"I hope you're enjoying yourselves?" Walker asked.

"Very much so," Bryn replied.

"I'm so happy you could come," Colson said. He patted his stomach. "And next time you're in the mood to bake, I'll gladly take an order of those cupcakes again."

I giggled. "I'll remember that."

Eden gave me a smile—a sly one that I suspected was her specialty. "The toro nigiri and the hamachi and jalapeño are my favorite. I know you didn't order either. I'm going to send some over."

I wasn't even a little surprised that Eden had looked at our ticket prior to coming to our table. Nothing slipped by her. She was one sharp lady.

"I can't wait to try them," I admitted.

The siblings said goodbye to us and left, and Lockhart leaned into my neck, holding my lower back as he whispered, "I won't be home until late. I'll text you."

"You'd better."

I could feel him smile, the way his scruff brushed my cheek before he put his lips in front of mine and kissed me. He lingered there, not nearly long enough, and pulled back.

"I'll try to check in again," he said. "But if I don't get the chance, make sure to find me before you leave."

I nodded. "I will."

"Enjoy your dinner, ladies."

The second he was gone, Bryn fanned her face. "The two of you are so ridiculously hot, I can't stand it." She grinned as she glanced toward her left. "Speaking of hot, I wish Beck was here. Those few minutes at the bar in Musik when I got to meet my pretend boyfriend wasn't nearly enough." Her eyes turned to full-on hearts.

"Lockhart said he has an away game."

"Bummer." She took a drink. "Girl, I've never seen so many good-looking people in one room. Do you have to show a photo of yourself before you make a reservation?"

I laughed. "That's because half the people in here are famous. It's the most popular restaurant in LA at the moment."

Everyone online was talking about Toro. It had filled my social media feed from the moment they opened—and for good reason. This restaurant was absolutely breathtaking. It felt nothing like Charred or Musik. But like those two, it was an experience from the second you stepped inside.

One that hit every one of your senses.

And one that made you remind yourself that you weren't here for the ambiance, but for the food.

The interior was decorated in all different shades of blue and silver—metallic and matte. Multiple textures had been used—from the floor to the ceiling to the linens and lighting. When combined, you didn't feel like you were swimming in the middle of an ocean. You felt like you were sunbathing on the sand in Fiji; the sound of the waves lapping the shore was humming in your ear, and the warmth of the sun was wrapping its rays around you.

We'd only had two dishes so far, the tuna tartare—which Bryn ordered wherever she went—and the oysters, flown in from the Damariscotta River in Maine.

Both were positively divine.

"I think our next course is coming," I said to Bryn as a food runner, headed right for us, halted at our table.

He set two small plates between us. "The toro nigiri and the hamachi and jalapeño, from Miss Eden Weston," he said. "Enjoy."

"Oh, I'm going to." Bryn picked up her porcelain chopsticks

from a small fish-shaped holder. "Take a picture. Hurry. I'm about to devour this, it looks so good."

My phone was already on the table, and I positioned it over the two plates, snapping several shots from different angles.

"You're good. Dig in." I lifted my chopsticks off the fish holder and picked up the nigiri, moaning the second the fatty tuna hit my tongue.

"Right?" Bryn sang. "Like, couldn't you eat a hundred more of these?"

"At least."

I tried the hamachi next. It had been cut in thin slices, all placed in a circle, soaked in a brown sauce with pieces of cilantro in the center. On top of the fish were disks of jalapeños.

I covered my mouth as I chewed and blurted out, "Oh my God."

"I don't know about you, but I'm dead. This is the best food I've had in a long time, and we haven't even gotten our main courses yet."

I nodded in agreement, and as I swallowed, I let that news pass through me.

It hit my chest and stomach, and it came out of my lips in a smile. "Bryn ..."

"Yes?"

I rubbed my lips together, trying to mask what I was feeling, even though I knew my best friend could see right through me. "They did it. Like, they really, really did it."

"Fuck yeah, they did."

There weren't any lights on in my office. The only thing aglow was my monitor, the room completely silent as I read over the review I'd just finished writing.

My boss had told me to use my words.

I'd done just that.

But those words were honest. They were the most accurate portrayal of my experience—from the way I had felt when I walked into Toro to the fullness in my belly when Bryn and I left. I skipped over nothing, not a single detail, and accompanying those words were a series of photos that I'd cropped to protect the location of our table and any hints of Bryn, but I'd added no filters and done no Photoshopping.

I was giving them the real Toro. What they did with that information, how they decided to react, that was up to them.

Satisfied with my read-through, I attached the document to an email, and I sent it to my boss. I grabbed my phone, and on my way to my bedroom, I typed Lockhart a text.

ME

I miss you.

LOCKHART

I miss you more.

ME

Are you still at the restaurant?

LOCKHART

Yes, I'll be here for a while.

ME

Will you be up for having breakfast in the morning?

LOCKHART

If it involves you, I'm up for anything.

Where do you want to go? Or do you want to come to my place?

ME

I was thinking … maybe you could come to my place.

LOCKHART

YOUR place?

ME

I think it's time. 😊 I'll text you my address. See you at 9?

LOCKHART

9? Is this really you? Or did Bryn steal your phone and I'm talking to her?

ME

Asshole, LOL. I can do early when I need to. And I NEED to see you EARLY.

I love you, and I'm endlessly proud of you, Lockhart.

LOCKHART

I love you too, baby.

The sound of a text woke me. I had no idea what time it was, but at some point during the night, I'd turned off my TV and pulled the blanket up over my head. I reached for my phone on the nightstand and saw Boss on the screen.

BOSS

Toro was as perfect as you described. I agree with every one of your words. Brilliant review.

THIRTY-SEVEN

Hart

BECK

In the plane, on the way back to LA. How'd last night go?

EDEN

We were sneaking footage of the game every chance we got. The whole kitchen at Toro erupted when you scored the winning shot. I think I might even have it on video.

BECK

You guys are one hell of a cheering squad.

COLSON

I'm not going to lie ... I could sleep for a week.

BECK

None of you have answered my question, LOL.

ME

Dude, Toro has hit the level—the one we dreamed of. You can't even get near the entrance.

WALKER

Or the bar.

COLSON

Or the dining room.

EDEN

Reservations are scaling faster than we anticipated. Word is spreading. We're currently booked 6 weeks out, and once we open for lunch, I assume those time slots will fill up too.

WALKER

There's only one thing that can change all of that.

BECK

Dear Foodie. Her review drops tomorrow, right?

COLSON

Yes, sir.

WALKER

I'm ready to start fucking drinking. There's so much riding on this.

As I lay in bed, the bright morning sunlight filtering in through my blinds, I focused on Walker's last message. He was right; there was a lot riding on this. And there wasn't a goddamn thing I could do about it. I couldn't even tell my family, aside from Eden, that I was torn up over the thought that Sadie could fucking shred us in her review. That she had every right to have an opinion, and it might or might not be in our favor.

I couldn't ask her to throw me a bone. I wouldn't put that kind of pressure on her.

So, I was helpless.

And that felt strange as hell.

> **EDEN**
>
> We can't control what happens with Dear Foodie, so let's not stress about it. Besides, I have a feeling it's all going to work out.

Eden ...

I shook my fucking head.

She wasn't the positive one out of the group. That was Colson. She had said that because she knew Sadie's identity, and she knew that Sadie had gotten special treatment, and my sister was hoping that would sweeten things up.

But that didn't mean shit.

Eden had to know that too.

> **WALKER**
>
> What gives you that feeling, Eden?

> **EDEN**
>
> My gut—and you guys know that thing never steers me wrong.

> **BECK**
>
> Do we think things have been running well? Smoothly? Have we gotten many complaints? Are we feeling good about operations? Staff? Menu? Food supply?

> **WALKER**
>
> Our staff will forever need extra training—that's true for all our restaurants. I'm pleased with the menu, however, I might tweak certain ingredients and preparations. Food supply—I've got that shit mastered.

EDEN

The reviews I've read complain about normal things—the food took too long to come out, they were promised an 8:00 reservation and weren't seated until 8:30. Bitching about our prices—we get that at all our restaurants. A few said our food was cold. (It's fucking sushi. Did they want their raw fish warm?) There will always be those who come in with the intent to destroy us. No matter what, we can't please them. Overall, I've seen nothing that's alarming.

BECK

All right, it's time to rate it. The same way we do every time we open a restaurant in our home state. Come on, guys. Give me your number. 5 being the highest. Go!

COLSON

5.

EDEN

4.5.

WALKER

I'm already 2 shots deep, by the way.

ME

It's not even 8 in the morning, Walker.

WALKER

So?

ME

4.5—there's always room for improvement.

WALKER

4.

BECK

Damn, Walker, really?

WALKER

We all know things will never be perfect at any restaurant.

ME

But a 4?

WALKER

Ask me again in a month. If my rating is still the same, we have a fucking problem.

ME

Can I bring anything?

SADIE

Just you.

You know ... I should tell you to wear the jacket.

ME

What jacket?

SADIE

The one you asked me to wear to your office. Now, wouldn't THAT be something?

ME

If you want me to show up naked ... just ask.

SADIE

Food first. Naked after.

See you soon. 🖤

"Well, those are absolutely gorgeous." As I stood at the door, Sadie reached for the bouquet of flowers I'd picked up on my way over, which had caused me to be a few minutes late since I'd asked the store to combine three premade packages into one.

But what I liked, when I saw them, was that they were all in different shades of red.

A color I fucking loved on her.

"Not nearly as gorgeous as you." My lips went to hers, and I breathed her in. "Good morning, baby." I handed her the bag I was holding. "I picked up some champagne. I wasn't sure if you had any. Mimosas sounded good to me."

"Funny, I picked up some too. But in case we finish off my bottle, now we have a second bottle to work our way through."

"I like how you think." I'd gotten a hint of the aroma as soon as she opened the door, but now that I'd been in her doorway for a few seconds, I was really getting a good whiff. "What in the hell are you baking in there?"

She smiled. "Homemade cinnamon buns. I've been tweaking this recipe for years. We'll see how this batch turns out. They'll be ready in"—she looked at her watch—"five minutes." She moved to the side of the door. "Stop standing out there and come in."

I stepped inside, and once she closed the door, I followed her into the kitchen.

"Nice place."

The space was bright and cheerful—just the way I would expect Sadie to live—with light colors, mostly in pinks and white.

"I've grown out of it, which is funny because it felt huge when I moved in."

She reached for a vase in the top cupboard. When I saw her on her tiptoes, still unable to reach it, I came up behind her and grabbed the glass from the shelf, setting it on the counter.

"You're the best," she added.

My hands briefly went to her waist, my mouth to her neck.

She was in a pair of leggings and a tight tank, clothes that let me feel her body, rather than a bulky top that I'd have to lift and a pair of bottoms that hid her ass. "God, I've missed waking up to you."

"You have no idea how much I've missed it." She stopped moving and put her hands on mine, leaning her back into my chest. "Let's end that streak tonight."

"Please."

She tapped my hand. "Done." She unwrapped the plastic from around the flowers and soaked them in water and turned toward me. "Let me give you the short tour." She circled her hand in the air. "Kitchen, obviously."

"Oh, I'm familiar with your kitchen."

"That's right." She laughed. "Sometimes, I'm so lost in keeping the lives separate that I forget when there's crossover, like right now." She gave me a sideways smile. "You know, aside from my parents and sister and Bryn, you're the only person who's ever been here. This is quite a moment for me, Lockhart. Sharing this part of my life with someone I love."

I couldn't get enough of her stunning blue eyes, gazing at them while I said, "I'm so happy you're letting me see this side of you."

Her shoulders slowly lifted. "Me too."

I took a glance around even though I already knew what it looked like. "You live on a film set."

"It looks that way, doesn't it?"

"I'm sure it feels that way too." I pointed at her living room, where mountains of boxes were taking up an entire wall. "Is that stuff that brands send you? Products they want you to influence?"

She sighed. "Yes, but that's the carryover." She brought me to the first door off her hallway, which ended up being her office. "Because this room can't handle another box."

Her desk took up a corner, and in another was an area that she had set up for photo shoots. The rest was boxes. At least fifteen high, and there had to be over thirty stacks. I didn't know how she worked in here. The chaos alone would make me unproductive.

"Jesus Christ, Sadie. You're busting out of this condo."

"I know, and it's getting worse by the day." She ran her hand down the arm of my hoodie. "I've had to get a storage unit, and that's where everything ships to now. The post office doesn't have a box large enough for me."

I watched her take in the disaster.

"I've thought about getting another storage unit, but I honestly don't know what to do. I know I can't keep living like this. I need more space."

While she was gazing around her room, I was looking at her. "I have an idea."

An idea that I'd been thinking about for a bit.

An idea that I was going to present to her when we traveled to Portsmouth and Charleston in a couple of weeks.

"Please tell me you're about to solve all my problems? I need that. I'm honestly at a loss for what to do. Do I sell this condo and find a bigger one? Do I get a house? Do I get an office and move the boxes there? Do I—"

"You move in with me and use this condo as your office."

She pulled her hand off my arm and crossed hers over her chest. A few seconds ticked by before a smile appeared on her lips. "You're asking me to move in with you?"

"I am."

Her brows rose. "Are you sure about that?"

I chuckled. "As it is, you stay several nights a week at my place, and you've already started leaving a few things there. I hate when you're gone. And we only live about ten minutes from one another, so the commute would be nothing."

She jutted her lips out in a pucker. "All very true."

I grabbed her hand and brought her into the living room. "Get rid of the furniture and use this room as storage." I used my finger to draw in the air when I said, "You can have racks along each wall, everything labeled and organized. That way, when you need something to film with in the kitchen, it's close by and easily accessible." My hand dropped to my side. "You can use your office as an actual office. And your bedroom, although I haven't seen that yet, you can make into a space for your photo shoots. If you find yourself needing an assistant, they could also work in your bedroom." I held the base of her neck.

"I have two wardrobes. Even the closet in my bedroom is too small."

"Two? You mean, one for cold weather and one for hot?"

"No." She laughed. "Like one for Sadie and one for Dear Foodie, and they don't mix. Ever."

"I wouldn't have even thought of that."

"I used to keep all of Dear Foodie's clothes in the closet in the second bedroom, but now that's filled with boxes too."

"Baby ..." I surrounded her neck with my other hand and moved us closer together. "You don't have to live like this."

She was quiet as she nodded.

I tilted her face up to mine. "But I don't want you to move in just because you need more space. I want you to move in because you don't want to wake up another morning without being next to me."

Her arms rested on my shoulders, and she rose up on her toes, gaining a few inches. "I absolutely despise not waking up next to you. But do you know what I love?" She brushed her fingers through my scruff.

"Tell me."

"The things we do together in your house. Cooking. Relaxing. Sleeping. Showering." She smiled. "Swimming."

I laughed. "I wouldn't call what we've done in that pool swimming."

"True." She giggled.

"Your beautiful house has always felt like home to me, Lockhart ..." She rubbed her lips over mine, back and forth, slowly. "I would love to live there with you."

"It's settled, then. Let me know when you want your stuff brought over, and I'll hire the movers."

"I don't think I need a mover. I'm just going to bring my clothes—not Dear Foodie's clothes. My accessories, bathroom stuff. It shouldn't be more than, say, fifteen boxes."

"Fifteen boxes?" I huffed. "I'm getting a fucking mover."

She poked my chest. "You're too much—" Her voice cut off at the sound of a bell. "The cinnamon buns are done." She rushed into the kitchen, slipping her hands into mitts, taking out the tray from inside the oven. "These need to cool for a few minutes, and then I'll top them with icing."

"Now that's just mean."

She looked at me over her shoulder. "You want a little preview?"

"You really need to ask?"

She waved me over, and I resumed my position behind her, holding her waist, my chin resting on top of her shoulder. She pulled off a small corner piece and held it up to my mouth.

I surrounded her fingers and sucked off the dough, immediately moaning, "Sadie ..."

She turned around and watched me chew. "You like it?"

"If this is without icing, I can't even imagine what it will taste like with icing." I closed my eyes, my head falling back as the richness of the cinnamon took ahold of me. "Do yourself a favor and don't ever bake these for Colson. He'll start asking you to make them weekly, and if Walker gets wind of this, he'll probably try to put these on the menu somewhere."

She laughed. "I don't know if they're *that* good."

"They are. Trust me."

"Thank you." She blushed and put her hands on my chest, rubbing them in a circle before her palms slid up my neck and to my face. Her tongue traced the corner of her lips. "You haven't asked."

I hid my smile. "Asked what?"

"Asked about the elephant in the room."

"What elephant, Sadie?"

She gently hit me. "Lockhart, you know what elephant I'm talking about. The review for Toro."

"I'm not going to ask."

"But I want you to."

I shook my head. "I respect you far too much for that. The review posts tomorrow, and whatever it is, whatever it looks like, it won't have anything to do with you and me. That's business, and this"—I held her tighter—"is what really matters."

"Fine, then I'm going to tell you." Her smile was almost sinister.

"No—"

"It was the best meal I've ever had in LA."

I let that sink in. And when it was done sinking, I let it fall all the way to my gut, where every bit of anxiousness had been living since the opening of this fucking restaurant. "What? Are you kidding?"

"I haven't stopped thinking about it since I left. Neither has Bryn. We've literally been texting about it nonstop."

"Sadie—"

"In this moment, right here, I'm not Sadie. I'm Dear Foodie. And I'm telling you that you have an absolute treasure in Toro. There's nothing like it. There won't ever be anything like it."

She stroked her thumb over my lips. "I had a meal that I will never forget, and those are the words that are getting published tomorrow. I didn't write from my heart, I wrote from my experience. I didn't write as Sadie, your girlfriend—soon-to-be live-in girlfriend. I wrote as Dear Foodie, and I've never published anything more honest in my life."

"Baby ..." I searched her eyes, pulling her against me so there was only air between us, and as I held her face to mine, positioning my lips over hers, I whispered, "I love you. Sadie, that is. Dear Foodie—she's all right." I chuckled. "But it's this side of you that I've fallen for. This side who I'm going to spend forever with. This side who's going to be my wife."

WALKER

I FUCKING LOVE HER.

EDEN

I told you!

BECK

It's posted? Already?

ME

I've never seen a review like this one ... holy fuck!

BECK

Dude, I'm reading it now. She's obsessed with Toro. I'm blown the hell away by what she wrote.

How are reservations?

EDEN

Coming in by the truckload. I'm worried the system is going to crash.

> ME
>
> I hope it does. That'll just earn us more press.

COLSON

"There are meals that leave you satisfied, and then there are meals that leave an impression, like the vows at a wedding, something you think back on. Something you know you're never going to forget. Toro was that. A moment that I would like to relive weekly. And I will be—reliving it weekly, that is. It was THAT impressive."

DAMN.

> ME
>
> Dear Foodie, we love you hard.

EDEN

I'll second that.

COLSON

Third.

BECK

Fourth.

WALKER

Have you found out if she's single?

EDEN

Walker, go back to the kitchen …

EPILOGUE

Hart

Ten Months Later

"I'm going to come!" Sadie leaned her head back over the edge of the hot tub, her arms spread across the top, holding herself steady, her lips wet from the steam of the water.

And from licking them.

And from biting the shit out of them while I fucked her.

Her mouth was directly in front of mine, sucking in some air, moaning, "Lockhart, I'm going to come right now!"

As always, I could tell. Which was why I'd positioned her legs around my waist, why I ground her clit with my thumb, why I had picked up even more speed. I was bucking my hips forward and back, giving her added friction with each stroke, the water slapping every side of me.

My thrusts were achingly deep.

Hard.

Sharp.

Fuck, I was going to come too.

I reared back, pausing there for just a second with only my crown inside her. I let the tingles build in my sac, feeling them take hold of me—through my body, into my shaft, working toward my tip—and when I couldn't stand it any longer, when I couldn't hold off my orgasm for another second, I buried myself into her pussy.

That wetness.

That fucking tightness.

All it took was that one drive, and I lost it.

"Sadie!"

She was matching me scream for goddamn scream. "Yes! Fuck! Ah!"

Our bodies were so locked together that I could feel just how hard she was coming. Not by her moans, although that helped. Not by her breathing, despite that giving it away too. But by the way she was pulsing, gripping me from the inside, contracting around my dick.

"Oh my God!" she cried.

"Agh," I hissed as her body began to loosen and mine became drained, the final jerk of my hips finishing off the last of my cum, and I wrapped my arms around her.

"*Mmm.*" She nuzzled her face into my neck, and out of nowhere, she laughed. "Now I see why when we're home, you always choose to have sex in the pool instead of the hot tub. The cool water is definitely a better pick over hot water. I'm semi-dying in here."

"I can take care of that."

I carried her up the small stairs, lifting her out of the bubbles, and walked us over to the private bean-shaped pool, both directly outside our villa. The change in temperature was appreciated, given how badly I was sweating.

"Much better." She kept her arms circled around my neck.

"About tonight ... I know we have a sunset cruise planned, and the captain is picking us up in about two hours, but I thought we could take a walk on the beach first."

"I would love that."

It wouldn't just be any old walk on the sand of Egremni Beach on the island of Lefkada in Greece, where we were vacationing—a path I'd predetermined with the event coordinator of the Cole and Spade Hotel we were staying at. A path that would be covered in rose petals and candles. And at the very end of that path, I would be getting down on one knee and asking that all-important question.

So far, I'd gotten everything I wanted. Sadie living with me and using her condo as her office, traveling with me when I needed to hit the road to scout out new locations for restaurants or to view the properties that Jenner Dalton had found us. And watching my beautiful girlfriend live out her dream of being a successful food influencer.

But she wasn't just successful. She was now the top influencer in the food space, and her career was on fire. She had a full-time assistant, got offered brand deals multiple times a day, and had recently accepted an offer from a large publishing house to release a cookbook, featuring all her unique desserts. Her preorder sales alone had already made her a *New York Times* Best Seller.

It was time to take things to the next level.

It was time for Sadie Spencer to become my wife.

I rested my forehead against hers, and as I was about to carry her out of the pool, I heard my phone ringing inside the villa.

"Fuck me. What do you think that call is about?"

"I don't know. Your family? But you made it very clear that

unless something was burning to the ground, you didn't want to be bothered." She smiled. "You hard-ass."

"That's because they'll call to talk about the fucking weather. Or to ask about the weather. And I love them, but no weather talk until we get back."

She tightened her grip around me. "They miss you—that's all."

The ringing stopped and immediately started again.

"I suppose I need to get that, or they're going to keep calling until I eventually pick up." I was still inside her, and I easily slid out. "I'll be right back."

I climbed out of the pool and went in through the open glass door to the bedroom, my phone on the nightstand. I lifted it, our corporate office line showing on my screen, and I held the phone to my ear.

"What's up—"

"You're not going to fucking believe this," Walker said.

"Believe what?" I headed back outside and sat at the edge of the pool, dipping my legs in the water.

"Hart, we just got the best news ever," Eden said.

There was excitement in her voice, something I didn't hear often.

I put the phone on speaker mode and said, "All right, hit me with it. I'm ready."

"Toro LA got Michelin-rated," Colson said.

Sadie had her back to me, her arms looped through my legs, but she released me and turned around, her mouth hanging open, lips shaped in an O.

"Hold on a second," I voiced. "We got *what?*"

"And it gets even better," Walker announced. "Hart, they gave us three fucking stars."

"Three stars, Hart," Eden sang. "Not one or two, but three!"

Sadie started jumping up and down in the pool. "Eden," she said close enough to the phone so that everyone could hear, "I told you it was going to happen."

"Sadie, not for a second did I believe you." Eden laughed.

Sadie was smiling at Eden's comment, and it reminded me of the time that Sadie had told me they were going to be besties. My sister was good at acquaintances. Letting someone new in? That wasn't her style. But slowly, she had embraced Sadie, and they'd spent many nights at Eden's house, sharing bottles of wine, talking until they fell asleep on her couch.

Sadie could be herself in front of Eden. She could show my sister both sides of her, and she didn't have that luxury with just anyone. And Eden could let down that callous edge she'd built up over the years, finding comfort in Sadie because Sadie had proven to her that she could be trusted.

That was what mattered most to me—Sadie, my family, the way we were all together, working as one.

But, shit, we'd hit a goal with Toro, and that meant everything to me too.

I ran my hand over the top of my wet hair. "Michelin-rated," I echoed, the news really sinking in. "Now, that's so fucking badass."

"It sure is," Sadie replied.

"I assume the team is going to put out a press release and get all the food outlets chirping about us?" I asked. "And somehow tie in Horned so it gets a boost too—not that it needs one, but it can't hurt."

"Already on it," Eden confirmed.

"I'm hosting a team dinner at Toro in a few nights," Beck said. "That'll give us even more press, and I'll make sure all the guys post about it."

"Good." I rubbed the side of Sadie's face. "We'll celebrate when we get back."

"Have an excellent rest of your trip," Colson said.

We said goodbye, and I hung up, setting the phone behind me on a chair so it wouldn't get wet when I slid into the pool.

Sadie immediately surrounded me—her legs around my waist, her arms around my neck. "So, I'm going to do something, and I don't want to hear any *chirping* from you."

"Oh, yeah? And what is that?"

She smiled. "We made an agreement, and I'm going to break it."

My eyes narrowed as I gazed at her. "What type of trouble are you about to get yourself into?"

"No trouble at all." She gave me a quick kiss. "But Dear Foodie's favorite restaurant was just awarded three Michelin stars, and her audience *needs* to know that."

"No more posts—we agreed."

She climbed up, like my body was the trunk of a tree. "Let me celebrate you. Let me brag about you." She paused. "Let me do this—not for you, but for me." She laughed when I still hadn't said anything. "You know, as my boyfriend, I think you're obligated to nod and smile and let Dear Foodie do whatever she wants."

Boyfriend now.

Fiancé later tonight.

At least this would appease my raging beast of a brother who still bitched that Dear Foodie had stopped posting about us after her review of Toro.

"All right." I held her harder, tickling her waist, listening to her squeals. When she quieted, I added, "But you only get this one pass, and you're using it on this—don't forget that. Because the next time you try to break our deal, you're going to get punished."

She pulled at my lip, nipping it between her teeth. "If

you're talking about the kind of punishment I think you are, then I'm going to post about The Weston Group every day."

I moved my face into her neck, my hand slipping around her until it was gripping her ass. And while a breeze sent me a faint hint of her fruity jasmine scent, I growled, "You're so fucking naughty ..."

Interested in reading books about some of the characters mentioned in *The Arrogant One*?

Beck Weston's Book: *The Wildest One*
Jenner Dalton's book: *The Billionaire*
Macon Spade's book: *The Playboy*
Cooper Spade's book: *The Rebel*
Brady Spade's book: *The Sinner*
Ridge Cole's book: *The Heartbreaker*
Rhett Cole's book: *The One*

ACKNOWLEDGMENTS

Nina Grinstead, every time I go to write this paragraph, I think back to the last time I was in this exact spot—which was probably around two months ago, LOL—the morning after I hit my deadline, when my eyes are fresh, my brain is rested, and I think of every moment that's happened in between. Moments we've accomplished together. Moments that make us speechless. This is a dream and everything I've ever wished for—because of you. To more of those moments, for us, forever. Team B, also forever. I love you so much.

Jovana Shirley, you are everything. My comfort at the end of a hard deadline, knowing I'm handing my baby to the best person ever. You're what makes me smile when the polish settles and it's time for the book to shine, and you're this constant support, sending me words of encouragement, clapping over my accomplishments, cheering me on. What that all means, how hard it hits me, how it puts me straight in my feels —that. So, so much of that. I've said this a million times before, and I'll never stop saying it because I mean it with my whole heart: I can't be me without you. Love you so, so hard.

Ratula Roy, to summarize what you do and what you mean to me is impossible. It's all so layered, going back a ton of years and a million tears and just as many books. There isn't anyone I'd rather text at three a.m. than you, and there isn't anyone, aside from you, who will write me back two seconds later. There isn't anyone who sends me vegan cupcakes when they know how badly I need them. And there isn't anyone who picks me up and keeps me up when I'd rather be curled in a ball on the floor. Only you. Love you forever.

Hang Le, my unicorn, you are just incredible in every way.

Judy Zweifel, as always, thank you for all that you do and for being so wonderful in every way. I adore you. <3

Christine Estevez, I LOVE YOU. You are such a light in my life, and you're forever putting the biggest smile on my face. I appreciate you so much.

Vicki Valente, you're the best—I hope you know that. Thank you for everything.

Nikki Terrill, my soul sister. Every tear, vent, virtual hug, life chaos, workout—you've been there through it all. I could never do this without you, and I would never want to. I've been saying this for years, and I ALWAYS will: Love you.

Pang, I treasure you. In all the ways. And I'm so, so lucky that you share your incredible talent with me. Love you.

Melissa Doughty, my Maine sister who's really a soul sister, you're such a light in my life. I'm so blessed to know you and get to work with you. <3

Kim Cermak, Josette Ochoa, Kelley Beckham, Sarah Norris, Christine Miller, Valentine Grinstead, and Daisy—I love y'all so much.

Erin O'Donnell, I love you, I love you, I love you.

Brittney Sahin, I cherish you, and I cherish us, and I hope you know that. Having you just a phone call away means more to me than you'll ever understand. Love you, B.

Kimmi Street, my sister from another mister. Thank you from the bottom of my heart. You saved me. You inspired me. You kept me standing in so many different ways. I love you more than love.

To my ARC team—To the moon and back, I appreciate you all. <3

Mom and Dad, thanks for your unwavering belief in me and your constant encouragement. It means more than you'll ever know.

Brian, my words could never dent the love I feel for you. Trust me when I say, I love you more.

My Midnighters, you are such a supportive, loving, motivating group. Thanks for being such an inspiration, for holding my hand when I need it, and for always begging for more words. I love you all.

To all the influencers who read, review, share, post, TikTok —Thank you, thank you, thank you will never be enough. You do so much for our writing community, and we're so appreciative.

To my readers—I cherish each and every one of you. I'm so grateful for all the love you show my books, for taking the time to reach out to me, and for your passion and enthusiasm when it comes to my stories. I love, love, love you.

ALSO BY MARNI MANN

THE WESTON GROUP SERIES—EROTIC ROMANCE

The Arrogant One

The Wildest One

The Mysterious One

The Irresistible One

The Forbidden One

SPADE HOTEL SERIES—EROTIC ROMANCE

The Playboy

The Rebel

The Sinner

The Heartbreaker

The One

THE DALTON FAMILY SERIES—EROTIC ROMANCE

The Lawyer

The Billionaire

The Single Dad

The Intern

The Bachelor

HOOKED SERIES—CONTEMPORARY ROMANCE

Mr. Hook-up

Mr. Wicked

THE AGENCY SERIES—EROTIC ROMANCE

Signed

Endorsed

Contracted

Negotiated

Dominated

STAND-ALONE NOVELS

Even If It Hurts (Contemporary Romance)

Before You (Contemporary Romance)

The Better Version of Me (Psychological Thriller)

Lover (Erotic Romance)

THE BEARDED SAVAGES SERIES—EROTIC ROMANCE

The Unblocked Collection

Wild Aces

MOMENTS IN BOSTON SERIES—CONTEMPORARY
ROMANCE

When Ashes Fall

When Darkness Ends

When We Met

THE PRISONED SERIES—DARK EROTIC THRILLER

Prisoned

Animal

Monster

THE SHADOWS DUET—EROTIC ROMANCE

Seductive Shadows

Seductive Secrecy

THE BAR HARBOR DUET—NEW ADULT

Pulled Beneath

Pulled Within

THE MEMOIR SERIES—DARK MAINSTREAM FICTION

Memoirs Aren't Fairytales

Scars from a Memoir

ABOUT THE AUTHOR

Audie® Award–winning and *USA Today* best-selling author Marni Mann knew she was going to be a writer since middle school. While other girls her age were daydreaming about teenage pop stars, Marni was fantasizing about penning her first novel. She crafts unique stories that weave together her love of flawed beauty, mystery, intense passion, and the depths of human emotion. A New Englander at heart, she now resides with her husband in Sarasota, Florida. When she's not nose deep in writing, crafting her next tale, she's fulfilling her wanderlust heart, sipping wine, boating in the Gulf, or devouring fabulous books.

Want to get in touch? Visit Marni at ...
www.marnismann.com
MarniMannBooks@gmail.com

SNEAK PEEK OF THE WILDEST ONE

The Wildest One, the second book in the Weston Group Series, features Beck Weston. It's a sizzling hockey, billionaire romance that's releasing July 10th.
Here's a sneak peek ...

Beck

There was only one thing that smelled as good as pussy, that was the scent of victory. And at the end of a long game, when I could stand in the middle of a bar and hold my beer in the air, shouting to my team, "To another win for the Whales," that was the most indescribable feeling. The air thickened as my teammates moved in closer, huddling around me, repeating the words I'd just voiced. Which I followed up with, "And to fucking destroying Boston—for the second time this season."

"Five to one," my left defenseman called out. "I'd say that's a shutout."

"Almost a shutout," I countered. "But I'll take it." I looked at each of their faces. "I'm proud of you guys!"

"And to our captain for getting us a long-needed break," my right wing declared.

"Use it wisely," I ordered. "Cheers!"

"Cheers," they all repeated.

I kept my beer high, booze sloshing over the sides of most glasses while we attempted to clink them together. Once they hit, I took a long sip, the huddle loosening around me, giving me just enough space to move out and position myself along the front of the bar. I was placing my back against the bar top, getting a full view of the room, when my goalie joined me.

Landon clasped my shoulder. "You know, you've got some balls to give a toast like that while you're in a bar in the center of Beantown."

I shook my head, laughing. "You know I give zero fucks." I moved to the right and left as if we were in a boxing match and I was dodging his punches. "What, is someone going to fight me? Here? In front of my entire team? Come on, man. There isn't a single motherfucker in this bar who could even lay a finger on me."

Landon had transferred to LA a season ago after spending two seasons in Boston. So when I'd taken it upon myself to encourage our coach and manager to switch up our travel schedule to spend tonight and the next two evenings here, rather than Washington DC—the team we were playing next—Landon was all for it. I noticed that when the East Coast fellas came to play on the West Coast, they never entirely gave up their love for home.

I wouldn't know.

Aside from attending Michigan State, I'd spent my whole life in California.

"Beck, you don't know this city like I do." He released my shoulder and held his beer with both hands. "The dudes around here will fight at the drop of a hat—even less. If you give zero fucks, I assure you, they give even less. Shit, they look for reasons to raise their fists."

I dragged out my exhale longer than I needed to. "I fight for a living. I train for hours every day, just like you. I'd like to see them try to beat my ass." I gave him a smile. "Hell, I'd welcome it."

"You're a fucking animal."

"That's why they call me the wildest one." I wrapped an arm around my chest. "Enough about that. You played a good game tonight, buddy." I unraveled that arm to pound his fist.

When he pulled his fingers back from tapping mine, he ran them over the top of his blond hair that hadn't been cut all season, his strands popping off in every direction, like one of those spiky plants. Our team, like most, were superstitious— some didn't cut their hair, some didn't shave, and some didn't do either. When I was home, my barber came to my house every week to trim me up, but my face was an entirely different story. My beard had been growing since pre-season.

"The game started off a little shaky." He pulled at his open collar. "I didn't think we were going to get the win."

"Our defensemen just needed to get their bearings. That's why I pushed to stay here. I can't fucking stand flying cross-country and playing the same night—and I know we had no choice with our schedule, but tonight we had an option to either crash here or fly out, so I put my foot down." I gripped the back of my neck, working out a deep ache in the muscle, feeling the ends of my hair that were still the slightest bit wet from my post-game shower. "We're tired. We're sore. We need a rest."

"Ain't that the truth." He rubbed his thumb over his mouth. "I didn't think Coach was going to change his mind"—he laughed—"but I should know better. When it comes to you, Captain, he always listens."

"Not always"—I punched his arm before my hand dropped —"but I put up a solid argument. He knows we need a minute. We've already been on the road for four days. After the next few games, it'll be close to two weeks. That's a long ass time to be away. When we have a small break, like this one, I want to capitalize on it. Come the DC game, we'll be ready to play."

He hit his beer against mine. "A-fucking-men to that." He pointed at several of our teammates standing on the other side of the bar. "Except something tells me they're going to do anything but rest while we're here."

The group, our second line, was pouring back shots of something clear—tequila, vodka, whatever.

"I got them the break," I huffed. "What they decide to do with it is on them."

Once he took a drink, he ran his fingers through his beard, the scratching of his whiskers drowned out by the music. "Do you know how I'm going to spend it?"

"There's no question in my mind." I smiled at my friend. "How many women do you have lined up? One for each night we're here?" When he said nothing, I laughed. "More?"

"Just one—and that one is more than enough."

"She's an ex?"

He rubbed his lips together. "Not quite that. Just someone I used to mess around with." He dipped his head. "How are you going to spend these three nights?"

Considering it was after midnight, technically there were only two left.

And my mind had already mapped out every hour that I didn't have to spend on the ice or in the weight room.

"I'm going to finish this beer, jump in an Uber, go back to the hotel, and sleep until tomorrow's practice."

His head fell back as he laughed. "I don't believe that."

"Why?"

"Because she can't take her fucking eyes off you."

I glanced forward, assuming that was where *she* was located. "She—" My voice cut off as a flash of black and gold came across my vision. "Oh fuck, yes." But it wasn't those colors that were keeping my attention locked.

It was the red of her hair.

Long strands that framed the most beautiful face I'd ever seen. The sexiest lips puckered around a straw as she sipped her pink drink, silver nails sparking as she held the glass. Creamy skin and a small, sloped nose, eyes of an unknown color because they weren't on me. They were on the woman she was standing next to. The redhead's black and gold sweatshirt hung open, a tight shirt beneath that was tucked into her jeans, showing off the most perfect-sized tits and a narrow waist, her jeans a little too baggy to show her legs, but I was sure those were just as fucking delicious as the rest of her.

"Sounds like you've suddenly changed your mind. That a boy. Since we both know there's nothing better than having sex after a game to let out that pent-up aggression." He nudged my arm. "And by the way she's eye-fucking, I don't think that's going to be hard."

"What are you talking about? She's not even looking at me."

She was still gazing at her friend, unaware that I was visually feasting on her, which gave my stare all the freedom to sweep up and down, devouring her body.

"Huh? She's staring at nothing *but you*." He paused. "How do you not see what I'm seeing?"

I blinked several times, making sure my vision wasn't messing with me, and when I was sure it wasn't, I said, "Who are you talking about, Landon?"

His eyes widened as I looked at him. "How do you *not* know who I'm talking about? The blond at three o'clock."

Three o'clock.

I shifted my gaze until I found the short-haired blonde who was doing just as he said, eye-fucking every square inch of me, and I immediately looked away. "Nah, man. She's not for me."

"You were looking at someone, practically fucking drooling. Who was it, then?"

"If I was going after anyone, it would be her." I nodded toward the redhead. "Twelve o'clock." I let out a moan. "Tell me you've seen a woman more gorgeous ... I dare you."

"Damn. She's hot as hell." He leaned in closer. "I was with a redhead once—it was a night I'll never forget. What I'm saying is, get your ass over there and buy her a drink."

I chuckled. "If I go over there, that's just how things will turn out—a night I'll never forget. I told you, I'm getting the fuck out of here and going to my hotel room. Alone."

A grin spread across his face. "Are you sure about that?"

"I'm positive."

"Why don't you look at her again and then repeat those words to me."

Twelve o'clock was where my stare shifted and the second it did, I realized why Landon wanted me to take this second glance.

The redhead was finally looking at me.

And those eyes—*fuck*. I could see the blueness from here. Along with a hint of the most beautiful smile.

She had an unassuming style and a kind of softness I craved in a woman, but never got, because most were like the short-haired blonde, overdone and edgy.

Two blinks. That was all the time the redhead gave me before her stare returned to her friend.

But it was a long enough span to make my goddamn dick hard. To make my hand clench my beer as though it were on her waist. To make the need in my body grow like the puck was in my possession and I'd just passed the blue line on my way to the goal.

"I dare you to tell me you're not going to go over there and at least talk to her."

I ground my teeth. "Stop using my words, asshole."

"But notice you didn't disagree."

I slowly filled my lungs, using the same speed to let the air out. "You're killing me, Landon."

"No, brother. I'm saving you."

"From what?"

"If you leave Boston without knowing what she tastes like, you'll never forgive yourself."

I laughed.

"What, you think I'm kidding?" he pressed. "I know you. The second we get on that plane to fly to DC in a couple of days, you're going to bitch and moan how you passed up a chance of a lifetime and—"

"How do you know she'd even say yes?"

"The only person who can get her to do that is you." He shook his head at me, grinning like a fucking fool. "I think she'd be all yours." His brows rose. "Are you going to prove that to me? Or are you going to go back to your hotel room, alone, and make one of the biggest mistakes of your life?"

Click HERE to pre-order The Wildest One.

Printed in Great Britain
by Amazon